*Mr Nicholas*

# Mr Nicholas

*Thomas Hinde*

**M**

ISBN 0 333 29539 0

*First published 1952*
*Re-issued 1980 by*
MACMILLAN LONDON LIMITED
*4 Little Essex Street London WC2R 3LF*
*and Basingstoke*
*Associated companies in Delhi, Dublin,*
*Hong Kong, Johannesburg, Lagos, Melbourne,*
*New York, Singapore and Tokyo*

*Printed in Great Britain by*
ST EDMUNDSBURY PRESS
*Bury St Edmunds, Suffolk*

# Chapter One

THE RAIN FELL continuously on the bonnet and against the windscreen of the car. Sometimes for a moment it beat on the road, raising a low mist, but more often it fell steadily without strength. As the cars passed their tyres hissed on the concrete. At the start of the by-pass the line of French poplars looked wet and dirty, and stood without movement, failing to hide the black corrugated tin of the factory. Though it was five o'clock in June the low clouds made it seem like evening. Sitting in the front seat, listening to the rain on the roof, and the hum of the windscreen-wiper, Peter Nicholas thought that he might have felt excitingly warm and safe if the rain had been more violent and his clothes thicker.

They drove slowly behind a gravel lorry and he watched yellow water running out of its back. On each side semi-detached houses extended, the details of their bow-windows and polished tile doorways blurred by the rain so that they appeared identical. The few people who stood on the kerbs in mackintoshes were like figures on an exhibition model to show that real people lived there, and Peter wondered if they sometimes went home to the wrong house. A gust of wind blew rain over the window and he turned the handle but it was already tight. If he had been warmer he could have ceased to resist the depression and enjoyed it, and, of course, if he could have forgotten that Mrs. Pawthorn might at any moment say something cheerful.

Not that she was invariably cheerful. At present she seemed to realise that he was depressed and to be putting herself in sympathy. He turned his head to look at her, carefully so that she would not notice. She sat upright with her hands near the top of the wheel, as if to make room for her large bust, and she kept still. He had the impression that she was doing it to be friendly and was annoyed. The half of her mouth which he could see seemed like an accidental opening, as out of place as the other features on her face. He could see where her peach coloured make-up which spread evenly over it began behind her cheek bones. When she turned towards him he turned away but not quickly enough.

He wondered who she was and was depressed that he had not wanted to know till she annoyed him. A friend of his father, the letter had said, who was driving from London and would give him a lift. She had talked about the weather, the war, and the shortage of sugar, not briefly to start a conversation but at length. Usually he took months to decide about people, but he had already decided about her. Perhaps he was becoming quicker with practice; more probably he was discovering types; because people were partly like others you guessed they were identical.

Presently he became aware of the silence and wanted to speak, but everything he thought of seemed too friendly. He was alert and the silence in his head came in waves. When he did not expect it she said, "I'm so glad your father's better."

Even people who knew them well still said this, though his father's illness had ended, he thought, about four years ago. He found it difficult to remember exactly when. Perhaps a nervous breakdown was like that; four years ago his father had been ill and at some time since then he must have recovered because he was well now; at least what people meant by well. Peter became aware that Mrs. Pawthorn was looking at him and thought for a moment that she had intended the irony and was waiting for his smile; but then he was sure that she was watching to see if she had guessed right and his father had in fact got better.

She said, "You are so lucky to have such nice parents."

"Do you know my mother?"

"Well no, but everyone I know says how nice she is." She

would not have admitted it if he had not asked her. It wasn't exactly deceit; it was leaving people with a false impression.

"But I used to know your father well, though it's some years now . . ."

When he did not answer she said, "How do you like Oxford?"

It almost seemed a question which did not predict an answer and he thought for a second of explaining to her. Half an hour before he would have done, because he found it easy to say what he thought to someone who had not yet shown that they were biased. He wanted to impress them and it was not till later that he realised they only understood answers they expected, and could imagine them before he spoke repeating to him what he would say with a different meaning. He could imagine Mrs. Pawthorn being impressed at the wrong moments. He said, "Very much, thank you."

It sounded like a snub so he said, "It's not like before the war, you must work; but you don't have to work hard."

He had said it too often and each time he expressed it worse. He was surprised to think that it was still true. He sat watching the rain on the windscreen, aware of the dampness of his feet in his thin socks. When he smelt her scent he moved away from her in his seat.

She said, "What are you doing?"

He sat still, wondering what to say, surprised at her familiarity—but of course, she was talking about Oxford. He tried to think what he was doing there: a certain amount of drinking, some painting, a little acting. It was a moment before he realised that she meant work.

He said, "Law."

"I think that's sensible because it is a training for something."

"Yes," he said, "that's true." He wanted to explain that he hated law, that he didn't want to be trained to be another solicitor earning adequate money, living in a fairly large house, breeding a moderate number of possible solicitors.

9

But first he must tell his parents. It had seemed easy at Oxford. Already as they drove nearer to Rodenham he began to think that he would not do it at once. He could hear them saying, "Well what *do* you want to be?" kindly, wanting to find out. They would not realise that he might never know, or understand that he might not want to be anything. They could not imagine a person without an occupational label. He might tell them he wanted to paint, but then, if they did not laugh they would understand that he wanted to be an artist and suggest an art school. He did not want to leave Oxford. He did not even mind reading law if he was not expected to become a lawyer. Sometimes he felt they were stupid not to realise this, but he knew that he should tell them.

They passed the gravel lorry and climbed the long hill away from the houses. Below to the left the unfinished brick memorial was indistinct through the rain at the top of its low rise. It would probably never be finished because too many people thought it ugly or misplaced. They got very excited about these criticisms, forgetting that no one looked at memorials which were beautiful and central. Only the tower had been built and its top was incomplete, but it seemed tall and made the cars on the sea coast holiday road beneath appear like insects. Grass grew up to its walls except where a thin approach of concrete slabs led to the Gothic doorway, which was out of proportion to its façade. Peter suddenly had the impression that it was very old and wiped the steam from the window to see it clearly, but they turned and were climbing to the Hill Road.

Mrs. Pawthorn said, "I used to live here as a child. It's a lovely part of the country." She looked at him but he went on watching the raindrops on the windscreen. "Don't you think so?"

"There are so many houses it doesn't seem like country."

"Yes, but there are so many nice people."

"Oh yes." He had never thought of them like that. He began to adjust his opinions.

She said, "Do you like Rodenham?"

It was the same question but he pretended not to notice. Rodenham was impersonal and he was prepared to talk about it; and he wanted to answer so that she should cease to look at him across the car and look at the road.

"It must have been wild when it was all heath?"

"Yes, it must." She seemed to applaud, and not to realise that he was asking her.

She said, "I expect you've lived here a long time?"

"Only a few years." He was surprised that she did not know.

"You must tell me all about it. It will all seem strange to me." She looked at him with wide eyes, smiling like a child waiting for a story. Peter looked back. He thought of saying, "I find it provincial," but he did not mean that. He must say something because the car was moving slowly to the right across the road. "Suburban," was equally wrong, and sounded smug. Then from the corner of his eye he saw the other car. He seemed unable to look away from her. He could not tell if she had seen it. It came quickly towards them. His hand was pushing at her buttock. He said, "Smug—I mean look out." Her plump arms turned the wheel suddenly with surprising strength. He waited for the impact, but they passed, and turning in his seat he could see through the back window the other driver leaning out of his car to his waist, his arms working. Mrs. Pawthorn was saying, "I was so young that I can't remember much, except a lot of pine trees, and my mother saying, 'Kissing's not in season when the gorse is not in bloom'." She smiled as if suggesting that they should share this nearly naughty idea.

"It's not a place you can describe," he said. "I could tell you how it seems to me, but it will seem different to you."

"I quite agree," she said. He almost thought she was

mocking. The country fell steeply from the Hill Road, giving the view over many counties which people came from London and the suburbs to see on Sunday evenings. The wide concrete parks for their cars were empty and reflected the grey sky on their wet surfaces. In the centre of one was a tea van but no cars had stopped and its shutters were closed. Beyond to the south the rural valley was full of rain and the tops of fir hills were hidden. There was nothing to show that they were already surrounded by houses with rockeries. To the north the grey and black of the city was on the horizon. Peter felt that the weather suited the place. The sun suggested too much. He found himself waiting for Mrs. Pawthorn's next question. Presently she said, "Can you drive?"

"A little." At another time he would have said, "Hardly at all," but she made him unwilling to admit a failing.

"I suppose your father taught you. He's a very good teacher."

"No, it wasn't him."

"You must have some practice; one never learns without practice."

Peter said nothing. It was too late when she began to stop.

"You can climb over me," she said but he disliked the idea and went round behind the car in the rain.

She explained the gears to him and he listened, not saying if he knew. He changed quickly into top gear and then drove fast to avoid using them again. She made him defiant and he tried to make the rain beat on the windscreen as if there was a storm. They went down from the Hill Road round a sharp bend and he felt the chassis of the car shift sideways on its springs. He could hear her beside him give the beginning of a nervous giggle; he didn't look round. In the next village there was a cross-roads and he drove at it fast sounding his horn, but there was nothing crossing. He drove up the rise between the green-houses and the imitation Tudor inn, and he tried to pass a lorry but a car was coming so he drew back using the brakes suddenly. Out of the corner of his eye he could see her sitting up, her plump arms bent in alarm. He stopped near the hospital on the outskirts of Rodenham, beyond the ferro-concrete church, before the dip which smells of gas. She was laughing to herself, and looked at him sideways, and laughed again. He felt deflated, and smiled at her slightly, but it wasn't his joke. Then she was smiling with him and he was confused, and no longer sure that she had been laughing at him.

She drove through Rodenham and out along the Beckford road which is flanked by medium sized houses with gardens and pine trees. "I'll drop you; our cottage is a mile further on. Will you be at home much these holidays?"

Peter could not decide about her. She went on talking till he was certain she never thought, and then did something which convinced him that she did. After that for a while he was prepared. He said, "I shall probably be in Sussex for two weeks, and perhaps abroad for a month, but otherwise here."

"You must come and have another driving lesson."

Peter walked slowly up the private road. The rain had stopped but the sky was grey; the water had made courses in the sand and left small heaps of fir droppings. At the bottom on the left was the Lt. Commander's house, who when on leave could be seen organising his gardener. Opposite, the retired Gas and Electricity Company manager lived in a new half-timbered house, and, next door, a retired Indian civil servant. Through the gates Peter could see his wife on the veranda hesitating to take out her blind Scotch terrier. Above this were pines and rhododendrons as far as the gate of General Binforth's drive. He kept Mongolian pheasants, and every evening sounded off on a bugle, and they came flying down from his trees to feed. Originally he had done this standing at attention on his front door-step, but the people who lived in the same wood on the next private road had complained so now he did it in his green-house. At the top of his drive near

13

the porch stood a Boer War field gun. Peter went on up the hill, beneath silver birches and firs, between banks of rhododendrons with the wet remains of purple flowers, towards Pine Knoll.

Because he was cold and tired he almost wanted to be there, and also because even now he thought he would enjoy it. He had felt the same about school holidays and they had failed because he had not been able to decide what to do. Sometimes he had woken on the first morning knowing that he wanted to stick in all his British Empire stamps, or make a garden, but sometimes he had not been able to decide, and on the second morning it had been harder because a day had been wasted and it was more important to decide correctly, and on the third still harder. But he already knew that this vacation he wanted to paint. It was easy, if he left out a few things, to suggest that he should be glad to be coming home.

He went up the cinder path, past the ash heap and the creosoted coal shed, towards the back door. The house was ahead and above him, the windows and grey stucco of the top two floors showing over rhododendrons. From the other side, on the tennis court, when the sun shone Pine Knoll sometimes looked pretty, and usually he had the energy to go round that way, hoping also to get in unseen by the drawing-room window, which gave him a sense of advantage, but the rain had started again. There was a light in the kitchen and he saw his mother's head and large shoulders go past the window. He thought of sitting in the coal shed to regain his breath, but how absurd if someone found him. If he went round the outside of the house she would probably see him. The rain was cold on his neck and he shivered and went in.

She was in the larder clattering tins, but she heard him at once. "Is that you, darling?"

She came out smiling at him. She held a plate and her bare arms were goose-flesh below her brown woollen jumper.

He said, "What a foul day," and then saw that she had put

14

the plate on the table and was coming to be kissed, and tried to kiss her cheek but she tried to put her mouth on his and half succeeded so he let her kiss him, doing nothing. It was silly to pretend.

"What a foul day. Have you had tea, or will you wait till supper? How are you, darling?"

"Wait, I should think," he said.

"And how is Oxford? Have you had a good term?"

It was the sort of question which he did not want at once. If only she would wait and try to find out without asking. Sometimes he thought of saying, "Dreadful," but she would hear and be sympathetic. It was when he said, "Not too bad," while he thought unwillingly of a fuller answer that she hurried on. Already she was hesitating for her cue. He said, "Quite fun."

"And you met Pussy Pawthorn all right?"

"Yes," he said. "Who is she?"

"She was one of the Miss Weights. I'm not sure which. I don't think her real name is Pussy—at least it may be—perhaps it is. I've never seen her—anyway not to remember, though father says I met her once." He could imagine her being persuaded that it had happened. "He knew them in Devon." She began to move about again, pouring a bottle of milk into several small jugs, arranging plates of bacon and bread to be fried.

"Supper won't be long. Father's upstairs."

"Who's Mr. Pawthorn?"

"Some American, I think."

She went into the larder and he thought he had stopped her cheerfulness and realised how easy it had become to do this, but she called, "Find yourself some sherry," and, coming back with eggs, "We're going to have a bottle of something."

He wondered why and almost asked, but said instead, "Where's Owen?"

"With Brian on the hillside making fireworks, I expect."

15

Her cheerfulness was indiscriminate. She disapproved of Owen's fireworks. He was only seventeen and she still tried to take care of him, in a way which she had given up with Peter since he had become twenty. And she disapproved of Brian Binforth who had been caught stealing books from a bookshop. It had been hushed up and before it was discovered Owen and he were already friends.

Peter said, "I'll go and find him," but he could hear his father coming downstairs, clearing his throat and spitting into his handkerchief, crossing the hall, his shoes beating on the tiles, towards the kitchen.

"Hallo, Peter, how are you?" He came at him, looking him in the eyes and they shook hands. It was like a *Tom Brown* scene. It was what his father wanted, except that he should have answered, "Well and healthy, thank you father," staring back.

"Have a good term? What a revolting day. I say, I don't think much of Oxford's performances on the cricket field." He seemed to fill the room with noise. Peter felt his half enthusiastic answers being forced from him; but he tried to make them sincere, for it was obvious now that it had all been planned by his mother. He could imagine her saying, "Let's have a bottle of something to celebrate when Peter comes home," and reminding his father when he forgot to buy it. He could imagine her arranging bacon and cheese omelette which he liked. And somehow she had arranged that his father should be friendly.

"Come and have a drink," he said, and Peter tried to ignore the suggestion of threat and went with him across the hall into the drawing-room. His father put glasses among the willow pattern china on the mantelpiece, poured out sherry, and brought it to him.

"All the best. Have you heard about my meeting? The local Rotary Club. Quite nice fellows but typical bourgeois. None of them properly educated. They had this young bounder down from Sheffield to give them 'The Workers' Angle.' He started talking this peace nonsense and no one did anything to stop him so I got up and said, 'Mr. Chairman, we haven't come here to listen to political propaganda'."

His father paused and Peter realised it was the end and said "Huh." He could not help half believing. He instinctively interpreted a different meaning into every sentence, trying to distinguish what had happened from what his father said.

"What did he do?"

"Who? The Chairman? Oh he's one of these dreadful 'All things to all men' people. You'll never get anywhere in this world if you're like that. He had the decency to thank me afterwards for what I said. Anyway there wasn't any more peace nonsense; I stopped that. At a proper meeting the audience should have walked out. Oh yes, you're perfectly entitled to walk out if a speaker doesn't stick to his subject. That's what these people don't understand."

"Mm."

"Have another glass. Take one to mother. What's that? Supper's ready? Supper, supper." He began to shout jovially about the hall. "Owen, where's Owen? Tell Owen somebody, supper's ready. Supper, supper, what's for supper?" His voice became muffled as he went into the dining-room, his feet sounding on the linoleum and board floor. Peter ran down the lavatory passage and slammed the door. The window thumped and the noise tingled in his ears, but no one heard and as soon as he listened again he could hear his father calling, "Is anyone coming to supper?"

He sat below his favourite family portrait, which looked down with seven others on the small square room, and he talked about wine.

"This is a jolly good claret. The average claret is only fit to fill your pen with. Burgundy, you don't want to drink too much burgundy, very liverish. No, I don't like those dry white wines."

17

The rain beat on the window and Peter felt warm and comfortable, and became a little drunk. He was noticing distinctly things which he normally did not notice: his father's grey side whiskers twitching at the bottom as he chewed his omelette. He said, "What about Sauterne?" and waited, almost amused, for his father to say what he usually said when they had this conversation.

His mother sat beyond the silver candlesticks. She said, "We've been asked to the Binforths' sherry party. I'm sure they'll include you if we say you're at home; won't they?"

"I'm sure they will, my dear. I'll ring up the old General. He'll do anything for me."

"And we've got a tennis party on Saturday when David is back."

Peter realised with surprise that for weeks he had not thought of his youngest brother. He said, "That's early for Harrow."

"Yes, they're being allowed home."

"Why?"

His mother did not answer and Peter became aware of a secret. He emptied his mouth and said, "Why?" as if he had not already said it.

His father said, "Some boy has died of this paralysis disease so we're having David home." Peter was aware that his mother and father had taken the decision together but that she had not trusted herself to remember why.

"It's typical of school doctors. They treat chickenpox as if it was typhus and here they had this boy dying and they said it was rheumatism." His father emphasised the word *dying*.

"Partly I blame the school. The boy was playing soccer two days before and when he complained of a pain in his chest they gave him an aspirin."

The strong movements of his jaw suggested his mind working on the next thing to say, but before he could go on Owen came in.

"Hurray," his father shouted. "Home at last. How was the moon?"

His mother said, "Your supper's in the oven."

"How was the moon?"

"Underneath a dish cover."

"Owen, I asked you, how was the moon?"

"All right thank you."

"Go on, old boy; mother says your supper's in the oven."

He was wearing an open Aertex shirt and corduroy trousers held up by a leather belt which made him seem even thinner than usual. It made his stomach concave, and he had long arms and a long thin neck. When he came back carrying his plate Mr. Nicholas said, "Well, one of your brothers is home."

"Yes," said Owen. He looked down the table and said, "Hallo," and Peter said "Hullo." It was easy to plan an unembarrassing tone because he was a little drunk. He felt that he could find words for anything. He understood Owen's embarrassment because he and Owen never publicly admitted that they did not hate each other as they had at twelve and fifteen. He understood his mother's happiness because her plan was succeeding, and he was afraid for it. When his father started asking him intelligent questions about his term Peter knew this was not because of his interest but to make the conversation his own achievement in interrogation.

He said, with slight unwillingness, "I'm afraid watching cricket bores me. Playing is all right sometimes, but there are so many more interesting things to do." It was a mistake.

His father said, "You mean your acting and your painting," ticking them off.

"And less definite things, talking."

"Yes, we used to do that, sit up all night talking about the problems of life." Peter wanted to laugh at the way in which he made anything anyone else did seem dull by putting it in a category.

19

For a moment his father said nothing. Owen was eating and his mother had gone out. His father's jaw had stopped and there was silence except for his audible controlled belches; and in the half-dark room Peter felt that he was sharing something with his father and that anyway to quarrel with someone so transparent only showed his own intolerance.

His mother came in with coffee and switched on the light. She said, "Have we told him our idea?"

"No."

"We're thinking of clearing the wood." She announced it cheerfully, like the tennis party.

"The beech wood?" he said. He wanted to be certain, but he should have kept quiet. His quickness gave him away.

His father said, "All that untidiness beside the tennis court."

He wanted to say, "You mean the young oak trees." The phrase made him a little dizzy with satisfaction, but he controlled it. If he took one side his father would take the other. After a moment he succeeded in not wanting to interrupt, but then felt angry at needing to confuse his opinions in this way.

"Why?" he said.

His mother said, "It'll make some jolly good Christmas logs."

"That isn't the point, my dear. All that growth spoils our view of our valley."

"I shouldn't have thought that mattered."

"What do you mean?"

"It's mostly houses."

"Now, old boy, that's not true." Peter started to think whether it was true.

"The old General knows what he's talking about. He says these hills need opening out." Peter wondered if the General did know what he was talking about, but it was incidental and his father was saying, "One doesn't like to ask people to tennis with that mess round the court."

"Surely," Peter said, "you must get permission from the

Town and Country Planning Committee to cut down trees?"
He had meant to reserve it as a final argument but he had
suddenly forgotten the others.

"Really, old boy," his father said, pausing and smiling at
him till he was embarrassed, "do you seriously think that
applies here? A whole army of inspectors couldn't enforce
it." Peter didn't answer.

"No, old boy, I can assure you that if we decide to cut down
a few small trees nobody will stop us."

There must have been several hundred, but what was the
good?

Mrs. Nicholas said, "I think it's stopped raining. Have
some more coffee?"

"No thank you."

"Nothing's settled yet, old boy."

Peter laughed once and got up and walked away into the
drawing-room and sat in an arm-chair holding a newspaper
but not reading. It was the right noise but he had not made it
loud enough. The others washed up in the kitchen and he
could hear the continuous drone of his father's voice coming
periodically to an upward intonation before his mother's
"Yes." They were talking about him.

When she came in he went on looking at the paper, expecting her to say something but she sat at her desk, so after a
moment he said, "Where's father?"

"I don't know," she said wearily.

He looked up but she went on writing, so he said, "What's
the matter?"

"Why must you?" she said.

"What?"

"Go on like this?"

"You don't think I want to, do you?"

"Why do it then?"

He was sure he was not to blame. He began to argue
indignantly, but his father came in.

He walked about beyond the sofa, his hands in his breeches pockets, looking at the carpet.

"Incidentally," he said, "we should get rid of our tree rat trouble."

"What trouble?"

"All those beastly grey squirrels."

"But what trouble?"

"They're not real squirrels at all, just rats with tails." His father made everything a battle. If he wasn't forcing his opinion on someone he was exterminating the remains of wild life on his three and a half acres. It was easy to feel how he wanted to win but hard to know how he enjoyed arguing when the other side had stopped, or shooting when the few rabbits and jays would inevitably be driven out as the houses thickened and the residential district spread.

"If you can't have red you might as well have grey. I think they're pretty."

"You think they're what?"

Peter was too embarrassed to repeat the word.

"Well I don't."

After a pause Peter said, "Well I do." It was much too late and sounded sulky.

"That's rude, old boy."

Peter said, "Yes, I suppose it was." It was an admission, a gesture, and he felt warm and self-satisfied. It was an approach to being frank with his father and that was close to friendship.

"Well then I think you should apologise."

Peter got up and walked carefully out of the room. His father said, "Peter, I'm speaking to you." He went upstairs to his room, and shut the door and lay on his bed.

He put his head in his hands and felt weary of dislike, and honestly thought it was not his fault. His mother's attitude recurred to him annoyingly for he had always assumed that she sympathised.

He supposed he had expected this, but not so soon. Perhaps

22

in reverse of normal order things would now improve but he could not imagine it. Because it had happened so soon he could go into another room and see that they were quarrelling about a triviality; but he knew that in a week he would not be able to do this, and already he could understand himself feeling that it was not trivial because it was an example of his father's attitude. He lifted his head and heard steps on the stairs and sat on the edge of the bed preparing himself.

His father came in and walked to the window, and Peter looked at the coco-nut mat. He was aware that his father was also looking at the floor.

His father said, "We can't go on like this, old boy." His voice was hoarse with genuine emotion.

"No." Peter was angry that his eyes wanted to water.

"What's it all about?"

"I don't know."

"Why can't we get on as we used to? I can remember a year ago you and I walking up and down the lawn discussing things together, and everything was pleasant and friendly. Can't you?"

"Yes." Peter could. It was useless to explain who had done the discussing.

"Well what's happened?" Peter didn't answer.

"Your mother and I have looked forward to when you would be grown up and we could share things. This is going to be a great disappointment to us." His father was looking at him but Peter didn't look up because his eyes were watering.

"After all it's not right that we should quarrel. We ought to be father and son standing up to face the world together."

"Mm."

"There are so many better things to be thinking about."

"Mm."

"We want you to help us with David, and with Owen who hasn't had the same chance. And what a silly thing to quarrel about, a grey squirrel. Well, shall we make a blunderbuss?"

"All right." It was difficult to say and Peter cleared his

throat and blew his nose and wiped his eyes with the back of his hand, thinking that in the confusion his father would not notice.

"Shake hands."

Peter half got up, and misjudged so that his father's hand gripped his fingers. It was hot and dry.

"Right you are, old boy. Come down when you're ready and have a drink."

Peter lay on his back on his bed. There certainly were better things to do. He felt willing to agree to the phrase because he knew that he and his father did not mean the same things.

He went downstairs at once. His mother was smiling towards the door as he opened it, and his father gave him a glass of sherry.

His mother said, "All the best," using his father's phrase without his conviction.

His father said, "Happy holidays to us all," and tipping back his head emptied three quarters of his glass; and they sat down and talked about the tennis party, and the sugar ration, and *A Tale of Two Cities*.

Presently Peter went away to find Owen. He stopped outside the drawing-room door, thinking consciously, "Do I want a book?" and listening. There was silence and then he heard his father say, "I had a good talk to him, my dear. I think I made him understand." Peter went quickly upstairs.

Owen was lying on his bed, his chin in his hands, looking at a book with many black and grey photographs and sentences printed thick black for emphasis. Peter recognised it as *The Seven Hundred and Seventy-Seven Wonders of the World*. He said, "Huh," trying to show neither contempt nor unlikely interest.

"What are you looking for?"

"Nothing special; chemicals and things." He shut the book, aware of what Peter thought of it.

Peter said, "How's school?" For a moment it was the only thing he could think of.

"Oh that."

"Don't you like it?"

"I don't mind it." Peter waited for him to go on but he seemed stuck for words.

"Whenever I do anything father says it's the school. And if I don't know anything he says, 'Haven't they taught you that?' and goes on about grammar schools being a disgrace."

"He can't blame you."

"No, he doesn't."

Peter wanted to say, "We've just had a row," to show his sympathy, but he had been too much part of it to call it that yet.

Owen said, "What was he saying to you?"

"It was about the wood."

"Oh yes, he's been meaning to cut that down for weeks."

"Why does mother agree?"

"She didn't till this business about Mr. Belvene."

"Who's he?"

"The man who lives below the wood. He's got some disease. He sent a message by Mrs. Jenning who also cleans for him that it cuts off his sun."

"Why didn't mother explain that?"

"Because father says it isn't true. He went and looked one day at lunch time and said there was lots of sun and anyway the man should write an honest letter and not send hints by a charwoman."

"Why does he want to do it then?"

"He likes the idea, I suppose."

"And mother thinks it would be kind."

"Yes."

Peter leant against the dressing table looking at Owen's books which were pushed tightly against the wall and arranged exactly by height so that he could see the gap for *The Seven Hundred and Seventy-Seven Wonders*. He felt excited that they understood each other.

# Chapter Two

PETER WATCHED the line of sunlight on the wall close to the window. He had the impression that he had been watching it for a long time with his eyes half open, and suspected it had been something else. The sky through the window between the tops of two large pines was blue without a cloud. He wondered why there was no noise of traffic on the main road and no sound in the house, till he remembered that the sunlight was usually half way across the wall near the bookshelf before he saw it.

He pushed back the bedclothes quickly before he had time to think of reasons against, and was still surprised he had done it when he had put on trousers and a sweater. He wanted to be in the sun without speaking to anyone and went softly downstairs. A spring creaked in his mother's room, and he stopped, but there was silence, and silence from his father's room. Sunlight was coming through unusual windows on the stairs and had even got into the hall through the open pantry door, making an orange patch on the red tiles. When he opened the French windows the cool fresh air came against his face so that he was aware of his sleepiness.

The grass of the lawn sprayed up his trousers and wet his pyjamas, but he didn't care and ran to the edge where, coming suddenly round a bank, he disturbed two blackbirds playing on the drive. They rose with absurd, unnecessary noise startling him, and several smaller birds which flew into the rhododendrons. He walked round the house and softly up the cinder path. Small brown birds were making short flights between the birch bushes and pine seedlings, and he tried to see them but though they were only a few feet away and he could hear their twittering of mild alarm they always settled behind leaves. The coal shed, against blue sky and curiously marked with pine shadows, was no longer ugly. The cat on the back door-mat stretched, smiling at him, and gave a wriggle as if about to come and rub against him, but instead rolled on its back to be tickled.

He stood still for a moment, and then, determined not to find that there was nothing to do, set off quickly round the other side of the house. He went across the lawn, this time avoiding the wettest grass; he could only have been away a few minutes for the shadows of the firs were as long and the patches of sunlight as surprisingly small; and he went up the slight rise to the tennis court.

In the day magpies, and sometimes a green woodpecker were there but now it was deserted, as if a cat had walked by. Perhaps it was still crouching in the laurels, but it made no noise. The sunlight fell straight on the wood making the young oaks and taller beech trees seem flat and colourless. Peter did not cross the empty court but walked round the edge, through the wire netting gate.

The ground sloped steeply and he held on to trees. The beeches and oaks were thin with no branches below their tops but the Spanish chestnuts sprouted from the ground like bushes. In places the sky was almost hidden but there were wide gaps where bilberries grew on the ground. It wasn't really a wood, but a fringe at the top and a fringe at the bottom connected by clumps. After a few paces it was possible to see below, through the last trees, parts of Mr. Belvene's white-washed house.

Mr. Belvene's lawn was over a fence below a steep bank. It was very small and enclosed on three sides by trees and on the fourth by his house. Possibly at midday the far side did get a little sun.

Peter went along the fence, through the bottom of the wood to its far side where the trees were small and there was heather. It was this edge that he liked. The rest was a background, a barrier from the house. He could remember running here, across the tennis court, through the upper trees, holding his breath till he could cry in the heather. In the summer he had read here, lying in the shade of the bushes, and stayed though he could hear his mother and father calling him in the house and on the tennis court, and only when they had stopped run quickly along the fence and answered from another direction. The sun was already bright among the bushes at the top and he knew that in a few hours the wet heather which sprayed his face and soaked his trouser legs would be steamed dry and warm.

It was the uncertainty that he hated. He almost wanted it to be decided that the wood should be cut down so that he could say what he thought. His arguments or agreements seemed equally to produce the wrong effect, till he wanted to say, "Why not burn the rhododendrons too?" but as soon as he thought of the words he was afraid they would give his father the idea.

He leaned away from the tree stump and began to climb the hill. He had been looking at the bright sky among the small trees at the top so that the ground seemed dark and he went clumsily, brushing against bushes and catching his feet in the heather. At the top he was dizzy and walked slowly through the trees to the tennis court. Steam was rising from the bushes around, and the sun was already misty so that it seemed to be some different early morning. Peter walked slowly across the court, down the grass rise, over the lawn towards the house. He was surprised to see through the open French windows people moving in the drawing-room.

A tall man sat in an arm-chair, and his mother at a corner table was pouring tea. She bent over it closely as if by showing her large back and buttocks she could pretend for a moment that was not there. When Peter made a noise with his feet in the veranda she turned her head quickly and said, "Hallo, you're bright and early. This is Mr. Belvene." She forgot to stop pouring and the tea ran over the edge of the cup into the saucer.

Peter said, "Good morning."

Mr. Belvene did not answer. His right leg was extended across the carpet as if he was lying in the chair, and his left bent as if ready to make an escape, but it had fallen sideways. Peter wondered if he had heard, and tried to think of something else to say.

His mother said, "Would you pass this," and didn't say which cup but went on making calculations above the tray.

"No not that—oh, it doesn't matter."

Peter said, "What a lovely morning."

Mr. Belvene started, and his hand holding his tea began to shake so that the cup which was not exactly centred rattled against the saucer, and Peter helped him put it on the arm of his chair. His hands and wrists were thin and brown, and presently Peter realised from the slight bellows action of two small areas of his cheeks that he was breathing hard.

"Did I give you sugar?" his mother said. "What a lovely day. I'm afraid it's too bright to last. You never can tell."

She sat in an upright chair sipping her tea and got up quickly and said, "Excuse me a moment." She had remembered the porridge.

When Peter looked round Mr. Belvene had stood up. He said, "Must be going."

"Oh, must you?"

"Mm," he said with a short frown as if that was the previous subject and he was trying to think of something else. Peter went after him through the French window. He walked with a thin stick. On the edge of the lawn he remembered and said, "Terrible hill." He seemed to realise that he had been an embarrassment and try to excuse himself.

Peter said, "Yes, it's very steep," and Mr. Belvene gave a short frown and pointed with his stick to ask the way.

"Straight down the path keeping left." Peter watched him

29

go, wondering if he should go with him. He walked back to the house and sat on the sofa. After a moment his mother came in.

"How's the porridge?"

"Just starting to make." She saw no implication. "Where's Mr. Belvene?"

"Gone. What did he come for?"

"I don't know. He didn't say."

"Did you ask?"

"No."

Peter said, "Did he ask about the wood?" He wanted to show her that he knew.

"He didn't mention it."

"I suppose," he said, "if he really wants it cut down we ought to."

She said, "No, why should we?" meaning why should we hurt your feelings, surely there is a compromise. It was stupid and gave him a chance to be annoyed.

"Of course we must."

He got up and walked into the veranda. The mist was thick but the sun still showed through it like a white coin so that he could not decide which would win. He heard his mother pour out a cup of tea and carry it upstairs to his father's room. He went into the hall and heard her saying, "We've just had old Belvene to call."

"What? Who?"

"Mr. Belvene."

"Good God, now? Before breakfast? What did the old fool want?"

"He didn't seem to know." She said it with artificial callousness to suit his taste.

"Be a darling and pass my dressing-gown."

\* \* \*

Peter sat on his bedroom floor, drawing shapes, but they

30

weren't good and he rubbed them out. For a time he worked on one, but when he held it away the detail was out of relation to the rest so he went on to another, but he could feel the same thing happening. It was as if he needed not inspiration or draughtsmanship but energy to lift his head away from the board. He began to rub it all out, but started to draw again before it was clean and stopped, and made himself go on rubbing, and the rubber caught the paper and tore it. He sat gazing out of the window at the sunlight in the white mist. It was difficult to tell which would win.

He wished he could have become indignant at his work, for that usually improved it, but because he knew this his indignation would not be genuine. Presently he began on new paper. His father's arguments kept recurring to him and he thought of answers. He could always think of answers afterwards. He thought: Carry on then, if you want General Binforth to decide what you do with your trees. This particularly pleased him and he repeated it to himself with various emphases, and improved it. He wished the opportunity could recur, but knew he would not use it.

Presently his father came in and Peter thought there was something to hide but couldn't remember what.

"I hear we had a visit from the old boy at the bottom of the hill. What did he want?"

"I don't know. It was hard to tell."

"He's a peculiar fellow."

"Yes."

"I should think he rotted his liver away in India."

"Mm." Peter wanted time to think. He said, "What's wrong with him?"

"Hardening of the arteries probably. That's what they mostly get. You're busy sketching are you?"

"Yes."

"Right, well I'm just off to order a taxi to meet David."

Peter went on drawing, carefully, forcing himself to take

31

out what he did not like. He had wanted to say something but had not wanted to disturb his father's friendliness.

★   ★   ★

Mr. Nicholas carved the mutton with enjoyment. It pleased him to stand above it and cut heavy slices and pile them on a plate, not letting himself realise that there were too many, till Mrs. Nicholas said so. When he cut well he became conscious of himself as if he was demonstrating grip and stance to a class of carvers.

"Just like the school," he said, "to put David on a train which arrives in the middle of lunch."

"How much cabbage?" said Mrs. Nicholas.

Mr. Nicholas did not hear, and Peter wondered which opinion he was leading to.

He said, "Who's going to help with the court this afternoon?" looking round expectantly.

"I'm quite willing," said Mrs. Nicholas. Her self-sacrifice was usually not noticed but if it became excessive they told her it was silly. When his father said, "My dear, you have lots to do," Peter was startled because it was almost what he had been going to say, and wondered if he would have sounded as careless.

"I'm asking the boys." His father worked a piece of gristle from his mouth to his fingers.

Peter said, "I'll help," trying to sound neither enthusiastic nor reluctant. He wanted to behave correctly to make his position tidy. Presently he was going to say one thing to his father and he wanted to give no other offence.

"What about Owen?"

"I might."

"Are you going to play?"

"I don't suppose so, I might."

"But I thought we'd asked your pal Brian."

"Yes. He has lessons."

"Anyway I think you might give us a hand, old chap."

Occasionally Owen tidied a room or collected logs, if it was to be obviously his own achievement, but if he was made to help mow the lawn he took a long time with the cuttings box while his father waited to go on, and emptied it in an unusual place, and handed it back the wrong way round, and if his father told him to pull plantains he pulled about three in half an hour leaving the roots. Sometimes his father sent him to bed and then he made it clear that he had been hoping for that.

Because Owen did not like tennis he did not play and Peter wished that he also could refuse for he did not expect to enjoy it, but it was difficult to associate the cheerful laughter which came across the garden from the court and convinced him he was missing something with the tennis parties he played in; and anyway the next might be different.

Owen was not underhand. Peter could imagine his father saying, "Owen can at least look you in the face. Peter is shifty-eyed." And he realised that although he was ridiculing his father's phrase he was adopting his prejudice.

Owen did not answer, and his mother, noticing the tension said, "Jolly good dinner, though I say it myself," and they remembered to congratulate her.

For a moment no one spoke. Peter was surprised at the silence and thought it was because his father was busy with his meat. The edge of his plate was piled with chewed lumps impregnated with cabbage. It was only in such rare silences that Peter realised how little conversational effort anyone else made. Sometimes he tried to think of something to say, discarding ideas as he realised where they would lead, but now he didn't try. He was waiting to talk about one thing but he would not start it.

Owen said, "By the way, there's dry rot in my bedroom." Owen often discovered dry rot in the house. It gave him a sense of power to announce it and watch what happened. But he looked for it anxiously.

His mother said, "Is there really?"

His father stared at him with alarm and impatience.

Owen said, "Yes really," as if he might mean it.

Peter said, "One of the legs of my bed is rotten." He wanted to end the conversation by making it a joke, for he began to be afraid no one would mention the wood, but he wished he had not made it so obvious.

"As a matter of fact," his father said, "the whole roof is falling down. I saw seven chimney pots come off this morning."

"Not our roof?" said his mother.

Peter said, "Yes our roof."

"No, my dear, it's a funny joke." He wasn't sarcastic, he was explaining. Peter cut hard at a piece of meat, the knife slipped and his plate moved off his table-mat knocking over his glass. The water ran quickly across the table. His father shouted, "Look out my dear," and stood up pushing back his chair so that it howled on the linoleum. His mother lifted her plate hitting the cabbage dish. Owen beat on the table with his spoon and sang, "La, la, la."

"Stop that noise. Can't you help and get a cloth. No, no, not your table napkin."

"All right, I'll go." His mother fetched a swab and mopped the table and floor.

When they were eating again Mr. Nicholas said, "Seriously Owen, is there dry rot in your room?"

"Yes, seriously."

"And the leg of my bed. . . ."

Peter was glad to hear the door open before he finished and David came in.

"Hallo," David said. Peter had forgotten how much insincere cheerfulness he put into that word. Though he was only sixteen, and a year younger than Owen, he was as tall and larger. He came towards the table smiling, and Peter looked away and tried not to hear him kiss his mother.

"Hallo, old boy."

"Hallo, Dad."

"Have you had a good term."

"Yes, thank you."

"Take lots of wickets?"

"Quite a few."

"Make any centuries?"

"Eighty-six was my top score."

"Did you hear about my cricket match? For the local team? They asked me to play for them. I said to the captain 'I haven't held a bat for five years; go on, put me in number eight or nine.' The other side had a fast bowler, the sort of pace these local lads don't like. They started to walk away to leg. The score was one for one, two for one, three for two. There were seven wickets down for seven runs. So I said to myself, either I shall be out first ball or I shall hit a boundary. I knew that the important thing was to knock this fast fellow off his length." He paused. "The eighth wicket fell at fifty-three. What was it I got, my dear? Four fours and five sixes?"

David said, "Huh," with enthusiasm.

Though his father was glad to see him and meant to be friendly he could not help being a bore. At least Peter assumed that David was bored; perhaps he wasn't. The mistake he made was to assume that David had feelings like his own, but it was difficult not to because David did not provide alternatives.

His mother was putting vegetables on his plate. "We've got a tennis party tomorrow," she said.

"And a rolling party this afternoon," said Owen. He said it looking down and his father said, "What? What's that?"

"Perhaps on his first day. . . ." his mother said.

"Actually," said David, "I thought the court looked in jolly good shape." He put his mouth close to his plate to fill it easily and hide his confusion after speaking.

Peter said, "It won't be soon."

He was aware of his father's head thrust forward and black against the window, its adam's apple outstanding, and the large shape of his mother's shoulders. Over the garden the sun came through the mist and lightened the heather and birch leaves but made the room seem darker. The grandfather clock made a small noise in the hall.

David said, "Why?"

"We're going to cut down the wood."

"Oh Peter," said Mrs. Nicholas.

"Aren't we?"

"What, the chestnut trees?" David said.

His father said, "We've been thinking about it."

"It won't be so easy to see the ball," David said.

Mrs. Nicholas said, "Must we start this again?"

"No, my dear, we'll talk about it later. Nothing's been decided yet."

Mrs. Nicholas gave David another helping and presently fetched the coffee. The sun on the garden became brighter as if a final film of mist had disappeared.

"As a matter of fact," Mr. Nicholas said, "the background is something we hadn't thought about."

\* \* \*

Mr. Nicholas, like the other tennis hosts of the district, wore white trousers and shoes and a white shirt for the game. A principal row last summer had been about whitening tennis shoes and Mr. Nicholas had strongly defended the practice. But he gave the impression that he was patronising, not submitting to convention. The others seemed to become smaller, less personal when they dressed to play, like priests performing worship. Perhaps Mr. Nicholas did not seem impersonal because he also wore a canary yellow cricket cap, the badge of his school house Old Boys' team.

He locked his bedroom door, and ran downstairs across

the hall into the drawing-room where Mrs. Nicholas was at her desk and Peter reading a newspaper.

"Anyone arrived? Where's David?"

He went across the lawn into the sunlight near the court and began to teach David strokes, demonstrating each slowly and often, so that Peter, watching through the French windows was aware after the second time that duty, not interest, was making David attend. In the distance, without words, it was less embarrassing than ridiculous, a little ape-like. He was very keen to make David a tennis player.

Peter said, "Who's coming?"

"Brian."

"Is he?"

"We thought it would give the boy a chance. People never invite him now they know."

"I should have thought everyone stole a few books. It's easy to do by mistake."

His mother thought he was criticising her and went on, "We thought it was bad for him not seeing—you know—decent people. He'll start finding his own friends." She was quoting. "Also it may tempt Owen to play tennis." She smiled as if a little regretting the device.

Peter said, "It hasn't," but he didn't want to argue and went on quickly, "Who else?"

"Captain Cambridge."

"Oh no."

"Well he almost asked himself."

"Yes."

"He's not such a bad little man. I've had several talks with him lately and he really seems to care about—you know—the things that matter." His mother changed to the embarrassed voice in which she spoke about God.

Peter didn't answer, agreeing to avoid the subject.

Something moved on the edge of the lawn and he looked up and saw Captain Cambridge. He had apparently come up the hillside through the rhododendrons for a piece of creeper was drooping from his green felt hat. Thinking that he had not been seen he was rearranging it over one eye. He reset his ruffled silk scarf, and smoothed his coat which he was wearing with white flannel trousers like a schoolboy without a blazer. The rounded lumps of his face seemed as if they had once grown hair but gone bald.

He came towards the house and when he saw Peter said, "I say, old fellow, your bloody path—excuse me, my dear lady. I was just about to tell your son that I'd had some difficulty in detecting a track up your herbaceous mountain."

His father came across the lawn. "Hallo Humphrey," he said, and they shook hands. "Come on now, Peter, we can make a men's four."

They walked towards the court, Captain Cambridge who had short legs hurrying to keep up. He remembered his creeper, tried to draw attention to it, but Mr. Nicholas was thinking about partners, and when no one was watching he took it off and dropped it.

They played a set, and then another with the daughter of a local fruit canner, an enterprising grocer whom Mr. Nicholas considered financing. Soon Brian, and two not quite middle-aged ladies arrived, and then two other local daughters. They were not particularly ugly but it was difficult to think of them apart from their parents. Sarah had the Admiral's eyebrows and Doreen her mother's strong jaw. It never occurred to Peter that they might be attractive. Anyway they were daughters of his father's friends and so he supposed accepted his father's opinion of him, for he never imagined that they might also not believe their parents.

They sat in a half circle on canvas chairs near the edge of the grass and watched.

"Have you played much this year?"

"No, hardly at all."

38

When Mr. Nicholas was not performing they listened to him watching.

"Well played, David," he said, and to them, "That was a fine shot."

Captain Cambridge said, "Yes, damned fine." He sat beside Mr. Nicholas in a lower chair.

"Well up," said Mr. Nicholas. "David is pretty good at those."

Mr. Nicholas had a way of taking sides so that he called the score loudly when his side won a point but otherwise did not mention it. If his side played well he said, "Good shot," and if the other was successful he said, "Bad luck." And what he said at one end of the court could be heard at the other. Sometimes Peter, when playing against him began to try to win to annoy him, but long before he succeeded he realised that this was Mr. Nicholas' real success; for Peter knew that if he tried and lost he would be annoyed himself. Mr. Nicholas, in the sets in which he was not playing, took David's side.

"Your boy's got quite an idea how to volley," said Captain Cambridge. He had taken off his coat but wore his silk scarf and his hat for shade.

"That was a foot fault," said Mr. Nicholas.

Brian wore a green plastic sunshield and served with a professional follow up so that it was difficult to tell when his feet crossed the line.

"I believe you were right," said Captain Cambridge. "I was thinking that what David probably needs is to watch some first-class play."

"I learned by practising against a wall," said Mr. Nicholas.

There was a pause while they watched.

"You're dead right, about the importance of practice. I remember Fenton telling me. . . ."

"Foot fault," said Mr. Nicholas.

"You'll put him off," said Owen. He sat on a box, his

Aertex shirt and corduroy trousers looking dirty against so much white.

Peter said, "Was it?"

"My dear boy, I can see, I'm sitting opposite the line."

"Talking of foot faults," said Captain Cambridge, "Did you ever know Admiral Fenton. Good fellow. Well I remember him . . ."

"*That* certainly was," said Mr. Nicholas.

"Brian always does that," said Owen.

"It's time he was told if he always does it."

Peter walked away quickly. As he went he heard his father say, "That sort of thing spoils the game for everyone else."

He walked round the court, through the bushes on the far side, to a small patch of heather. From here he could see over General Binforth's wood, over the Lt. Commander's roof and the Baptist chapel, across the valley and the tops of fir trees and many other medium sized houses, to the heather covered opposite slope. There the tanks practised, moving like camouflaged beetles, and their engines came across the valley, a continuous, faint hum. After a time they went up the slope, showed like tiny models for a moment on the skyline, and disappeared. Three minutes later came the explosions. Sometimes they seemed soft so that you mistook them for wind, sometimes heavier, and six months ago they had begun to rattle the windows of the house. When the range was opened there had been three local petitions and a letter in *The Times* about a tumulus. Peter watched for the mortar bombs in the air, which he had seen on clear days, but the dust was already rising. The explosions were heavy and exciting so that he wanted more.

Owen was going through the bushes towards the house and Peter called, "Look at this," so that he would come and talk.

"Have you noticed how much more dust there is?"

"Yes." Peter believed him, recognising his own device of telling the truth because it put you in a stronger position.

Peter said, "What happened?"

"He stopped the game and warned Brian. He did it very tactfully. 'I say Brian old chap, I'm not sure that you quite realise what you're doing.' Anyway Brian won't come again."

They watched the dust cloud rising above two trees on the horizon.

Owen said, "Bloody funny about the wood."

"I suppose it was."

"He won't cut it now."

Peter agreed, and began to laugh, realising the joke. "What a wonderful reason: to see the ball better. And it was David's idea."

"That wasn't what worried David."

"Wasn't it?"

"Well a little perhaps, but more the conker trees."

"But there aren't any." Peter was annoyed that he had not realised.

"One row along the top."

"But they don't have conkers."

"They will."

"Surely he grew out of that years ago?" Peter remembered David going on his bicycle at six in the morning to find conkers which had fallen in the night before the village boys, and his mother praising them, and David ripening half-white ones on his window-sill, and several thousand in a wholesale cereal box which had stuck together with green mould.

"Does he still collect them?"

"No, but he still likes them." It was only Owen's guess but Peter believed it. He was prepared to accept what he was told about David, feeling that he had no instinctive understanding.

Presently Owen went away. As Peter went back on to the tennis court the explosions came again and Mr. Nicholas, sitting on a step ladder opposite the net called, "Love forty, damn those guns," and one of the ladies tittered. He umpired with obvious fairness.

After tea Mr. Nicholas played several sets and it was possible to see that he had once been athletic though he now bent at the bottom rather than the knees and left the impression of large hands reaching too far. He came off the court smiling and lifting his canary cap.

"Not bad for an old man. Go on, my dear, you make up a set now. Come on, Humphrey, we'll get some drinks."

When they came back Peter, on the court, could hear him saying, "This fellow from Sheffield ... to give the workers' angle. Well I got up and said.... At a proper meeting...."

"I agree with you," said Captain Cambridge.

"The Conservative party round here will never be any good with its present chairman."

"Now there you're right. Did you hear about him and the election allowance? Let me tell you that one. Mark you, there's no proof, I should be the first to admit it. But there is a hint, a possibility, I might almost say a suggestion...." Captain Cambridge began to take deep breaths and settle to his platform manner.

When Peter came back to the same end Captain Cambridge was teaching David strokes. "What you want, young fellow, is to watch some first class play."

Mr. Nicholas was standing above the ladies with his back to the court. "The trouble is that no one will be bothered to give a lead. It's all too easy: twenty thousand majorities every time. It would do the old fools good if they got a Socialist member...."

"Cider? Sherry? That's what I'm having...."

"You see, I've been thinking a good deal about this. It's no use us imagining that Lord this and Lady that will pay up indefinitely. In some way we've got to attract the working classes."

The ladies listened.

"If I could find enough keen people I should certainly do

something. It would be well worth while. Cider? Sherry? Is this a serious proposition? We'll ask Major Dale."

The set ended and Peter was able to watch Major Dale's approach. At most hours after midday there was a suggestion of a totter about Major Dale's walk, but it was under control. He came slowly, and it seemed that even if he fell down sideways he would give a quick wink and go on looking ahead with no embarrassment. Anyway he was short and would not have far to fall. He had not been a proper Major but an engineer or something.

"Major Dale, don't you think that it's time someone put a stick of dynamite under the arses of the local Conservative Party?"

"Sir, I couldn't agree with you more." Major Dale grinned quickly at the ladies.

"Now if I did something would you help? Something which would interest the working fellows round here; that's the important point."

"Peter," said Major Dale, "while I take note of your father's political wisdom, would you mind easing that decanter from his grasp and putting just a few drops in a glass for I have a tickle?"

"What do you want? Sherry? Gin? Now, old fellow, we're asking your opinion."

"Well the working classes aren't quite my line, but . . ." pausing for laughter. Major Dale had a way of answering Mr. Nicholas very seriously so that he made him seem a joke, but surprisingly Mr. Nicholas did not mind.

"Come on, Major, you know what I mean."

"Oh, I know what you mean; that's one thing I say for your father, it's always clear what he means." Peter chuckled. "No, I'm serious. In this age of mass education, adult education, sex education—but, sir, as you were saying, there's nothing like the working classes; I mean they—they—well they work and. . . ."

43

Peter walked away to let down the net and hide his giggles; not that the Major was very funny, but because he knew that he should not laugh the desire became uncontrollable. He supposed that his father tolerated Major Dale's innuendo because he missed much of it since he was attending to his own next remark; also because it was not unkind.

He walked on slowly till he came into the light of the sun which was beginning to throw the shadow of the wood across the court. The small white cumulus clouds, made in the hot afternoon, had ceased to move, receded, grown thinner, and become tinged with orange. The grass was almost damp. To his left he suddenly saw, between two bushes, David and Captain Cambridge on the lawn. They seemed to be looking at the roof of the house. David was shielding his eyes with his hand and Captain Cambridge pointing with his arm bent. The bottom of the bushes hid their feet and they stood still so that they seemed like a picture, and Peter had an impression that he should not be watching. In the wood's shadow the group at the drink table was not easy to distinguish and their voices less insistent but the clink of the decanter stopper was distinct. He heard his father say, "Come on, Major, you're just the man we want," but it was faint and inoffensive without the familiar gestures. The Major's reply was lost and there was laughter but Peter felt no desire to be there. It seemed that despite their noise they were not moving, and he wanted to go quietly off the court, away from the house, leaving them there in the evening.

# Chapter Three

MR. NICHOLAS usually had breakfast in bed, brought to him on a tray by Mrs. Nicholas, but sometimes for a week or even a month he came down to it in his dressing-gown, and on the fine days after the tennis party he began to do this. It was as if twelve hours a day in other people's company had become too little for what he had to say. Not that he always talked at family breakfasts and perhaps this was why he gave them up, finding that they depressed even him. He ate porridge in loud, wet spoonfuls and read the *Daily Telegraph*. But his reading was not restful because they were aware that he was hunting for material to quote or contradict. Soon after he had asked for his second cup of coffee he seemed to be able to contain no more, folded the paper untidily, passed it to someone else not noticing who, and began to express himself. It seemed, however, on these days, that the paper did not satisfy him, and he gave it away during the toast and marmalade and talked about the Club.

"My dear, I've got Major Dale to be our secretary. He only needed a little persuasion. The Major will do anything for me. The truth is he was afraid that Mrs. Major wouldn't allow it. Pass the sugar, old boy.

"We've got an open meeting at the end of the week when I shall give them the idea. Peter will you come and lend a hand?"

Peter said he would, realising that he was still flattered to be asked to help his father.

"My dear, I said we'd cope with the teas, is that all right?"

Peter said, "Are you having afternoon classes?"

"No, old boy, we're having a cricket side."

"Isn't there a local team?"

"In the league, yes, but lots of these local chaps won't play for it. As soon as you introduce cups and competitions you spoil the game. They don't want to take it so seriously. Besides, the fellow who runs the Beckford team is a bounder and they've no use for him."

"Who will you play, the local Labour Party?"

"I don't suppose they could raise a team. No, there are twenty other sides within five miles."

Peter suspected that there weren't but he didn't know. He suspected that his father didn't know. Sometimes he remembered one of his father's statements and checked it and told him the correct answer but his father said the book was wrong or listened and changed the subject having honestly forgotten what he had said. Peter drank his coffee, gazing out of the window at the bright morning sun on the trees.

"My dear, we're going to call ourselves the 'Defend Britain Club.' Major Dale suggested the 'Blue Blades,' but he entirely agrees that this is better. We want to be very careful. It's extraordinary the strength of the unions even in a place like this, and some of these paid agitators would seize on that sort of name to put the idea into their heads that it was just a trap."

Peter walked through the veranda on to the lawn. The sun was already hot and though the white smoke of the boiler chimney went in a thin line to the west there was no wind near the house. He heard his father's slippers on the tiles of the hall and he came into the veranda, carrying his coffee.

"This is what your grandfather used to do: always carried his coffee away from the breakfast table. Then he wasn't wasting time. Your grandfather was a very busy man."

Peter didn't answer. He wanted to stand in the sun and let it warm him. It would have needed such a small effort to have looked at his father when he first spoke but now it seemed impossible. He moved one foot slowly in front of the other, watching the shadow of his slipper on the daisies.

46

His father said, "You see, for people like myself it's no joke seeing the mistakes that were made last time being made again. Most of my best friends were killed in the first war."

Peter swung his foot so that he turned away and then half turned back to avoid rudeness. He didn't want to pity his father's loneliness. Perhaps he might have done if he had been allowed to discover it for himself. But anyway he did not believe in it. His father demanded appreciation and would always find people to give him that. But Peter realised uneasily that his father's loneliness, though it was loneliness for flattery not friendship, might be as unpleasant as his own. And that his own was only different because he wanted the less direct flattery of knowing people whom he admired.

His father said, "It's no good thinking that if you treat people kindly they won't hurt you. That's all wishy-washy idealism. That was the mistake that fool Wilson made. If there's one man to blame for our present troubles . . ."

Peter had heard it before. There was no sense of discovery in his father's conversation. Sometimes with great effort and tact he managed to agree sincerely with him about some obscure political question but at the next argument his father started again with his old convictions. "By the time you're my age, old boy, you've made up your mind about most things that matter." It was true; the same sequence of ideas came out. If you disagreed with them you could not change them. If you agreed there was nothing to do but say yes. It was not conversation but applauded monologue.

His father began to ease to his subject. The long "er"s in the back of his throat with which he kept continuity while searching for a word became more frequent. The sentences expanded and as he made one point he was preparing others. It was good, till he became aware of it and consciously added subordinate clauses.

Peter said, "Mother's calling," and went quickly away. His hurry was impolite and he should have gone back to hear

47

the rest, but he locked himself in the downstairs lavatory.

Presently the upstairs door slammed, the seat fell, and the pan began to echo. Peter knew from other occasions that his father was being heard in other rooms of the house. The explosions, rising through various climaxes, lasted about ten seconds. Then there were sounds of completion and would presumably be silence for twenty-four hours. It was disturbing and Peter came out and went quickly upstairs.

The bathroom door was opening but he hurried past, up the second flight to his bedroom. He heard his father's steps on the stairs and sat on his bed, studying a postcard reproduction, but it was too small, and his books were out of reach, so he dropped it and lay down and stood up, fiddling on the mantelpiece. When he listened again the steps had ceased, they must have been going down.

There was a prepared canvas on the dressing-table and he picked at a piece of fluff but it was stuck and his fingers made a smudge and he started to pick again but turned his back. The sun shone into the room making it hot and yellow and he drew the curtains but that was depressing so he drew one back; then the light fell on the washstand and his unfinished painting so he half drew it again. The wooden rings ran with difficulty on a wooden rod and he had to lean across his table and jerk and lean back before he overbalanced. His slippers slid on the linoleum and his stomach fell against the table edge. He stood still wanting to shout to relieve the pain.

Presently it was better and he thought he heard a noise and listened. Perhaps his father had been standing all the time a few paces from his door. He went softly on his toes and opened it suddenly but the upper landing was empty and silent except for the faint sound of a pan moving in the kitchen so he went back and sat on his bed.

He was trying not to see his painting, and made himself look at it, and was depressed by its olive green. It was impossible to work by the light in his room. A bad workman

48

blames his tools—but that was as silly as the rest of his mother's proverbs. No artist used a south light. Then he remembered that he had put on the green in the evening when there was no sunlight in his room.

But he was not prepared to blame himself. The atmosphere of the house was impossible. His father, by not listening when other people spoke or noticing when they were silent, produced the same insensitiveness in them. They did not talk too much because they had no chance, but they ceased to notice what other people were thinking. Everything was explained in good plain language, several times. Not that his father openly advocated good plain painting—and if he had it would have produced the opposite—but Peter ceased to trust subtlety because he ceased to expect that there were people who would notice.

Perhaps his painting would seem better from further away. He propped it against the wall but it slipped on to its back and he hunted for his hammer to hang it. It wasn't in his tool drawer. He looked under the papers on his table and in his cupboard. When he found himself tipping up his boots for the second time he stopped, and remembered that he had not seen it these holidays. Someone had taken it.

The air on the stairs was hot and smelt of dust for Mrs. Jenning had been brushing them, and he held his breath. If only people would leave his things alone. He wouldn't mind if they put them back. He checked himself, hearing his father use the phrase, but his mother was turning up her smile to him as she bent over pastry decorations.

"Do you know who's taken my hammer?"

He was aware that only at home was he conscious of rights and possessions. Everywhere else making a good impression was more important.

"I'm afraid I don't." She was friendly and concerned. If only she would take offence, that would stop him, make him self-conscious. Surely she must have heard the ill temper and accusation in his tone. If only she would put her own valuation on the loss of a hammer instead of taking his. Just occasionally she was peevish whatever he said, but usually however rude he was she replied with after-church good temper. Peter went away before he should say any more, upstairs to his bedroom, and found the hammer on his bookshelf where he remembered putting it.

He knocked in a nail and hung the picture but it was too high, and put it lower but that was worse so he put it back in the first place but the plaster crumbled and the picture fell into the grate scratching its surface on the scuttle. He hit it several times with the hammer, and shut the door so that no one should hear and held the frame on edge and hit it, splitting the joints. Then he lay on his bed.

Presently he got his drawing board and, lying with it against his knees, his back against the head of his bed, began to draw with a soft pencil. He rested his hand on the paper because it was shaking and drew a long line which might be the top of his father's hair. He drew the side whiskers and the chin, and the disproportionate adam's apple. The rest was not so good for he was trying too hard, but adequate; his talent for caricature had led him to painting. He was particularly pleased with the look of business-like impatience. He added a tiny body with clumsy hands standing on top of his mother who lay on her face and was meant to be smiling tolerantly; but that was cheap and he shaded her into the battlements of a castle.

When he went downstairs into the drawing-room David was sitting in an arm-chair uncomfortably, his tummy forward, as if there was a cushion in the small of his back. The wireless was on low but he did not seem to be listening. Peter went through the French windows on to the lawn and walked slowly in the sun, and lay on the grass. Mr. Nicholas was out and Owen at school so the garden was empty. There was no wind and the blue sky was cloudless, and soon he was warm and moved into the shade. It was lunch-time before he became restless.

Peter carved the cold meat, and his father came back before he had finished and stood close to him waiting to be given the knife and fork.

"Right, shall I come, old boy?"

Presently he said, "Well, what has everyone been doing this fine summer morning?" and no one answered.

"David, what have you been doing?"

"Nothing in particular. I had a look at the court."

Peter waited for his turn, but his father said, "Now Peter, will you be available to play for us on Saturday fortnight?"

★   ★   ★

After lunch Peter walked on the lawn. The sky had become evenly covered with grey clouds, and every few minutes there was a small cold wind. Presently he sat in the drawing-room reading a paper. Owen was at school and his mother had gone to a diocesan conference, taking David with her to visit a stamp shop in the county town, and the house was silent except for his father's slippers moving occasionally upstairs. After a time they went across the passage, the door of his room shut, and Peter imagined him getting on to his bed, covering himself with his eiderdown, and reading. His father had a strong hibernating instinct. Peter went into the work room and began to clear a corner.

He took the deck-tennis off the bench, swept shavings on to the floor, and moved Owen's model ships carefully across the room; three identical destroyers side by side on a square of cardboard. He put the dart board in another corner and cleaned a space against the wall for a canvas. His father's slippers were moving again upstairs. He found a sheet of glass, wiped it, and laid it ready on the bench for a palette. He heard his father's steps on the stairs and stood still, preparing to defend what he was doing.

"Is that you, David?"

"No, it's me."

He came to the work room door. He was wearing his red dressing-gown and held it together with one hand near his neck.

"Peter, can you come a minute?"

It was without the usual threat, and Peter said, "Yes," and gave the glass an unnecessary wipe.

His father said, "Up here," going to the stairs and Peter followed. His dressing-gown brushed the banisters and the wind made a noise in the half open window on the landing but otherwise the house was silent and Peter was conscious that they were alone in it. He suddenly realised the enormous cheerful effort his mother made so that no one else had to try. When she was away there seemed no restraint or end to his quarrel with his father and he wanted to make one. Quarrelling alone seemed absurd and a little frightening. On the top landing they stopped and his father said, "Now, can you hear anything?"

He seemed to wait anxiously for the answer. Peter listened but there was silence, and listened again expecting small continuous noises to become audible but there was still silence, and then the wind in the trees.

"No, I'm afraid not. What sort of noise?"

"Come over here. A curious hum."

"Can you still hear it?"

His father said, "Try over here." He was not listening, as if his own ears were out of order.

Presently Peter heard something, a higher note than he expected, and said, "Sh," and listened, but it had stopped. His father bent and pulled open the top drawer of the chest on the landing.

"Was that where you heard it?"

He began to take out its contents in untidy handfuls, piling them on the top and floor. There were lantern slides spilling from a cardboard box, electrical plugs and sockets, rolled pictorial maps, bundles of receipts, and a lot of tow. At the bottom were .22 bullets, collar studs, tiddly winks, and grey dust. Peter noticed that his father's hands were shaking, and helped him pile it back.

His father pulled out the second drawer.

"Terrible rubbish," he said and began to take it out, but stopped as soon as he could see the bottom, and piled it back. They packed carelessly and the drawer jammed so they pushed on top until something cracked at the bottom that made it fit.

The bottom drawer contained receipts, and letters in bundle tied with coloured ribbons.

His father said, "Terrible, terrible rubbish." He pushed on one side, and Peter helped him straighten the drawer and shut it.

"Did the noise you heard seem to come from there?"

His father said, "I think so," as if he didn't.

"I don't see what could be in there." Peter thought it might be behind but wasn't going to say so or his father might want to look. He had ceased to believe that there was a noise, and was anxious to work or it would be tea-time.

"Don't you bother, old boy."

"Well, call me if it starts again, but till then I don't see what we can do."

"No." Peter could sense his mind racing but could not keep track.

"We did look in the top drawer?"

"Yes; anyway, what could it be in a drawer?"

His father stood in the centre of the landing holding his dressing-gown shut with one hand, and Peter hesitated near the top step.

"Right you are, old boy." It was the normal phrase of dismissal, but his father was thinking of something else and not watching to see how it was obeyed.

Peter went down slowly and on the middle landing heard

53

his father start to follow. He went into the work room and continued clearing the bench. After a time he finished and went upstairs to collect his paints and brushes. His father's door was shut and he went past softly, imagining him under his eiderdown propped against the bed-head, reading an historical romance. As he came to the top landing there was a small noise and his father was bending over the bottom drawer of the chest.

The bundles of receipts had been pushed to one end and he was hunting at the other.

Peter said, "Have you found it?" trying not to seem surprised or critical.

His father said, "No." He said, "I'm looking for a picture," but he was too slow.

Peter went past him into his room, and collected his tubes and brushes. When he came out his father had left the drawer open and was going downstairs. Peter went after him and could see over his shoulder that he was tearing up a brown photograph. He put the halves carefully on top of each other with his clumsy fingers as if he was doing something delicate in gloves and tore them again, and carried the pieces into his room.

At four o'clock they had tea, which his mother had left laid, and ate some of her cakes. Afterwards his father went upstairs and Peter went back to the work room. A little later he heard her come home. As soon as she opened the back door she called, "Hallo," cheerfully. He had heard it so often, the same tone, the same place, the same squeak of the back door handle. She was always glad to get home and always anxious to share her pleasure. Her voice echoed and then there was silence. It seemed to Peter that the house had asserted itself while she was away and would not at once let her impose on it again. The rectangular cream rooms in the grey daylight had acquired unusual shade and atmosphere. Even she seemed to notice it, and didn't say to herself as she usually did,

"Answer came there none," but began to do things in the kitchen and larder and occasionally he heard a tin move. His father's bedroom door opened and he called, "Is that you, darling?" He came downstairs, and Peter heard them kiss in the scullery. When she asked him how he had got on he said something short which Peter could not hear.

*   *   *

An hour later the Pawthorns arrived, talking as they got out of their car, and his father took them to the billiard room, and Peter went too because he could not work and wanted a drink.

The billiard room was large and usually sunlit with a view over the lawn to the tennis court and the wood, but to-day it was dark and Mr. Nicholas drew the curtains and turned on the light. There were nineteenth century prints of Harrow, his grandfather's arm-chair, his grandfather's desk, and a three-quarter-size billiard table.

His father said, "Do you know my boy, Peter?" and Mrs. Pawthorn said, "Of course."

They shook hands, and she said, "Hallo," smiling at him as if they were too intimate for names. When she smiled hard there was something Chinese about her eyes.

"Why haven't you come for your driving lesson?"

"I seem to have had no time."

"Pawps, come and say hallo to Peter."

Mr. Pawthorn was short and wore rimless glasses. He was gazing across the room at the curtains, and started when she spoke, so that gin slopped out of his glass. He shook hands and said, "How do?"

They had also brought Mrs. Morton who sat in the arm chair with her head back and her white arms laid out. When Peter said, "How do you do?" she lifted one, dangling a hand at him, and said, "Charmed," so that he thought she was making fun of his politeness.

"We found Mrs. Morton walking along the white line on the main road," said Mrs. Pawthorn," and just as we drove by she sat down so we picked her up." Mr. Pawthorn chuckled violently and stopped suddenly as if he wondered whether he should. "I expect she was looking for Squadron Leader Morton."

"Stuff," said Mrs. Morton from the chair with her eyes shut.

Mr. Nicholas moved about preparing the balls on the table. "Now then, how shall we play? What about Mr. Pawthorn and Mrs. Morton?"

"Well thanks awfully," said Mrs. Morton, "but do you mind frightfully if I miss this one? I've sprained a finger."

Mrs. Pawthorn giggled, and Mr. Pawthorn giggled, checking himself again, and Mr. Nicholas said, "Come on then, Peter."

They played several games and in between they had gin with a little water. When offered a third glass Mr. and Mrs. Pawthorn said "No thanks," and Mr. Nicholas, said, "Oh, come on, one more," so they had one more and after that didn't refuse.

During the third game Major Dale arrived, and Mr. Nicholas poured him a gin. "What an inspiring sight," the Major said. "Four mature, sensible adults—mature, shall we say—spending their evening poking white and pink balls with sticks. Oh, they enjoy it, don't get me wrong, as the moving films say; I enjoy it, but it *is* curious when you think about it. Do you ever listen to the wireless, Peter? Nor do I, but my wife does. She has it on all day; she says it's something for the visitors to listen to. Have you met my wife, Peter? She's nice, you'd like her. She and I understand each other very well, very very well. Pretty shot, sir."

Major Dale had a way of putting his phrases in inverted commas and almost laughing at them so that if anyone else laughed they were laughing with and not at him.

"Your father's good at billiards, isn't he? He shapes nicely. I expect he practises before breakfast in his pyjamas. Do you wear pyjamas, Peter? So do I. My wife tells me all the best modern ladies wear them, so I wondered if I ought not to. Have you noticed how things go by opposites, Peter? All my brothers, and fathers and grandfathers and great-grandfathers were Admirals—well near enough, and they gave me sailor suits and a nurse who sang sea shanties, but I went into the army." He leaned against the window ledge, looking at Mrs. Morton who lay in the arm-chair with her eyes shut.

When the game ended they played several more including Major Dale, and he talked about billiards, and life, and the speed of light. "Have you ever thought," he said staring excitedly at Mrs. Pawthorn, "that the light from that little bulb could get to the moon and back while you're thinking of your shot." Mr. Pawthorn paused with irritation. He liked silence while he played. "Carefully sir," said Major Dale. "Higher, lower, too much. I'm afraid he'll miss. Have you ever thought of the odds against a cannon? All the rest of the table for the balls to roll in."

Mr. Pawthorn became pink, his skin showing through his white hair. "Shut up," he said, and looked up in astonishment at himself, and dropped his cue, and went on his knees to find it.

They heard a car on the drive. "My lady," said Major Dale. "I know her by her tyres."

"You mustn't go," said Mr. Nicholas. "I'll tell her to come up."

Peter moved the curtain and saw him appear on the drive. "Won't you stay and have a drink?" She stood on the running board gripping the wheel with one hand. She looked about forty. She was said to be a planter's daughter whom Major Dale married when in a Malayan rural district. She said, "I'm afraid we mustn't. It's after seven and our party began at six."

Major Dale had followed Mr. Nicholas downstairs and got in beside her, and they drove away.

When Mr. Nicholas came back he said, "By the way, you must all join our club."

"Is it licensed?"

"Be quiet, Pawps." Mrs. Pawthorn giggled and looked at Peter, and Peter giggled.

His father explained to them about the Defend Britain Club. "We're going to have talks and debates: try to get some of these local fellows to open their mouths a bit. And we've got a cricket team."

"Is Peter a member?"

"Yes, Peter'll play for us."

Mrs. Morton's glass fell off the arm of her chair and they all looked round but she didn't move.

"I'm afraid one of your guests is asleep."

"Nonsense," said Mrs. Morton, and got up suddenly. She came towards Mr. Nicholas with her head forward and whispered loudly, "Where can I find it?" Mr. Nicholas led her on to the landing.

"Peter's biff," said Mr. Pawthorn, and they finished the game. Presently Mr. Nicholas remembered Mrs. Morton, and went out and hit on the bathroom door and called, "Are you all right?" but there was no answer. Peter and the Pawthorns watched from the billiard room and when he came back bumped each other getting out of the doorway.

"She must be in there."

"How do you know?"

"The door's locked."

"You dirty old man!"

"Do you think we should call a doctor?"

"Your biff," said Mr. Pawthorn, and they played another game. After a time Mr. Nicholas said, "I wonder if we should call a doctor?"

"She may not be there."

"I shall look."

"Isn't your father a dirty old man?"

From the billiard room doorway they watched Mr. Nicholas hit on the bathroom door. "Are you there?" The door opened, Mrs. Morton put her head out, said, "Yes," and shut it.

In the middle of the next game she came back and put on her coat.

"Excuse me," she said, "it's Squadron-Leader Morton's birthday."

"Wait for us."

"Come on Mr. Nicholas, come on Peter."

Peter watched them getting into the Pawthorn's car, laughing and pushing. Mrs. Pawthorn drove, and she called, "Come on Peter, lots of room," but he said he had promised to go to a film. She let off the brake and they free-wheeled fast down the hill, brushing the rhododendron bushes, calling good-bye several times.

His mother was in the kitchen arranging sausage buns for frying. "Well," she said, "has that party of pleasure gone?" and his desire to talk and laugh about them evaporated as she used the familiar phrase, reminding him that she thought in familiar phrases.

★   ★   ★

Peter was in the drawing-room when his father came back at about eleven o'clock. His mother came to the doorway in her dressing-gown.

"Hallo. I'm afraid your supper's ruined." She was offended.

"All right dear, I'll have some cake."

"I'm off to bed."

His father said, "I've had an astonishing evening, Peter." He chuckled as he thought of it. "This peculiar R.A.F. man's wife."

"Mrs. Morton?"

59

"Yes, well she stands a lot without a sign, but to-night she overdid it. First we went to Pussy Pawthorn's and had port, then to the Hop Pole, and had beer and whiskey, and ended at the local on brandy. By then she was well away, making all sorts of suggestions to me—you know—pretty broad hints that she wanted me to - er - well, go the whole hog." He grinned.

"It's bad," he said, "that sort of thing. We always use the public bar, and it. does a lot of harm when the local working fellows see people of our class behaving like that."

"What happened?"

"Eventually old Pawthorn and I managed to get her into their car and drive her home."

"Did you find Squadron Leader Morton?"

"No no, he's stationed in Yorkshire."

His mother came in carrying a plate with two slices of iced cake, and a cup of tea, and Peter went upstairs and put on his pyjamas. When he came down to the bathroom his mother was in the bath, and he began to clean his teeth at the basin. He would be finished before his father came in. The bathroom was narrow with mustard-coloured shiny paint on which the steam condensed and ran down to puddles on the linoleum.

His mother said, "This is altogether too pleasant to leave." She meant the hot bath, but her flirtations with indolence were unconvincing; it was obvious that she would not enjoy staying there. It was as if she was trying to convince him that she had human weaknesses.

His father came in and Peter pretended not to notice.

"Old boy, I have asked you not to use the basin."

Peter turned round and went on cleaning his teeth into the lavatory.

"How long will you be, my dear?"

His knees and shins were bare below his shirt-ends and his toes turned up.

"Coming now," she said, and got out.

Mr. Nicholas sat upright in the bath pouring hot water over his thin shoulders and neck with a large sponge and blowing through his mouth and nose.

"Poor old Major Dale," he said. "His wife keeps him properly in order." The implication that he was more successful with his own wife was obvious. "Did you see her carry him off this evening?"

"No."

"I said to her, 'Now come along Mrs. Dale, surely you've time for just one drink before you rush away,' but oh no, she wasn't going to wait." He soaped himself vigorously, making white froth under his arms. "She's a hard woman."

"Mm," said Mrs. Nicholas, sadly. She did not like censuring people, but she agreed.

# Chapter Four

THE SUN SHONE again, at first between large grey clouds which sometimes covered it, then among small white clouds which never completely hid it, then from blue sky. The days became hot and the nights airless, so that a light sheet caused sweating, and there was little dew. For two evenings the clouds formed layers of red and black with green below and pink above, but after that the sun set quickly in a bright orange glow. Instead of appearing gradually through morning mists it came over the horizon, a large red circle and gave heat almost at once. The grass ceased to grow and turned yellow, and the tops of small beech trees hung downwards. The green paint of Pine Knoll, which always seemed to flake quickly as if on the hill top it was nearer the sun, could be watched after lunch forming blisters.

The house was silent, for Mrs. Nicholas was at church, and Mr. Nicholas somewhere with the Sunday papers. Peter took Julia's letter with him, out of the drawing-room windows into the sun, across the lawn noticing its hardness, to the tennis court, but there was no convenient shade so he went through the bushes and sat on the heather with a view over the valley to the range. He left out the first sentence, remembering from yesterday that it had seemed hostile.

She had invited him to stay a month before, in the half light quadrangle, when the sun had not risen enough to show the paper napkins and overturned candle-jars on the herbaceous borders, and the figures in tail coats and long pink and white dresses were mysterious and unindividual till they came peering at you, while Abraham Sing's Rhythmic Boys were playing *God Save the King*. For several days he had expected a letter in each post; but gradually he had realised that an invitation at five a.m. to someone you had met since midnight was only a friendly gesture. He had looked for her address, but that was lost with his ticket. He might have been able to find out whose party she had been with, but by then term had ended.

At home he had listened each day for the letters falling on to the mat during breakfast and fetched them, but he had ceased to expect hers. Yesterday the post had come early and his mother had put his on his plate; though he never saw her do it he knew from things she said that she read postmarks. It was in a blue envelope with small upright writing. Sitting in the heather in the half shade of a pine he read her invitation again carefully.

He could not imagine her family, or house. Supposing he went in a suit and they wore corduroy and Aertex. Supposing he didn't take evening dress and she had arranged a dance. But his suitcase was small and creased his clothes; and all his white collars were dirty. And if he went when she suggested he would miss his father's cricket match. He could not think of words to excuse himself. He discovered that when he tried to remember her he could imagine her long red taffeta dress and her bare shoulders and arms but could not clearly see her face.

He told himself that adventure was to the adventurous; but this was hardly an adventure; surely he could find one better and less embarrassing. He was aware that he was reasoning away his difficulty, that if he could not make the effort for the small he would miss the big adventure; but perhaps he didn't want adventures; perhaps he enjoyed adventure stories because they were about things he didn't do, and they were all embarrassing and frightening to experience.

By this time of the holidays he was usually anxious to go away, but recently his father had been busy with the Club, or at the Pawthorns', or the Red Lion, and when he was at home he sat in a deck chair near the veranda. Peter went through the bushes to see if he was there now, but the lawn was empty, and the house, standing in the hot sun with the French windows open seemed deserted. Across the court the vapour inside the petrol-can expanded in the heat and it echoed as if it had been kicked. Little sounds came from the valley, someone a long way off was hitting a piece of tin, a voice was singing from a wireless, in the distance there were church bells. From the path by the edge of the wood a large white poodle and a dachshund came on to the court. Peter had never seen them before and stood in the shadow of a tree, where they passed a few yards away, trotting behind each other, and never saw him. They went over a corner of the lawn, on to the drive, and away down the private road, as if they knew where they were going.

Peter went back and sat against a pine trunk, and put his hand in his pocket for Julia's letter, but he heard music. Looking down the hill over General Binforth's wood and the Lt. Commander's roof he saw the Salvation Army on the patch of gravel outside the Baptist chapel. They were singing a hymn which he presently recognised as *Tell Me the Old, Old Story*. Perhaps the distance was distorting it. When it ended they stood in a circle each going in turn into the centre presumably to say a prayer. Then they were in a half-circle at the side of the chapel and one was apparently chalking on it. Another figure appeared near the chapel door not in uniform, and faintly up the hill over the wood came fragments of shouting. The man near the door bent and seemed to throw something and then walked away down the road, perhaps for the police. The Salvation Army stood in a circle, sang a quick verse of the same hymn, marched to the bus-stop, and were carried off to Rodenham in a green double-decker.

A twig snapped behind him and his father was coming through the bushes, parting them inaccurately with his hands, holding his head back so that they should not flick his eyes.

"Hallo, are you the only one at home? What are you up to?"

His father put his hands in his breeches pockets, and stood, unusually restful as he sometimes was in the hot sun.

Peter said, "Watching the Salvation Army." His father started to think, and he hurried on, "They came and played outside the Baptist chapel, and one of them wrote a slogan on the wall, and a Baptist came out and argued with them and went to fetch the police, but they escaped by bus."

"Mm." He was not listening and Peter knew he had been too slow.

"When I was at Dorchester in the war they used to make their filthy row outside our barracks." In a sentence his father could put him in sympathy with the other side. "One Sunday morning a mad Irish lieutenant we had threw a lot of squibs into the stable yard where the battery horses were being watered and opened the gate. They came rushing into the road and put paid to the Salvation Army. I've never seen men run so fast. Afterwards"—Peter waited for it—"we picked up two of their trumpets squashed so flat that you could have pushed them under a door."

Peter laughed; when he could not think of anything else to say he asked, "What happened to the Irishman?" and re-membered asking before.

"Oh, he was sent to another brigade and killed later. Of course there's no doubt the Salvation Army has achieved some remarkable cures." Even his tolerance was dogmatic and familiar. Now there was a story about a sale of work and the best pair of socks he had ever had, and Peter was aware of it going on. He tried to think how he might excuse himself from the cricket match, but anyway there was no oppor-tunity. Conversation with his father moved heavily over a subject till it was exhausted and then by some obvious con-nection to another. There was no precedent for an un-explained change. Peter said, "Mm" periodically. When the anecdote was finished he said, "By the way, have you got a pitch for Saturday week?"

"Yes."

He had not waited long enough. The subject was still the Salvation Army and his remark an interruption. From across the lawn he heard Owen call "Telephone" from his window.

"Telephone," he said.

"What, can you hear it?"

"No, Owen called."

His father pushed through the bushes and ran across the lawn, consciously on his toes, holding down his money in his breeches pockets which flapped and jingled.

\*    \*    \*

After lunch Peter went to Owen's room to see his model. It was made of purple plasticine with dirty orange streaks, the result of mixing all the colours from several boxes, and set on a tea chest top. There were keys and jetties, coaches and engines, cranes, warehouses, and granaries. Cotton wool smoke came from factory chimneys, and the trucks were tightly filled with plasticine cows, sheep, horses and pigs. He had made the rails of match sticks divided into quarter thicknesses, and the wires of the cranes of thread. Tied up alongside the jetties were his three wooden destroyers.

"I like it."

Owen explained the details of the cranes and a grain elevator.

"What are you going to do with it?"

"Bomb it."

"What a shame."

"That's what it was made for."

"And the ships?"

"No I'll keep them at present."

Owen explained the biological differences of the animals extracting one of each with a pin to show him.

66

"I think it's good, I really do."

"I don't suppose father will."

"Why not?"

"He hates plasticine. Nasty messy stuff."

They looked at it again, and then went to find David.

"He's probably writing his diary."

"Is that what he does?"

"A lot of the time."

But his room was empty and they heard a tennis ball being hit in the garden and went downstairs, through the drawing-room, across the lawn. There were a few small white clouds in the sky, but not near the sun and there was no wind.

"He's probably playing against father."

"Or himself."

They came up the grass rise to the court and saw that David was alone, and looked at each other. They walked along the side and sat together opposite the net. When David said, "Hallo," they each waited for the other to answer till it was too late. David went on throwing up an imaginary ball with his left hand, pretending to serve. There was no resistance to his stroke so each time he overbalanced, and Peter and Owen looked at each other and giggled.

David said, "Did you speak?" not turning his head. He began to pick up balls and serve them hard. When the first three went into the net Peter and Owen giggled. He hit the next harder, and it struck the wire at the end of the court a foot from the top and Peter and Owen rolled on the grass, unable to stop their laughter.

They thought that David was going to fetch it, but he walked off the court leaving the balls. "It's all very well for you," he said, not looking round, and they could hear that he was crying.

They were surprised and told each other that they had not meant to be unkind. Peter began to walk back to the house,

He wished that Owen would not come too, for it seemed like a conspiracy.

David was in the drawing-room in an arm-chair looking at a paper, and Peter was relieved that his mother and father had not seen him. Then his mother was in another arm-chair, looking at them over her paper with pained inquiry. They went through the drawing-room together without speaking, and Peter was aware that David felt that they were still in conspiracy. In the hall he said loudly, "Well, I'm going to paint in the work room." It was much too obvious.

Owen said, "Will it disturb you if I work there too?"

"Never mind, I'll go upstairs."

"But didn't you want the work room?"

"It doesn't matter."

"You have it because you thought of it."

"No, really, I prefer my room." Peter ran upstairs; now he had offended Owen. It was rare that either of them gave way, but if one did he had the advantage, and could be justly offended if the other was not friendly. After that instead of a competition in consideration they began a competition in success. As he came to the top landing Peter was aware of a shadow moving in his doorway against the brightness inside, and saw it was his father.

He was holding the handle as if he had just opened the door, and did not hear Peter till he was close.

"Ah. Now then, Peter, we've got a problem."

Peter went past him into his room. The drawing board was on the dresser with the sketch of his father still pinned to it. He had thought that it might be flat, but it was supported by books and faced the doorway. He stood in front of his father and said, "Have you? What?"

"David can't play for us. Captain Cambridge is taking him to Wimbledon."

"Is he? What for?"

"To coach him at tennis. Nonsense, I think, but it's a kind act. Anyway, it leaves us one man short."

"Mm." Peter picked up a book and moved towards the door.

"Now, I've been thinking about our cousin Richard Nicholas."

"But he lives miles away."

"That's not the point. Is he any good?"

Peter could remember little about Richard except feeling ashamed when he was put in a rain-butt and cried. He had always explained him as a second cousin a few times removed. He found it impossible to remember him in connection with cricket.

"Quite good, I think."

"You should know; you were at school with him."

"He was younger than me and in another house."

"But can he play?"

"Yes, he can play. I'm sure he can play."

"He apparently spends his holidays at Lord's."

"Then I expect he's good."

"But you don't know?"

"No, I don't know. I can't remember. His breath smelt."

"That doesn't mean he can't play cricket. He probably needed a dose."

"As a matter of fact," Peter said, "I may not be able to play." He went on quickly, "I've been asked to stay."

"By an Oxford pal?"

"Yes."

"Have you accepted?"

"No, but . . ."

"Can't you postpone it?"

The idea had not occurred to him.

"Write and say it's quite impossible, you've an important game; he'll understand."

Peter thought, "Dear Julia, I have been pressed into my

69

father's political cricket team and for domestic peace would prefer not to desert." It seemed surprisingly possible.

"I suppose I could."

His father came past him to the chest of drawers and picked up the drawing board. He stood sideways, his face silhouetted against the bright sky through the window so that his expression was hidden. Peter tried to prevent his knees shaking, but they were curiously out of his control. He waited, staring at four drawing pins on his table which were almost in a square, and his mind kept moving the fourth half an inch to complete the pattern. He thought suddenly that a long time had passed and looked up, afraid that his father was watching him, but he held the drawing board, standing side-ways against the window.

"Is this yours, Peter?"

"Yes."

His father began to laugh.

"Did you do it from memory?"

"Yes."

His father looked at him and laughed. Presently he put it down and went to the door. "Well you get on and write that letter, old chap."

*　　*　　*

The sun between the fir trees warmed the cool air, shining on the damp leaves of small beeches and oaks, giving an impression of light among dark green. Across the lawn Peter could see Mr. Nicholas walking slowly in the warmth, stooping occasionally to dig out a plantain with his penknife. He had nothing to do for three hours till the Red Lion opened. Somewhere in General Binforth's wood a pheasant croaked and Peter was reminded of another garden, when the hot summer morning seemed to have extended hours from breakfast, and be no nearer lunch, as if it had receded into a timeless yellow day, and far across the vegetable beds had been their other empty house. The pheasant called again, and the morning was fresh, and Mr. Nicholas was stooping to dig out a plantain. He stood up and said something, but Peter could not hear, and went slowly across.

"Are you all set for this evening?" For a moment Peter thought it might be a special party, but it was only his father's way of giving importance to his own future. Each night there were parties in the residential district for the different groups of retired officers and business men. They were not exclusive but the result of attending too many was that one's own had to be bigger. The Binforths had described theirs as "Just a few friends."

Peter said, "It'll be large, will it?"

"No, I don't think so. The usual dozen." At the first hint of co-operation with his excitement his father lost interest.

"I think the Binforths are a good thing." His father didn't answer and Peter was aware of him preparing to patronise the idea. "Their Victorian manners." He let the sentence fall away, sick with himself for producing what he supposed to be his father's opinion for his approval.

"No, old boy, I don't agree. I and my friends at Oxford said what we liked to each other." It was always frightening to find evidence that thirty years ago his father had been modern. It was absurd to defend the Victorians against him and Peter didn't really want to for he could see that he was right: if you were a decent, good-natured person however rude you were it was apparent that you meant well. Politeness was a concealment for meaning badly.

"The trouble is," he said, "one can't always be good-tempered." It was like a Women's Institute morality hint. When he talked to his father he had learned not to say what he thought till he had put it in a form which would not be ridiculed.

"We didn't get upset," said Mr. Nicholas. "It's concentrating on the inessential things of life. You don't have time to worry about other people's tempers if you get on with the job." He dug with his penknife and flung a plantain into the rhododendrons. "People who fuss about other people's feelings always spend more time thinking of their own."

It was too nearly reasonable. Peter tried not to listen and keep his own opinions clear, but they were confused by his father's words.

"There are so many better things in life to think about. That's the trouble with these old fools who live round here: they haven't anything to occupy them. They potter about with silly little dogs."

His father was working himself into a state to refuse to go to the party, but anything Peter said would be material for contradiction. He stood rubbing the dry grass with the sole of his sandal, trying not to let himself answer.

"You'll find more people than not die in the first year after they retire.—Don't, old boy, you're ruining the lawn.—It's too much of a shock. They haven't the mental stamina. They just sit about and mope." Mr. Nicholas was immune, and Peter realised after a few moments that he was deflected into a period of self-approval.

That evening Mr. and Mrs. Nicholas went arm-in-arm up the slight ascent of the Binforths' drive, and Peter walked with them. On either side the wood and tall rhododendrons excluded the sun making the drive grey but the fir tops above were orange. On the gravel circle in front of the house Mrs. Nicholas stumbled, she was not used to such high heels, and Mr. Nicholas held her up, glancing to see if she had dirtied his suit. He led her past the cannon, a little away from its muzzle, past a line of twelve-horse-power cars, and left her on the porch steps, with the relief of an exercise completed, to ring the bell. No one answered so they went round the house and found General and Lady Binforth on a back lawn.

It was at once obvious that the party was not going properly.

72

The mistake had been to open the garden windows, for the fifty guests, sweating in the confinement of the drawing-room on the hot evening, had begun to go out, taking decanters with them. When few were left the Binforths had followed, but their party had spread over the hillside, on secluded lawns, among ornamental shrubs. Above them on the hill middle-aged gentlemen could occasionally be seen returning to the house for dishes of anchovies and cheese straws, and determined ladies came and went through the rhododendrons holding empty glasses, but most of their guests were somewhere out of sight in the surrounding bushes. General and Lady Binforth continually glanced side-ways as they talked to two friends; and they hesitated, not knowing whether to say, "So nice of you to come," or, "So sorry you must go," to the Nicholases.

Lady Binforth's dress was of thin material patterned with blue and black flowers, with many recesses and frills which extended to her chin and wrists. Over and amongst it were three ropes of pearls, and she wore rings on her fingers and long, intricate ear-rings set with diamonds. According to Mr. Nicholas who had once called at eleven in the morning she wore them to do the housework. "General," she said, "do find poor Mrs. Nicholas a glass of sherry."

"Certainly, dear." General Binforth looked about him. He had learned in years of civilian life to hide the irritation he felt when there was no subordinate to whom to pass orders, but he had not found an alternative. The small lawn was empty for the two friends had gone. The sun passing behind the house had left it grey-green, the bush-hedges curiously the same colour as the grass. The General began to lead them without conviction downhill.

"So you're at Oxford?" he said.

Peter was aware of his tolerance. "Yes," he said, "for two more years," but laughter came suddenly from the bushes and the General was not listening.

73

"Isn't it sad," said Lady Binforth, "that all these lovely, lovely rhododendrons are over," and while Mr. Nicholas agreed she went on gently, "mm, mm," with upward then downward intonation. "I was just saying the other day to the General, we are so sad, so very sad that we can't have these beautiful flowers all the year. Why is it that instead of inventing horrible new ways of hurting each other we can't invent beautiful new flowers for all the days of the year?"

"What about our climate?" said Mr. Nicholas.

"Yes, I suppose you're right, we can't have everything. If we have our lovely snow and holly we mustn't expect too much. What happy weather we are having. The General was just saying to me that the summers seem to get finer every year."

Near the bottom of the hillside they came to the rockery. Large stones went in irregular steps down to a pond where gnats were flying in a sunbeam. Standing alone on the top rocks was a decanter of sherry.

The General picked it up, took out the stopper, and turned happily, but there were no glasses. "We made it all ourselves," said Lady Binforth, "at least the General and Brian did. It took seven years. We got the rocks from the hillside by exploding it. I did so hate that, but of course I'm glad now. Are you disturbed by those horrid guns? Oh what a shame. We are so very lucky, we scarcely notice them. Perhaps it's the atmospherics. Now you must see our stream." They went to the bottom of the rockery, the General carrying the decanter behind him.

The stream flowed down the hillside in a series of little falls and pools, under a crazy pavement bridge, into the lily-pond. As they came to the bridge they heard a continuous hum, and the General, lifting a metal plate painted like a crazy paving stone, disclosed an electric motor.

"Mm," said Mrs. Nicholas with appreciation. She had no idea what it was for.

74

"We have to help it," said Lady Binforth.

"In fact there isn't a stream at all," said Mr. Nicholas. He began to laugh. The General, taking it for approval, grinned and explained that there were 800 gallons which circulated three times in twenty-four hours. "Extraordinary thing, need only cost a penny a day, but we usually leave it on at night for the birds."

Lower down, near where the trees began, there was a second pond, and Peter noticed Brian Binforth sitting by it. His feet were over the edge as if he was cooling them, and he was facing away, not moving, his grey clothes and even his red hair the colour of the shadows. When Peter thought of him later he could not decide whether he had been five or twenty-five yards away.

Laughter was coming down the hillside and they began to hurry back, up the rockery, past shrubberies and ornamental lawns, into the shadow of the house. "What fun this has been," said Lady Binforth. "We do hope you've enjoyed it as much as we have."

Outside the drawing-room a few guests were gathered, but inside the party had begun again.

Presently Peter got his back against the wall. Of the thirty or forty people in the room a few stood near side tables picking crumbs absent-mindedly from potato-chip dishes, but most seemed invigorated by the evening air and were talking and drinking as if they had just arrived. Lady Binforth stood near the General who crouched over a bottle-drawer, lifting and replacing empty bottles. They should not be shown undecanted, but the shortage was serious. When a Commander stepped backwards into him he stood up suddenly.

Between the curved cotton backs of two heavy ladies Peter saw Mr. Nicholas glance round and refill his own glass. The backs moved together but his conversation came across the room, and in one silence the only sound was his "er-er" in the back of his throat as he hunted a word.

In a near-by corner a large lady was saying to Mrs. Nicholas, "I'm so anxious to find him a nice home. He has such a sweet nature. What he would really appreciate, of course, is a young man for a master. I did think that just possibly your middle boy . . ."

On the dresser a telephone began to ring, frightening the people near it but inaudible across the room over the conversation. They fingered it, looking round uncertainly, and the General reached past them apologising. Realising that they should not be watching, and anyway unable to hear, they gradually turned away.

"Ours is awful this year."

"But have you tried the new hormone weed killer?"

The General was lifting his chin and calling over their shoulders for Mrs. Nicholas. Those near him looked away and shuffled. They were too crushed to move even if they had known her.

"It's not the weeds, it's the ants; it isn't any use killing them, they come again the next night, in armies. They're bigger than ordinary ants; we've measured."

The General climbed on to a chair, aware that he was showing initiative. "A call by telephone for Mrs. Nicholas."

"My wife, who's seen my wife?"

Mrs. Nicholas moved with embarrassment from her corner, conscious of the conversation stopping and heads turning.

Mr. Nicholas came towards her. "Is this my wife? Hallo dear, will you or shall I?"

"All right."

"You'll do it, will you?"

The General was leading her out.

"My dear, you're going to do it, are you?"

"Yes."

The General led her into the hall, the door closed, and the noise began again, growing quickly to new intensity.

"Hallo, Peter, how are you getting on? There's a full decanter behind the window curtain." Mr. Nicholas whispered loudly, bending so that Peter recognised his smell.

"Ah, is there?" Peter tried to think of something to say but his father was looking round.

Mrs. Nicholas came back smiling, but no one noticed, and made her way slowly towards them.

"Who was it, my dear?"

"David, he couldn't get into the house so he walked back to Captain Cambridge to telephone. It would have been twice as quick to come here." She could have known that he had been too shy, but she was saying what she expected him to think: fancy telephoning in the middle of a sherry party about a shut door.

"What did he want to know?"

"Where we'd hidden the key."

"You didn't tell him?"

"Yes."

"On the telephone. Mother dear, mother dear."

"Oh, was that wrong?"

Peter moved quickly away towards the window curtain.

The party rose towards its climax. Colonels talked to captains, the curate confessed his distrust of the English Hymnal to the Vicar's wife, and half a gate-leg table shut suddenly, dropping a lady; the Major who had explained each time he was offered a drink that his carburettor was set to a slow jet finally swallowed the dregs of his glass; General and Lady Binforth who had been saying good-bye for ten minutes with their backs to the door at last realised from the crush that no one could get away and with difficulty opened it.

Families crossing the gravel circle in short lines continued to talk to each other, while cars drove slowly among them, blowing their horns. The sun was no longer on the pine tops but the air was warm between the rhododendrons. Arm-in-arm Mr. and Mrs. Nicholas went down the Binforths' drive, across the private road, up the cinder path, to the back door. As they opened it, from below the hill, across the wood, muffled yet audible came the General's bugle call. The party had made him late.

Owen was in the drawing-room, stroking the cat on the top of the piano, but it would not settle, and ran along the edge, and jumped on to the closed key-board, its head down and tail waving, so he lifted it back, but it jumped to the floor and ran under a chair.

"Good party?" he said. He was watching for it in the shadows.

"Quite fun," Peter said. There was too much to explain. "The sherry was goodish when you could find it. Father managed to get merry." He was aware of Owen allowing for the prejudice of his answer just as he allowed for his father's prejudice. His father's drinking was no longer a discovery or a comment, but his own fixed opinion; something to be commented on. He wanted to escape from it, to talk impersonally about it, to show that he was aware of it and outside it, yet because it was still true he couldn't. He wanted to explain that it was still true, but because Owen, leaning against the piano, watching in the shadows, was critical he would not make the admission. In the evening light his expression was indistinct, but his silence indicated clearly that he knew better.

The cat's nose was moving between the hanging chair-covers and the carpet, and Owen crouched quickly and caught its tail as it turned, and it struggled with a long squeal.

Mr. Nicholas in the kitchen shouted, "Who's killing the baby?" Peter went into the dining-room and shut the door.

Owen had been bombing his harbour. He had stabbed at the jetties with a penknife, making aeroplane noises, and cut craters among the warehouses. One of the factory chimneys had fallen across the trucks, scattering cattle over the lines into the dock. With repairs he had made the battle last two hours, but now he didn't want to remember it. Finishing, not bombing, destroyed what he made, for then there was no more reason to think about it. Till then he never realised how much he thought about it, or how it was all the time an excitement in his mind.

Peter watched the orange shapes which the evening sun was making on the dining-room wall. It was the hour in the sick-room when the curtains had been drawn for night but the day went on outside and there was nothing to do but try not to want them to reach the washstand because they never did. Far away there was cricket on the playing-field but presently that too stopped; and somewhere beyond the silence the staff was dining.

They were coming across the hall, Mr. Nicholas calling to Owen, "Supper, old boy, come on," with cheerful authority, Mrs. Nicholas banging herself against the door before turning the handle; "Hallo, you are in outer darkness," switching on the light.

"Fish, fish, glorious fish," shouted Mr. Nicholas.

David carried it in. "Fish, fish," he said.

"Well, what unbeatable strokes has the Hump taught you?"

"Oh, lots," said David with a loud laugh.

"No thank you," said Owen as Mrs. Nicholas gave him potatoes.

"Just a few." Her kindness showed that she was aware of his depression. She asked to be snubbed.

"Have you learned to spin the ball by draw---ing your racket away?" He demonstrated with the helping knife.

"Oh yes," said David with a loud laugh.

"What do you think you've been offered?" said Mrs. Nicholas.

"I don't know, " said Owen.

"Guess."

"I don't know."

"A puppy."

"Mm." He wasn't going to be rushed into good humour. He became aware that he should be grateful.

"What sort?"

"Mostly terrier, I think." Near the window the drop of orange sunlight which had remained despite the electric light went out. Lowering his head towards his plate David took mouthfuls of fish and both vegetables. Mr. Nicholas bit on a bone, pursued it, failed to find it, and took out chewed fish with his fingers.

"What's all this, my dear? Nobody told me."

"You were there when Mrs. Rains spoke to us."

"I wasn't."

"You were, darling."

"Darling, I most certainly wasn't."

"Have it your own way." She didn't agree, but would not argue. Occasionally she knew he was wrong and was obstinate showing that normally she was genuinely persuaded that he was right.

"Darling, I ought to know."

"I expect so."

"No, my dear, let's get this thing cleared up. Who is Mrs. Rains?"

"It doesn't matter."

"Yes it does matter."

"She lives in Fir Vale Lane. We've often met her at parties."

"You may have, my dear, I haven't; but never mind about that. What did she say?"

"She wanted a nice home for a puppy and would Owen like it?"

"What sort?"

"Mostly terrier, she said."

"My dear, you weren't taken in by that? It's probably the most dreadful mongrel."

"Almost certainly," said Owen.

"Has it had distemper?"

80

"I don't know. If it's a puppy I suppose not."

"Is it house-trained?"

"I didn't like to inquire." She laughed uncertainly.

"Oh no, my dear, you're perfectly entitled to ask that. You look a fool if you take someone's dog for a kindness and find yourself with a £200 bill for new carpets."

"I don't think Mrs. Rains . . ."

"My dear, I'm not saying she would, but it's no good starting to think of a dog till you've found out these things."

"No good at all," said Owen. He ate looking at his plate. Mrs. Nicholas gave David more mashed potatoes.

"I suppose it's not a bitch."

"Oh no, she definitely called it a dog."

"My dear, that means nothing."

Owen tipped his chair. He had skill at being maddening and didn't hesitate to use it. He wanted the dog, but at the moment he wanted more to be unreasonably forbidden it. He heard his father's gathering excitement as his mind worked on the subject, discovering arguments, freeing himself from logic as he dispersed opposition, and he didn't want to calm it.

"Who'll look after it?" said Mr. Nicholas. "Owen won't be able to when he goes into the army."

The army was an unknown, which Owen did not like to think of, and he felt an impulse of hatred and tears.

Mrs. Nicholas didn't try to go on arguing. The idea had been a failure; she should never have suggested it.

"Mother's church functions give her enough to do without an animal to look after."

"I shouldn't mind."

"No, my dear, I know you wouldn't. You wouldn't mind if someone ran a steam-roller over you, but I should." His interest in the argument made him give the impression that she, like the carpets, must be preserved.

"Well, David, are you ready for a game?"

"Yes," said David with enthusiasm, and he went upstairs

with Mr. Nicholas to the billiard room. He made even what he meant sound artificial. It was impossible to imagine him laughing alone.

Peter began to clear away, trying not to look at the chewed pieces on Mr. Nicholas's plate. He put the dishes and cups on to the trolley and wheeled it into the kitchen.

Mrs. Nicholas was crying over the sink. That was the trouble, he went on being aware of her feelings till she showed them and then he realised that he had forgotten they made her happy or miserable. She kept her head turned away, sniffling; the washing-up water was too hot for her hands. He forgot that a happy family was not for her a convenient background, but the thing she had wanted.

★    ★    ★

Peter heard them talking from the bathroom and went quietly on to the landing. Light was coming from his mother's door which was a few inches open. Inside his father was moving about, for sometimes his voice was at the far side of the room, and sometimes near the door.

"Well, you must decide, my dear. The last thing I want to be is damping. If you think you can cope. . . . One mustn't rush these things. It would be a dreadful tie, have you thought of that? You couldn't go for a holiday."

"Mm." She was probably sitting at the mirror, interrupted while doing her hair.

"And what's it going to cost? I suppose dog biscuit is as ridiculously expensive as everything else. You say scraps, but the dog's got to have decent food. Then there's the licence."

"Mm."

"One must consider these things. Our finances are not going to get any better. You can never tell when the bloody Government will steal another lump. And we still have three sons to pay for."

His shadow fell on the wall inside the door and Peter moved quickly into the bathroom, but his voice receded, and presently he was saying:

"I agree with you, my dear; if it would only give Owen a sensible interest it would be worth while, but would he stick to it, or become bored with it after a week like his other crazes? And it's not going to be a sensible interest for anyone if it's a miserable little lap-dog. That's one thing I won't have. I may live in a suburb but I'm not going to have a lap-dog."

She didn't answer.

"Where's it going to sleep? I suppose it's a house-dog, because we haven't got a kennel. In normal times one could buy a load of deal and knock one up in an hour; to-day you can't get wood."

His mother didn't answer.

"Do we know that it hasn't got eczema?"

"Oh, I'm almost sure Mrs. Rains . . ."

"Yes, well you must decide, my dear. If you really think . . ."

Peter went quietly upstairs. He was surprised at her skill. She went on listening and agreeing, allowing him to talk himself into a good humour and find his own retreat; it was a remnant of cunning left after living with a household of men; it was surely unconscious.

\*　　\*　　\*

When Mr. and Mrs. Nicholas went to tea with Mrs. Rains Peter and Owen found Brian, and together they tried for a time to persuade two of the General's pheasants to swallow separate crusts of bread joined by string, but after absurd obstinacy one ate both and flew away with a loop trailing. Presently they went to the General's raspberry canes which had survived the drought, and later across the private road to look for strawberries in the Nicholas' garden where, since the gardener had left, the bracken was advancing. But while crossing the tennis court Brian remembered a juggling trick with tennis balls, and when this had failed they lay on the grass.

"I wish it would snow," said Brian.

"That'd shake'm," said Brian and Owen at the same moment, and they giggled and kicked up their legs.

They lay, saying nothing in the hot sun.

"I say, Brian, this is the tennis court." He had turned on to his elbow, his red hair hanging close to the ground, and was scraping a hole with a twig.

"It's an ants' nest."

"I know, but . . ."

"Let's play tennis."

"That'd shake'm."

A car came up the private road, turned into the drive, and stopped at the front door. While Mr. Nicholas paid the driver Mrs. Nicholas came towards them, and the dog ran in front. She was pulled a few steps, then lost hold of its lead and it ran across the lawn, up the grass slope, and stopped three yards from them its front legs forward, its head close to the ground, yapping. When they held out their hands it retreated in the same attitude and howled.

"Good dog," said Peter.

"What?" shouted Owen.

Its head seemed to have been caused by a spaniel and the rest by a wire-haired terrier.

When Mrs. Nicholas came close it stopped barking and waited for her, its two-inch tail wagging continuously, and began to jump at her hands, and missed and got tangled in her dress.

"He's rather sweet, isn't he?" she said, trying to disentangle him. "His name's Sambo. Good dog, Sambo. Sambo, stop it. Stop it, will you, Sambo."

Sambo stood still for a moment, his head sinking slowly as

if it was too heavy, but brought it up suddenly and ran barking at Mr. Nicholas who was coming on to the court.

"Be quiet, Sambo."

"Sambo, don't be rude to your father."

"Well," said Mr. Nicholas, "that's our good deed for the day. Has mother told you about it? After hunting round Mrs. Rains' rubbish dumps and muck heaps for half an hour we eventually heard a miserable whine and discovered him in an old chicken coop. I can't describe how revolting it was. He hadn't been cleaned out for months. The straw was solid filth. There was just enough space for him to squeeze his head out, and he had no water. That's the sort of thing the R.S.P.C.A. should stop instead of spending their time deciding whether it's cruel to put worms on hooks. I feel very inclined to go to the police about it. No, my dear, it would be an honest thing to do."

"Why was he there?"

"Some story about him chasing the postman, but that was all nonsense. No, it's my belief that if she couldn't get rid of him she meant to kill that dog."

"Here, Sambo, Sambo."

But Sambo had seen the cat strolling in the evening sun on the lawn and ran barking at it, and stood yelping below its fir tree, till Mrs. Nicholas took him away for a disinfectant bath.

After supper Mrs. Nicholas telephoned to Dorothy Mariner. She had known Dorothy since school where they had each called the other Dots, and still did. Once a week they wrote to each other about friends' babies and knitting patterns and family events. Dorothy often came to stay, and at Christmas gave them all presents, and she was called Auntie Dots. Peter could hear what his mother was saying to her from the drawing-room.

". . . . Yes, we fetched him this afternoon in a taxi . . . White and copper with the sweetest expression . . . Nominally Owen's but really the family's. . . . He didn't say much.

85

... Yes, in a Jeyes bath... Sambo.... No, white and copper ... Who? ... Dear David, oh, I don't think he's committed himself yet. We shall doubtless have some profound utterance in a month or two.... Bye-bye dear; longing to see you next week."

# Chapter Five

"DAVID, PETER, OWEN, come and say hallo to your cousin."

Moving his curtains slightly Peter saw them coming across the lawn into the veranda below. Richard was carrying a leather cricket bag in one hand which the small suitcase in his other did not balance though he held it away from his side, but he was talking and laughing and Mr. Nicholas was listening. His short fair hair gave an inverted-boat shape to the top of his head. Peter lay back in the sun on his bed and went on sketching.

After a moment he stopped and put on a shirt and went downstairs.

Standing at the French windows with the lawn and the hot day behind him Mr. Nicholas was saying, ". . . so a few of them got together and asked me to form a club. We shall do other things, of course: talks and discussions, make these locals open their mouths a bit, but the great thing is to get the cricket started. That will create an interest. This is our first match, four weeks to a day after our first meeting. Not bad?"

"Jolly good," said Richard.

"Hallo," said Peter. He was not sure what name to use.

"Hallo, Peter." Richard came forward and they shook hands. He had the sort of small features which do not get out of proportion between fourteen and eighteen but seem as neat as a scale model and the sort of fair skin which never grows spots.

"Peter's our artist-lawyer," said Mr. Nicholas. "He drew his father the other day. You must show it to Richard." There was no innuendo; his father did not say one thing when he meant another. He seriously thought it flattering.

87

"All in the family tradition," said Mr. Nicholas. "My grandfather, your great uncle, had several pictures hung at the Royal Academy as well as the largest legal practice of his day."

David was coming across the lawn from the tennis court carrying his racquet, wearing the white shirt and grey trousers in which he took exercise. He often tried to reintroduce public school habits like changing for exercise, which the Nicholases had forgotten.

"Come on David, say how do you do to your cousin. David is our athlete and classicist. Well, David, have you been beating the ball about?"

It was like a play of pre-war society. The sons of the house and their guests return from the tennis court and golf links, substitutes for the Victorian riding party, for cocktails and conversation before the butler calls them to lunch. It was the background of many of Mr. Nicholas's anecdotes and had seemed an exciting and pleasant part of being grown up. It was easy now to see that the conversation had been about the morning's sport.

Not that Mr. Nicholas had approved, but explained about house parties with skill: whisky-damaged officers talking politics, healthy young men spending their days hitting a stationary white ball and their leisure discussing it. He was able to see their futility since he wished to detract from a society which had controlled him, but he could forget it now, when he had the chance to control a similar society. He took easily the role of host, and would have re-created the whole set-up. But there were never quite enough guests, and Peter and Owen were always busy with selfish personal occupations, and there was no butler.

"I must nip up and have a bath," said David. Normally the Nicholases forgot to bathe after exercise.

Presently they went to lunch. The door and windows of the dining-room were open but they gave no draught. The sunlight was bright on the bleached window seat. In the warm air the pie did not steam so that it seemed uncertain whether it was hot.

Mrs. Nicholas sat down heavily. "Pff," she said. She had cooked it and the effort left her unwilling to do anything but eat it. "What weather," she said, remembering Richard. She hated it.

"Frightful," said Richard. His small healthy features shone, but the idea of taking off his coat on the first day of a visit did not occur to him.

The sweat stood in drops on Mr. Nicholas' forehead and on his upper lip where he shaved, and a drop had run down his chin.

"Look at Kent," he said. "To-day they never take the field with more than one gentleman. When your great-great-uncle played for the side there were always six and sometimes ten."

"Were there really?" said Richard.

"Sir Charles Nicholas, Deputy Speaker. Four years in the Oxford boat, also played for the 'varsity. You couldn't do that to-day."

"Your great-grandfather?" said Richard.

"No, my great-grandfather the surgeon was in the eleven at Harrow. He should have been head of the school but he was done out of it."

"Was he really?"

"The headmaster liked the boy who ran the nature society but my great-grandfather wasn't interested in bugs and didn't hesitate to say so; as a result the other boy was chosen."

"Mm," said Richard with sympathy.

"Five generations in the school. I don't suppose many families can equal that."

"No," said Richard. "Is that his picture?" pointing to the gold-framed oil painting of a dark-coated man with side whiskers above Mr. Nicholas.

"Where? Up there? No that's my grandfather, the Indian

judge; rowed for the school; brother of William Nicholas who won the Governors' Prize at Marlborough." Mr. Nicholas worked his tongue round his mouth between his teeth and his cheeks collecting escaped matter. The first course was over.

"More peas?" said Mrs. Nicholas.

"No thank you," said Richard.

"Come on, mother, you must feed our cousin properly. We rely on him for a century on Saturday."

*   *   *

On the following days Richard was a great success. He helped with the washing-up, taught Sambo to fetch a stick, and played billiards with Mr. Nicholas. They played after breakfast, tea, and supper, and often after lunch. Mr. Nicholas couldn't let it rest. Because he was not bored himself it did not occur to him that Richard might be. It had been the same with David who had played willingly at first but had gradually begun to make excuses. Richard did not become bored. Usually he suggested the next game, but if Mr. Nicholas called him he didn't wait to finish the sentence he was reading.

Richard always listened, and often laughed, and never looked as if he expected a drink when Mr. Nicholas took one. Usually Mr. Nicholas remembered him; it was one of his principles: "If a fellow wants a drink and you've got it, damn it yes, you give it him." Omar Khayyam was about the house in many small leather editions, and he had once spent a late evening reading it to Major Dale. But when Mr. Nicholas remembered him too often Richard politely refused.

Dorothy Mariner arrived on Friday in time for tea, sitting in deck-chairs on the edge of the lawn. The iced cakes on the plate stand had to be put in the shade of the veranda. Mrs. Nicholas had made them that morning. In the afternoon she had cleaned the silver and brass, placed flowers about the

house, two vases in Dorothy's room and five in the drawing-
room which now smelt like a florist's shop, and made the
scones.

"My dear, you're exhausting yourself." Mr. Nicholas
resented her exertions to please someone else. It was so easy
to see the selfishness of anything that he said that the explanation seemed too simple, but it was difficult to find another.
He was fond of her in the way that he might have been fond
of something inanimate like a useful car, though, of course,
what made her useful was that she was animate. Once, perhaps, he had loved her, but it was easy to imagine his attitude
only altered because to make love to, and take to bed, and be
loved by, had then been her uses.

"No I'm not," she said cheerfully, collecting the wedding
china from the pantry.

"We really must stop mother wearing herself out." His
indirectness suggested that he had once tried to be prohibitive,
but that about Dorothy Mariner she had been obstinate.

Across the lawn the broom seeds snapped in the heat.
Dorothy lay back in her deck chair, her knees apart. She was
exhausted by the journey and Mrs. Nicholas was letting her
'have her tea in peace.'

"A bit of jam sponge?"

"No thank you."

The untouched cakes were pathetic because Mrs. Nicholas
minded.

"Peter, a piece of fruit?"

"No thank you." Why need she take offence? It was too
hot to eat. But David in a deck-chair, his tummy forward,
accepted in turn a slice of each.

"Dear David."

Kneeling on the grass just outside the tea circle Owen was
playing with Sambo. When he ran at him, his jaws open,
trying to bite his hand he rolled him on his back, and he ran
at him snarling and he pushed him over backwards.

"Owen, for God's sake."

"What's the matter?"

"Well," said Mr. Nicholas, "how's London?"

"Hot," said Dorothy.

"Still full of foreigners? Last time I was there I didn't once hear English spoken in the streets." He was laughing, but he almost meant it.

"Mm," she said, agreeing wearily. She wasn't going to argue about London; she lived there.

"How's Mr. George?"

"Oh, he's Mr. George." She never put Mr. George into phrases. Between nine and five on weekdays she saw too much of him. Sometimes in stories about him she would say, "You know what Mr. George is like," but then instead of explaining him she would say what he did. Her gossip gave confidence that when your turn came you would not be mis-gossipped about. Mr. George might not be complex, but he was more than 'the amorous middle-aged business man,' he was Mr. George. Peter had only learned recently that Mr. George was often 'a trouble' to Auntie Dots.

"Pass it to David, will you?" Mrs. Nicholas held out the plate.

"No thanks."

"Come on David, don't be faint-hearted." Dorothy and his mother conspired to pretend that he was still under ten, the fat boy who could be tempted with toffees.

Retreating two yards on to the lawn Sambo began to give a regular hysterical bark.

"Shut up, Sambo, shut up." It was obviously meant for Owen.

"Poor dog," he said.

"Well," said Mr. Nicholas, "have you heard about my club?" He talked louder than anyone else so that conversation seemed to go on at two levels. Standing in the sun he drank his tea which was now cool in three swallows.

"Peter, fetch your picture to show our visitors. Peter's drawn his father. Damn cheek, I call it." He was laughing and greatly pleased. "Actually it's not bad."

Peter went upstairs. As he pulled it from under books he saw it start to tear, and couldn't decide whether to let go. Then it was in half. He tore the halves several more times and wondered where to hide the pieces, and put them in his grate and lighted them. They flared and he moved a heap of clothes hurriedly and tripped on the wire of his bed-side lamp which fell from the mantelpiece, its china base shattering on the fender. The ashes drifted about and he tried to collect them but they crumbled over the floor making his hands black. They would be found in the waste paper basket. He got a handful and carried them to the bathroom. The lavatory would have been better: they stuck over the basin and the soap, and he tried to wash them away but someone was coming upstairs.

"Peter. Peter, are you all right?" You couldn't break anything in the house but everyone ran to see what had happened with curiosity and alarm.

"Yes." He came on to the landing and went downstairs past his father, avoiding his stare.

"I can't find it."

"What?"

"The picture. It must be lost. I can't find it.

\*   \*   \*

"I realised long ago," said Dorothy, "that it was no good arguing with your father, or I should never see your mother again." She bent to smell a lupin in Mrs. Nicholas' flower-bed on the edge of the tennis court and straightened as if she had almost bent too far. She was enjoying the grass and the warm evening air and the orange sunset behind the pine clumps on the hills. She made Peter feel that normally he did not appreciate these things.

93

"He's a very difficult man, but then I'm not your mother."

Somewhere beyond the tennis court, over the chestnut palings where the Binforths' trees began, the gardener's child was singing. She sang, "One the object of our journey," and stopped. Presently it seemed that she must have gone away and then she sang it again in the same place. Why wasn't she in bed? Across the lawn the billiard room windows were open and the balls could be heard striking each other, and sometimes a loud laugh.

"He's the most self-interested person I know, but then so are you all."

"Yes," said Peter. He knew that, but was surprised that she did.

"I mean you get on with what interests you." So that was all she meant.

Half up the sky three small yellow clouds were lit by the setting sun. There was no wind to move or heat to disperse them. The day seemed to be going away without them.

The most self-interested people she knew. It was probably true; but she only meant independent.

Owen came on to the lawn and began to run round, the dog dragging at his trouser legs. He would tear them or tear out its teeth.

It didn't matter what she meant. Was it true? And if it was true did it matter?

"One the object of our journey," the child sang.

"But I do think if you want to go on living here it would be sensible to co-operate a little more." Dorothy turned to him and said it with too much purpose. The conversation which had been unusual and interesting suddenly fitted into the phrase, "Perhaps I could have a talk to him." He could hear her saying it to his mother.

He was astonished and frightened by the skill with which she mixed criticism and sympathy.

The clouds had faded into the grey evening sky. Across

the lawn the billiard-room light was on and from the open window came a loud laugh.

She seemed before she spoke to have imagined you listening, and then to listen with you. He wanted to explain to her that he was refusing to answer because she had made a mistake and not because he was offended.

Beyond the chestnut palings on the Binforths' land an adult voice was speaking and presently the child howled.

★   ★   ★

There was thunder in the distance at breakfast. Through the dining-room windows the clouds were black over the hills.

"All set for a century, Richard? Did you sleep well?"

"Fine thank you, Uncle Philip. Did anyone hear the cats?"

"Cats? We'll soon deal with them; can you use a twelve bore?"

Owen said, "Be careful of Deborah."

"Who? She must look after herself. She shouldn't invite her friends and relations without asking me. Anyway you've got a dog now." Mr. Nicholas looked round, smiling at his successful repartee and Richard smiled.

"I hope the weather doesn't spoil your tennis," said Mrs. Nicholas.

"What's that, my dear?"

"I hope the weather doesn't spoil David's visit to Wimbledon."

"Why should it?"

"I didn't say it would."

"But why should it?"

"It might."

"Obviously, but why?"

"I don't know."

He wanted her to mention the thunder so that he could reassure himself that he had not heard it, but she could only remember that she had made the remark to change the subject.

"Good morning, Peter." Mr. Nicholas had a way of saying this half way through breakfast to one of his sons who had not yet spoken to him and waiting for an answer.

"Good morning, Dad."

"You all set for the match?"

\*    \*    \*

Behind the bus in which they had come, and the tall elms which stood along the hedges of the flat surrounding fields the thunder clouds had receded into a dark layer near the horizon as if they had failed to break the fine weather but would try again. This was where Mr. Nicholas had once lived and his opponents were the Working Man's Club he had then founded.

The game was going to end in a draw, for their opponents had not time to make the runs and Mr. Nicholas's team could not bowl them out. But Richard was moving about on his toes, bent forward, ready to sprint at the ball. He was aware that while the rest of the side had failed he had made, not a century, but the highest score.

Mr. Jenning, the wicket-keeper, ducked and the ball went for byes.

"I've warned him," said Mr. Nicholas. "If he doesn't stand back as I tell him I shall make him take off the gloves and give them to you, Peter."

Mr. Nicholas spoke loudly so that the rest of his side could hear, and the wicket-keeper moved back a short pace, grumbling to the first slip. Mr. Nicholas had a way of working up hostility not only to the enemy team but to members of his own, and favouring others.

The spectators gathered near the pavilion began to call at Mrs. Pawthorn's dog which stood twenty yards on to the field looking at them over its shoulder.

"Get that bloody dog away." There were only a few more overs and little chance of winning. "Richard, I'm going to put you on to bowl." Mr. Nicholas was making the moment a crisis. It was easy to hear how he would later tell it: "By this time I could see that the situation was desperate so I said to myself, there's only one thing to do. . ."

"Richard, we've got to fool them out. I want you to toss up your slow stuff."

But the batsmen welcomed the change, hitting over or between the deep field, and began to score fast so that it seemed they might after all win. Richard bowled obediently, not implying that it was someone else's policy, trying to make it a success. When one of them hit a long catch it was dropped.

"God help you," said Mr. Nicholas.

At the end of the over he said, "Well bowled Richard." It was not a compliment, but a criticism of the rest of the team.

The dog came trotting towards the wicket, the two fieldsmen danced in front of it, their open hands stretched sideways making small embarrassed hisses and shoos, as if they were driving hens. Five or six spectators came after it on to the ground and it ran round them in a circle. It was long-legged with a brown-sandy coat which just curled, a hairy tail, and a horse-like canter so that it seemed to avoid them without effort.

"Who owns the bloody thing?"

The game stopped, the umpires and fieldsmen lunged at it, but when they came too close it shifted its circle to another part of the ground. Then it ran under the wire fence and stood in the middle of the next meadow, waiting for Major Dale. His small figure receded into the large field, moving with difficulty through the long grass, often stopping to listen for the giggles of Mrs. Morton and the Pawthorns. They knew what he had already had to drink.

In the hot evening the fieldsmen ran wearily after the ball and Mr. Nicholas, becoming aware of their criticism, continued to make Richard bowl. The batsmen walked down the pitch and hit where they pleased. If there had been more time they could have won. In the last over Richard took two wickets.

"Well done Richard. Richard's the hero of the match; half our runs and half our wickets."

There was beer in the pavilion and more at the Half Moon where the bus stopped in the village.

"Give some beer to Richard."

The passages and low inner bar were filled with players standing round the hatches and packed on the wall benches, looking inwards. Despite the crowd and the congratulations and Mrs. Jenning's singing which made it difficult to hear, they all seemed detached and were glancing down and away from each other when they spoke. Mrs. Morton stood near the bar, drinking pints of beer. Peter remained uneasily aware of them after they were swallowed in a way he did not with men. Looking sideways he accidentally caught the eye of the village storekeeper's wife. He turned away quickly but was aware of her excusing herself to the man she sat by, and rising from the bench to come towards him. He did not want to speak to her. She would say, "Isn't it nice to see Mr. Nicholas so much better again." He made his way quickly between groups to the door. The other small panelled room was empty except for two 'young louts'; one sat with his elbows on his knees, the other threw two darts at the board and one fell out, and he left them.

"What's yours?" said Mrs. Pawthorn, and Peter recognised her close to him in the congested passage.

"I'm not sure. Gin and something."

She went towards the bar, hunting with her plump hands for coins in her bag, and Peter wondered if he should have offered to pay. When she brought the drink he felt bound to say something. "How are you liking Rodenham?" It was so formal that she would probably be offended. She was always forcing intimacy on him.

"There's Major Dale," she said. "Let's give him a drink."

He was coming through the doorway and beyond him Peter could see Mrs. Jenning in the inner room with her elbows on the bar-billiard table, singing. Two of her sons had an arm each round her neck, and her black hair had fallen over her nose in a way which she did not allow when she scrubbed the Nicholas's kitchen. Major Dale came up the passage with his hands against the walls.

Peter gave him his drink and he looked at it, and at Peter, and drank it quickly.

"What a wonderful hat, Major."

He stared at Mrs. Pawthorn. He seemed to know a good reply but not quite remember how to say it.

"'Tis isn't it?"

"Let's get the Major a drink."

"Let me," said Peter.

The Major turned to him, placed a hand on his upper arm, and stared into his eyes.

"This hat was given me in '04 by my great-aunt. Just fancy an old man like me having a great-aunt in '04."

Peter moved back, freeing the Major's hand, and he stumbled, and Mrs. Pawthorn stopped giggling, and they helped him out of the door.

In the open he seemed offended, and pushed them away, and stood swaying slightly, saying nothing.

"I'm drunk," he said.

"Not drunk," he said.

"Can't somebody do something?" said Mrs. Morton.

"Oh, I do think it's a shame," said Mrs. Nicholas. She stood by the iron railings drinking a lemonade. "Oh, it is bad luck on Alice."

Alice was Major Dale's adopted daughter. She was

somewhere inside the pub. She was fourteen, with wide sandy hair and large breasts, and everyone said that she was devoted to him.

"Can't somebody do something?" They were all suddenly angry and critical. There had been a mistake and they wanted to blame someone. It was as if they had been shocked into a different sense of values in which drunkenness was unfunny. Mrs. Nicholas, of course, never thought anything else except in loyalty to Mr. Nicholas, but Mrs. Morton had been almost as incapable herself in the billiard-room on Squadron Leader Morton's birthday. Her attitude now made drinking like the school outing when you may do anything you like except be naughty.

Mrs. Pawthorn was trying to grin at Peter but when he wouldn't grin back she said, "Really, I had no idea."

Major Dale stood still between them as if he did not trust himself to walk. He started to dribble out of the corner of his mouth, down his chin where it formed a drip. Peter knew that he should do something, but didn't know what. If he treated him as a child he would realise it and be angry. He began to move forward, but a large friendly man pushed past and took the Major's elbow.

"Come on, old chap. You and I are going to have a nice sit down together, old chap." The Major stared at him, and then let himself be led away.

Several men were already sitting in the bus, breathing heavily. More were coming out of the Half Moon, draining their glasses, shaking hands and saying good-bye emotionally to friends made since the close of play.

"Our cousin, a most promising young player. Won the match for us."

When Alice came into the bus she stood behind Major Dale's seat. "They say you're drunk, Daddy, you aren't are you?"

"Er." He looked at her out of the corners of his eyes, then

reached at her with both hands across the back of the large man who sat outside, keeping him in place.

She moved away, and went slowly down the bus looking back at him, as if she didn't know where else to look.

"All aboard?"

"Where's Bill?"

"Let's go then."

"All right, driver."

"'Ere I am."

"Who's seen Bill."

"All right, driver."

"Who's seen the driver?"

"There he is, in his seat."

"So he is."

"All right, driver."

Mr. and Mrs. Pawthorn took Mrs. Morton in their car. They started behind the bus, and overtook it, blowing their horn, but later it passed them stopped, their bonnet-cover raised, standing side by side, their heads close to the engine. After a few miles they drove past it, blowing their horn, but presently the bus, travelling heavily along country lanes, overtook them stopped and peering into the engine. Everyone looked back and gradually the bus slowed and halted as if stopped by their united curiosity. When most of them had got out the Pawthorns drove past blowing their horn. Mr. Pawthorn was leaning out of the window, and seemed to be trying to get back, but Mrs. Morton was striking him behind.

"There was never anything wrong."

"Silly, I call it."

They went behind bushes and got back into the bus.

"But if there was nothing wrong, why did they stop?"

"It was a joke."

"Oh, it was a joke."

"Silly I call it."

The bus moved with frequent halts through the evening and

then the night, from the flat country back among pine hills and rhododendrons. After the second inn there was continuous song. After the third there were several continuous songs.

"Three cheers for Richard Nicholas."

"For he's a jolly good fellow."

"Happy birthday to you."

Richard was last down in the morning and there were grey bulges under his eyes looking out of place on his pink and white face. After breakfast when Mr. Nicholas called him to billiards he put down the *Sunday Times* and went, but forgot to answer cheerfully. After lunch he sat in a deck-chair in the sun with his eyes shut, and Sambo bounced on him, and he struck him on the nose to the dog's astonishment, and then sat up and stroked him, glancing towards the house.

That night Peter had also heard the cats. Every time he woke they were screaming and in the morning he had the impression that between midnight and dawn they had never stopped. When he walked on the lawn in the fine early morning he was almost surprised not to find fur and blood.

During the morning Richard remembered an engagement which would prevent him staying for the rest of the week, and he left after lunch.

"Who would have thought," said Mr. Nicholas, "that a thing like that would have happened to a boy like Richard?"

\*　　\*　　\*

Peter stood on the edge of the drive in the hot sun, looking across to the tennis court and the wood, and the blue sky above. To his right across the valley the pine hills were misty with the heat. If he looked round he could see the house, almost pretty with the sunlight on its red tiles and green veranda. They had not, he thought, been bad weeks at home.

Tomorrow he was going to stay with Julia, but the idea was too uncertain for him to like it. When he tried to

remember her face it had the wide jaw and thick features of a
certain cousin; and what would he say to her parents? He
wanted to see her again, but somewhere where there would
be no need to act.

Behind him on the lawn Owen was running with the dog.
It had been a great success and he often played with it on the
lawn. He held it on its back and thumped its chest till it
howled and scrambled up and ran away. His Aertex sleeves
were rolled on to his shoulders showing his long bare arms
and the dog ran at him barking, and he ran away, letting it
chase him, and then turned and chased it in small circles till
it rolled on its back. There was something didactic about the
way Owen played with the dog. He was just too energetic
to be doing it entirely for fun. Peter turned to shout at
him to stop, but that was the sort of intolerance his father
showed.

On the whole they had not quarrelled during these weeks.
Sometimes it seemed that they never need quarrel now because he could see so clearly how they began. It was only
necessary to avoid saying the little angry things you felt at
little infuriating things he did and he would never know you
had been angry; and if you did not say them there was no
need to go on being angry. He was working the dog backwards and forwards by a stick which it held in its mouth while
it made a strange high growl. He was deliberately provoking.

"Poor dog." Peter walked away across the drive.

"What?"

Peter walked up the grass slope on to the tennis court.

"What did you say?"

Dorothy was writing a letter on her knees in a deck-chair
under the overhanging branches of a fir. It was cool there in
the tiny wind which he had not noticed in the sun. He was
surprised to find her, and a little embarrassed as if she had
overheard what he had been thinking. That was the effect
she had on him; at first she was friendly as if she trusted his

motives, but one day he said something, looking at his plate instead of her, and she, looking at him, understood more about him than he had said. After that it didn't seem worth pretending. At first she laughed at the clever things he said, but gradually she laughed less because she saw their unkindness; and then she saw his careful attempts to be fair to people to prove that he was not unkind. As he came on to the court she smiled and he was pleased and smiled at her. It would have been easy if he could have disliked her.

"What weather," she said.

"Yes." He liked it. He liked the hot dry grass with bare feet, and the cool red tiles in the hall. He liked the way it made his mind clear, hearing what was said not a second late but immediately, understanding the difference between what was said and what was meant, and then, suddenly, with the consciousness of what was happening the dizziness which gave the whole hot shimmering day unreality. He liked the way it freed his emotions so that, when he knelt in the arm-chair with his face in his hands against its back and listened to Mozart, the urge to cry was real and not an awareness of what it might have been if he had not been full of food.

Dorothy, like his mother, hated it. They were too big. It was almost the only way they were alike. Dorothy was never quite calculable, and if you were foolish or wrong she said so. His mother agreed and admired too easily so that he ceased to care. He couldn't argue with his mother because long before necessary she was on his side so that he wanted to tell her her arguments, and once for fun took the other side, but she did not understand. He supposed he liked her. It was a silly word. In these weeks they had, as always, got on all right. They had scarcely made contact. He was perhaps sorry for her, but it was people who had a good effect on him that he liked. After twenty-five years of having a good effect on his father by unqualified appreciation she could not realise that her sons liked criticism; and anyway she loved them too much. But

104

Dorothy was critical so that however Peter disguised it he was always playing to her for appreciation.

Looking back from the tennis court to the lawn it seemed strangely like a stage. Some trick of hot air made the thick rhododendron bushes at one end waver like a cardboard screen, the house in the bright sun was flat and shadowless, and from the tennis court he seemed like an audience to be watching unobserved: "Exit Owen and dog. After a moment Mr. Nicholas enters, stands in the centre of the lawn, stoops to dig out a plantain with his penknife, and goes out round the corner of the house. This leaves the stage empty, and the audience with an uneasy feeling that there is significance in that plantain or the producer would have arranged something meanwhile for their diversion. Re-enter Mr. Nicholas still with plantain. He throws it into the rhododendrons and the audience realises that it has been had. But it still feels uneasy. . . ." It needn't. Mr. Nicholas had only been making sure that he threw the plantain in a safe place.

Now he was coming towards the tennis court, looking for someone to talk to, and Peter went quickly off the far end, down the edge of the wood. Not that, after the first days of these holidays, it had been difficult to talk to his father. They seemed to have agreed to avoid politics or anything controversial, and not to meet too often. It would be stupid not to be careful on the last day.

Peter went down the hillside and remembered how, a month before in the early morning the undergrowth had been rain-soaked, with the dazzling sun just showing among the bushes above. Now it shone on the hill face and the dry heather scratched his legs, and the outer leaves of the small trees were brown. He walked along the bottom of the wood, retracing the path he had then taken. He thought that there were no hateful people. When he was away from them he could not go on hating them. Sometimes he could dislike them when they hurt other people because he could imagine

105

how it felt to be hurt. But it was the people who hurt *him* that he hated, and that was why, by avoiding him, he could almost cease to hate his father.

And tomorrow he would be staying with Julia, labelled, "Julia's boy friend."

Mr. Belvene's small lawn was green, like a fairy circle in the centre of a dark forest, and completely in shadow. Peter did not turn up through the wood because that led back to the tennis court, but went along a winding path between young Spanish chestnuts and firs, up to the rockery directly below the end of the house. At the top of the rockery his father was waiting.

"What weather," said Peter.

His father was silent. His mind seemed like a flat pool, and Peter was aware of his remark disturbing it. One remark was sometimes enough to set it in violent motion. It had no middle state between violence and this ominous calm. Sometimes Peter made several remarks and went away before anything happened.

"I can't remember a summer like it." That was foolish because his father obviously could.

Glancing up Peter saw thick white smoke coming from Owen's window. It seemed unreal, like a piece of white paper stuck on a painting.

"Look at that."

"What?"

"Up there. Isn't it odd."

His father saw it. "Well, don't stand staring. For Christ's sake do something."

He was hurrying to the telephone. He thought the house was on fire. Peter followed slowly. He knew it was Owen's chemicals, but he didn't want to say so. He resented the information being rushed from him.

"It's all right," he said.

"Don't speak to me like that."

This was how they started.

He stood by the telephone at the dining-room mantelpiece and there was sweat on his upper lip and his hand holding the receiver was trembling.

Peter said "It's Owen's chemicals."

"He may have killed himself. Go and see."

Peter went upstairs, not fast, not too slowly. Owen's room was full of smoke and he was giggling and treading on bits of smouldering stuff.

"It's terrific," he said. "Five times as good as nitrate." He had frightened and delighted himself.

Peter leaned out of the window.

"It's all right," he said.

"What? What do you say?"

"He's all right."

Peter came back from the window. It would have been possible, he supposed, to co-operate with his father's alarm.

"The flash went up literally five feet," said Owen. "I still can't see properly."

Luckily it was over now, for he would stay upstairs for a time.

"God, look at that." Owen had found a wide singe on his sheet.

Peter heard his father's steps coming up the stairs and went quickly across the landing to his room. It would be stupid not to be careful for one more day.

They had supper and sat about waiting for it to be cool enough to go to bed. The French windows were open but there seemed no air in the drawing-room and the hot evening was taking hours to get dark. "Well, I think I shall go to bed," said David. He went gradually towards the door. He seemed to be waiting for someone to say something to stop him, but they didn't and at last he went out. Owen sat in the arm-chair near the window, tuning the wireless. There were distant symphony concerts, and sudden jazz, and once a cultured voice

107

said loudly, "... the inevitable outcome from the woman's point of view. . . ." Mr. Nicholas glanced up from his book; Dorothy paused, and went on writing her letter; Mrs. Nicholas shifted heavily as she knitted in the corner of the sofa. She crossed her legs and after a moment recrossed them and began to stretch one foot up and down behind her calf, and then uncrossed them. Presently she and Dorothy went to bathe and Owen went after them. "Well," said Peter, "I think I'll go to bed." Near the top of the first flight of stairs he heard the drawing-room door open and his father came to the bottom and said, "Peter, come and talk to me will you."

"Yes," he said, pretending that he could not imagine why. He felt the usual depressing excitement. His stomach seemed to turn over once and the sweat started under his arms. He had been foolish to think that he had avoided it.

He came into the drawing-room and stood waiting.

"Sit down, old chap." It wasn't an invitation to be at ease but to cease to irritate his father by standing about.

"Now then, old boy, what are we going to do about it?"

He didn't answer. He could think of too many possible answers and their answers and arguments beyond. None of them were any good.

"We can't go on like this."

"Mm."

"Well can we?"

"I don't know." He had lost the chance to reply now. For once his mind had been as clear as his father's; but it had been impossible to decide what to say. Now it was too late. He sat down on the edge of a chair. It had somehow become established that his father was going to talk. He no longer had the energy to put his thoughts into unembarrassing words and if he spoke his eyes would water. He honestly could not think what he had done, but he would be told.

"Either this is my house or it's not."

"Yes."

"Well which?"

Peter didn't answer.

"You see when you get to my age, old boy, with a family of your own it'll be your turn to say what happens."

"Mm."

"Well either we must agree about that or come to some other arrangement."

He didn't actually say, "I'll turn you out of the house." Each time he seemed to come nearer to saying it; but Peter could never believe he meant it.

"I didn't know that I disagreed."

"Oh yes you do, or you wouldn't behave in this way." His father used his answers to increase his temper.

"How do I behave?"

"Your whole attitude is disrespectful. And you incite Owen."

"I don't."

"Yes you do."

"I certainly don't."

"Yes you do."

It was like a prep-school argument without the chance to fight. The dog on the hearthrug went on sleeping, its head forward, one paw curled under its chin, and his mind kept trying to uncurl it. His father walked up and down, his shape crossing and recrossing against the sky.

His father said, "I don't know if it was you who made that mess in the bathroom?"

"What mess?"

"All that burned paper." He paused. "Anyway, it's not the first time it's happened." He waited but Peter said nothing.

"Was it you?"

"I expect so."

"You must know. Either it was or it wasn't."

"It was."

"Well I think you might have said so. It only makes more work for mother. I won't have this perpetual untidiness."

Peter said, "I thought it was only cleaning teeth in the basin that you objected to."

"Don't be silly, of course you didn't think anything of the sort. That's cheek and I won't have it."

The more he answered the longer his father would need to talk without being answered before the scene was over.

"You never used to be like this. I think your aunt Dorothy is right; you must have made bad friends at Oxford."

So that was what Dorothy thought of him. He had some-how forgotten that people talked about him when he wasn't there; not his father and mother, but people whose good opinions he wanted. He remembered the little overheard phrases which took him with a shock outside himself, and made him curl up and want to go away and never tell anyone again what he was thinking.

"If I had appeared at meals in your grandfather's house in the state you do he'd have sent me away to eat in the kitchen.

"Another thing," he said, "it's ridiculous that a man of my age should be turned out of his own drawing-room as I am by all this music. You know I can't sit in the same room with it. If you want your highbrow concerts you must have them somewhere else."

Peter didn't answer.

"And let's get this business of your drawing straight. If you want to draw my picture you don't go away and do a funny caricature in your bedroom; you come and ask me. If you asked decently I wouldn't mind sitting for an hour or two. I won't stand being insulted in my own house and it's time you learned that."

His father walked up and down across the French windows against the grey sky. The light had faded and his features were difficult to distinguish. The dog was still sleeping in the shadows of the sofa. It was time for the row to come to a reconciliation, but it seemed to hesitate.

Presently his father said, "Have a drink."

"Thank you."

"Well, old boy, you go away and have your holiday and think it over will you."

"All right."

# Chapter Six

THEY RACED UP the hill, over the dry grass and ant hillocks, between the two oak woods, and at the top they saw the castle again. She lay exhausted, her cheek against the ground, her bare arms laid beside her head, and he sat near her, breathing quietly. The sun was warm on his back, but the trees were making long shadows and the slope in front was already shaded. At its end, three hundred yards away where the land levelled, was the shadow of the horseman and monument beside them. Beyond, the elms and meadows of the park stretched till they merged in woods and hills, and on the centre of these instead of on a nearby rise as he had hoped was the castle, its stone walls lit by the evening sun like a tiny yellow toy.

They had been there in the hot afternoon. The old man in a hut at the entrance had sold them tickets, and they had walked on his gravel paths between his neatly mown lawns, and climbed the battlements, preserved in their ruined state by almost concealed Ministry of Works iron brackets. For half an hour Peter and Julia had been there alone. Then a man and woman had come in, neither old nor young, nor noticeably in love. There had been a sense of penance about their visit, as if they expected to be bored, and they had stood for a minute and moved on saying nothing. When Peter and Julia tried to get out by climbing down a wall the old man had shouted and made them go through the turnstile.

"I'd almost rather it was allowed to decay."

She agreed and ran ahead for a flower. She noticed chiefly things which delighted her, and Peter also ran and knelt beside her, glad to show that he was in the conspiracy.

Since then they had walked, and sat, and walked again

among the wooded hills of the park. It was a country of trees in full leaf and grass rides with timber railings where rabbits played, and a small stream which was not an appendage of a fence but ran alone between sloping fields of short grass.

"The sort of burn," he said, "from which Richard Hannay refreshed himself before setting out for another brisk twenty miles over the hills after a spy."

"Or some Lawrence peasant lay and watched the clouds." The cows moved lazily, confined by no obvious enclosure, and once they disturbed some sheep which ran off in a flock.

"They look as if all their back legs are off the ground."

"What a wonderful colour," she said, pointing to a corn-field.

"The sort of green I thought Van Gogh invented."

Later Peter knew they were lost, but would not say so because it would show that he was thinking of home and eight hours sleep while she was only aware of the smell of hay and the hot insect-filled evening. He almost hoped they were lost. When they came to the hill with the monument she had said, "Race you to the top," and he had agreed and won. Her loose hair lay over her bare arms and on her cheek and Peter thought that he had never been so fond of anyone.

When she had met him at the station he had not been sure. She had seemed just a friendly girl with a not unpleasant face. They had sat in the back of the car.

"Our local trains get later and later, ha, ha," her father had said, sitting in front driving.

"Really, I can't think where it'll all end, ha, ha." Then she had smiled at him and he had felt excited and happy.

In the ten days since he had gradually been less afraid each morning that when he met her at breakfast he would not like her. They had bathed in the river, and lain in the orchard reading, and sat up later each night when her parents were in bed, talking about books and music and pictures. She knew more than he did but not too much. Each day he had become more fond of her and tried to think how he might touch and kiss without offending her. As she lay beside him on the hill-top with her face in the grass he knew he had never been so fond of her.

She began to sniff and lifted her head, and said, "Have you smelt it?" He put his head down as close to hers as he dared.

"Smells like goat to me."

"I mean the grass."

"Oh, sorry," he said, and they laughed.

They climbed the monument which was of large uneven rocks and about fifteen feet tall. She took off her sandals and he climbed after her, watching her small figure and neat movements. Half way he thought she was afraid and asked if he could help but she didn't answer. At the top the horse was larger than it had seemed and they stood together under its belly looking over the parkland to the castle. The sky was blue without clouds; the heat of the day had passed and there was a sudden small wind but it ceased and the evening was still again. On the last rock as they climbed down she slipped and twisted her ankle.

They started quickly down the hill towards the castle, but on the lower ground it was often hidden by trees and hills. Sometimes they recognised clumps, but they had walked without system in the afternoon, turning back and circling, and could not remember which they had seen first or which way they had passed them, and gradually as the sun set they ceased to be familiar and became grey shapes. They had not eaten since lunch but Peter felt it wrong to talk to her about food because unless he mentioned it she didn't, and anyway when he was with her he had an excitement which made him enjoy going without it. He had the feeling described in *Youth* that he could go on for mile after mile, hour after hour, without rest. At first she would not admit that her ankle hurt but then she sat on a log and let him take her foot in his hands and bind it with a handkerchief.

On a lane they came to a pub and sat blinking in the yellow light of the small smoke-filled bar, avoiding the slow stares of three old men and two middle-aged women, who let it be obvious by their silence that their conversation had been interrupted, but presently let it slowly start again. They bought brandy, but she would only drink a sip and gave the rest to him. When they left and climbed a fence, and set out over fields he wanted to sing. It seemed too soon that they had gone up the last slope and were standing below the castle.

"It would be fun to get in."

He helped her up the outer wall and they stood together on the grass which on the inside was level with its top. The moonlit parts of the broken towers and ramparts were a clear yellow-grey, others were in black shadow, and it threw curious rectangular patches on the tidy paths and lawns. Below them stretched the country they had crossed, but they could recognise nothing except between woods on a distant hill the horseman silhouetted against the sky. Peter tried to think of something to say, but he was aware that she was thinking it too beautiful for literary allusion. He waited for her to speak, but when she turned towards him he saw that she wasn't going to say anything and he took her in his arms and kissed her.

As they drove home he thought he should have been afraid that he had offended her, but it had seemed too right; so right that he did not want to look at her. When he looked she smiled.

"What a wonderful place for our last evening."

"Yes," she said, as if she meant it.

"You must come and stay with us," he said.

The car went smoothly, and he changed gears with only a little noise.

"Scott would have written a poem about it," she said, and he wasn't sure if she meant the place or the event.

# Chapter Seven

IT WAS EVENING when Peter came home and the small pink clouds had lost their colour, and the sky which had been clear green and yellow was grey. He stood in the tiled hall and it was full of shadows with the window on the stairs a grey square and only a little grey light coming from the drawing-room doorway. The dining-room door was closed but there was yellow light beneath it, and beyond his father was telephoning. After a moment he stopped and came out.

"Hallo Peter."

"Hallo Dad."

"Someone I know has had an accident. I must go and see them."

Peter waited curiously but he did not go on. "Is it bad?"

"No." His father was putting on his coat, thinking of something else, and he went out through the kitchen. Peter went quietly upstairs.

From her bedroom his mother called, "Is that you, darling?" with surprise and happiness.

"Yes."

"Have you had a nice time? How are you?"

"Yes," he said. "Yes, very nice."

She wanted him to go in and kiss her goodnight.

"Tell you about it in the morning." He didn't mean to. Once he had been careful not to promise things he did not mean, as a defence against other people promising things they did not mean to him.

"Night-night."

"Night-night."

He went slowly upstairs and opened Owen's door. His

light was out and he was sitting on his bed putting on his pyjama trousers.

"Hallo."

"Hallo." He sounded friendly but it was difficult to know in the dim light.

"You're home are you?"

"Yes," Peter said, and grinned just before it was too late.

There was a pause, but it was no embarrassment to say nothing to Owen.

"How is home?"

"Much the same."

"Father was telephoning."

"Yes, he does that every night."

"Who to?"

"Mrs. Pawthorn. He shuts the dining-room door and then shouts so loud that I can hear it up here."

They laughed.

"He said there'd been an accident."

"Yes, there often is."

Owen got into bed and Peter went to the window and leaned on the sill. The mist in the valley hung half way up above the tree-tops like a white pancake and one chimney was adding to it. There was the sweet smell of wood smoke.

"How's mother?"

"Much the same. She works too hard. She won't do anything about her leg."

"What's the matter?"

"It's been bruised for months. She hits it on the kitchen table two or three times a day in the same place. It hurts her most of the time."

Peter was surprised, and annoyed that he had not noticed. He realised again that though Owen was as aware of his mother's foolishness he had more sympathy for her.

"What does she think about Pussy Pawthorn?"

"She doesn't say."

Peter went into his room and wrote to Julia. It was dark before he finished. Once he leaned out of the window looking at the moon. The smell of wood-smoke was strong in the night air and made him want to cry for the memory of holidays from school in tents. Presently he felt cold wearing only a shirt and went on with the letter. He thanked her as enthusiastically as he could without losing a sense of proportion, and he mentioned Kafka whom he had been reading in the train. He did not ask her to stay because there would be time for that, and to do it at once seemed wrong. He hesitated a long time before he signed it, "Farewell, Peter."

★   ★   ★

In the morning he came first to breakfast and went to look for it in the kitchen.

"Good morning darling."

"Good morning."

"Ready in half a moment." His mother moved busily, frying, making toast and coffee, stirring the porridge. He was flustering her.

"What time did father come back?"

"Four o'clock," she said. She laughed but without much amusement. He had the impression that she was waiting for him to comment but he did not know what to say.

Presently she said cheerfully, "Have you heard about the Hump?"

"No."

"We asked him to David's birthday party, we thought we ought to because he's been very kind to David, and he said he couldn't come because it's during his landlady's ten days' holiday when he has to go away; so we felt bound to invite him to stay.

"For ten days?"

"Yes. He's not really such a bad little man. Since he's been coming here to play tennis I'm sure we've improved him. Made him—you know—laugh at himself a bit."

Peter could hear his father saying it.

"It may be quite amusing."

"I suppose so."

Mr. Nicholas came down at eleven and stood on the lawn. The morning had become fine gradually, without haste. Only a few white and grey cumulus clouds remained in the blue sky and the wind which had been moving them steadily was now an occasional light breeze. The mortars were firing on the range and every few minutes the windows of the house rattled. "What a night," he said and grinned. He was at the stage of recovery when pride in his adventure compensated for his headache.

"What happened?" Peter tried not to sound too interested.

"Well you know this mad R.A.F. man's wife, Mrs. Morton. They wanted me to help get her home. The landlord like a fool had asked her into his back room when he was told she wasn't well, and then like an idiot given her another drink. He'd got her there and couldn't get rid of her. So I said to Major Dale, 'Come on, we've got to carry her.' Well you know what a pathetic little man he is. He kept dropping his end. However we eventually got her to the Pawthorns' car and drove her home, and put her to bed, and we were just going away when she came downstairs and began giving us whisky. That went on for hours, till eventually she had an accident, and we persuaded her to go to bed while we rang up the doctor."

"What was wrong?"

"A woman's accident. While we were waiting for the doctor she came down again and pushed us all out of the house saying that the Squadron Leader was driving from Yorkshire and would arrive at any moment." When he thought of it he laughed and Peter smiled.

"What time did you get home?"

"Four o'clock, but don't tell mother."

It was the moment to make an excuse and go, but Peter was always tempted to stay in case his father still had something interesting to say, and after that it was usually too late. A car came up the private road, turned into the drive, and stopped by the lawn, and Squadron Leader and Mrs. Morton got out.

They sat in the drawing-room facing the sunlit lawn through the open French windows and Peter brought drinks.

"Have you heard about New Thought?" said Squadron Leader Morton. He was short and plump with a black moustache, and the hot weather made him seem lightly greased.

"We're going to a session this afternoon," said Mrs. Morton. She was thickly but erratically powdered and there was a suggestion of extinct volcanoes seen through a telescope about her face.

"Is it spiritualism?"

"Oh no," said Mrs. Morton.

"Oh no," said Squadron Leader Morton.

"We tried that last leave. We went to seven séances in five days."

"New Thought has sessions, not séances."

"Two of your neighbours are keen members."

"Who?"

"General and Lady Binforth."

"They would be," said Mr. Nicholas. He had exhausted his satisfaction in his adventure and still had a headache.

"It's also called Theosophy."

"It's not, dear."

"It is."

"Dear, that's something quite different. Mrs. Spills runs that on Thursdays at six."

"Well, she gave me my booklet."

"Mrs. Graham gave me mine."

"But she's a Christian Scientist."

"Can I fill your glass?" said Peter.

"Thank you."

"Thank you."

"Wasn't Pussy in fine form last night," said Mrs. Morton.

"Yes," said Mr. Nicholas.

Squadron Leader Morton asked, "What's happened to old Pawthorn?"

"He works at the Jade Bowl, the antique shop in Rodenham," said Mrs. Morton. "You can see him sometimes standing in the window with a duster, his feet surrounded by eighteenth century china, looking quite lost."

"Pathetic when you think he once employed several thousand workmen."

"Did he?"

"Yes, in America he owned eight underwear factories, and nineteen cars."

"What happened?"

"He lost them. Also some discontented machinist slugged him. That's why he has three inches of rubber tubing in his tummy. It explains a lot."

"Will you have another?"

"No, really, well just half."

Peter filled their glasses.

The Squadron Leader went on to speak about champagne. There was nothing like it. It provided gaiety, *bonhomie* or whatever damn silly name you called it, but no hangover. He could not understand why everyone did not drink champagne all the time. Had they heard of the new Lagonda Fourteen. It was bang-on.

Presently Owen came in and sat near Peter.

"Peter," he said quietly, "what's the effect of gin on children?"

"Bad I should think."

"Oh dear."

"Why?"

"Elsie Jenning has just had some." Elsie Jenning was Mrs. Jenning's six year old daughter whom she sometimes brought with her, and who stood sucking her finger watching her mother scrub the kitchen floor. When her mother hit her on the toes with the brush she moved a pace, and sometimes when she got more than usually in Mrs. Nicholas' way she was knocked down but usually she stood still sucking her finger. Mrs. Nicholas never dared to suggest that Elsie Jenning did not come in case Mrs. Jenning should be insulted and not come herself.

"Did you give it to her?"

"Well she asked for it."

"How much?"

"Not much, about a quarter of a glass."

"Oh well," said Peter.

"A dinner glass."

"Darling," said Mrs. Morton, "you've got it all ballsed up."

"Excuse my wife's language."

"Where is she?" said Peter.

"I shut her in the larder."

Round the corner of the house, into the bright sunlight on the lawn Elsie Jenning came running. Her straight black hair had come out of the middle-aged style in which her mother fixed it each morning with two hair clips and was blowing about her nose. She carried a two pound pot of red jam. She stopped at the edge of the rockery and deliberately threw it down the steps. In the drawing-room it could be heard to land with a soft smash.

When Mrs. Nicholas came running to catch her she dodged, and came and stood at the French windows.

"Hallo, bright eyes," said Squadron Leader Morton.

Elsie said nothing.

"Hallo, Elsie," said Mr. Nicholas who had not noticed her before. "Be a good girl and run away now."

Elsie said nothing. She was staring at the Squadron Leader's moustache. After a long pause she said, "You old so and so."

She turned and ran out of the veranda with a high giggle and tripped over the mowing machine. For a second there was silence while she realised what had happened. Then she howled.

Mrs. Jenning ran and picked her up.

"Elsie, stop that silly noise." She shook her and Elsie stopped.

"What you do smell of. Elsie, what *have* you been eating? El . . . sie, you've been drinking. Wherever did you get it?"

"Master Owen," she said and fell asleep.

"Well!" said Mrs. Jenning staring round fiercely. She walked away, across the lawn, still carrying Elsie. At the corner of the house she stopped and turned. "Well!" she said. Later they heard them mount their bicycles and ride away down the back drive.

"Owen, did you do it?"

"There may have been a little in the bottom of the bottle." Mr. Nicholas laughed. It did not affect him.

"No more charwoman," said Peter.

"Nonsense," said Mr. Nicholas. "I shall go and explain to her that it was all an accident. Mrs. Jenning is a great friend of mine. She'll do anything for me."

"Two whole pounds of my new quince jam," said Mrs. Nicholas. She pretended to cry, but she almost meant it.

Possibly Mr. Nicholas went to see Mrs. Jenning, or perhaps he forgot, for she did not come back. Nor did anyone replace her. It was difficult to get charwomen in the district, where there were many more houses that could afford them than provide them. But none of the Nicholases really tried.

\* \* \*

The Flying Squirrel had once stood on the bend of a country lane, but the lane had become the main road from Rodenham to the nearest town, the County Council had straightened the bend, and during the war armoured fighting vehicles had broken off the Flying Squirrel's projecting corner. Peter walked slowly down the private road and down another hill, between the fir trees and shrubberies of large front gardens. Passing cars disturbed the dust at the road edge which blew about in the hot sun, into his sandals and in his face. He knew that this was an act of family disloyalty, because Mr. Nicholas had quarrelled with the landlord of the Flying Squirrel.

Its door was open, and Peter wondered if it was true, as someone had said, that it was against the law for a bar to be visible to the street. Inside, two men in suits and a taxi driver stood drinking. It was like all the pubs of the district: no one seemed to belong to it. They came there, but could too easily step into one of the buses which passed in both directions every fifteen minutes. Near the door a farm labourer with wrinkled face and hands, and high leather gaiters sat behind a pint of beer. It was difficult to think of any farm among the pine hills and three-acre garden residences. A few feet outside the door three men in shirt-sleeves stood on the gravel. They drank without talking to each other, as if they suspected that it was against the law to drink in public.

Presently two small women wearing hats came in. They stared at Peter as they carried their stout to a table and began at once to talk about him. He turned his back and stood, shifting his glass carefully on the bar with one hand, listening.

"Top of the hill," one said.

"Where the Major was?" Mr. Nicholas had bought Pine Knoll from an Irish Major.

"Him with the son what shot himself."

"All his doing, they say. Unkind to him he was."

They were talking softly and when he ceased to hear them

124

Peter turned to see if they were whispering, but they were both staring at him.

He looked away and felt himself blushing. After a moment they went on, but more quietly.

"I saw them carrying her, then she fell in the grass wriggling; she wasn't half wriggling. Such a shame, yes, yes, such a pretty girl, yes, yes, yes, such a shame."

"What was the matter?"

"They never did know. She died in three months."

Peter was aware of them staring at him again and made himself turn, but they were looking at their stout.

He finished his drink. The bar was gloomy and he wanted to go. The small bright patches of sunlight emphasised its darkness. They were talking again but he did not want to listen. He went out of the door, pushing past the taxi driver who stared after him and said something rude which he did not understand.

Going up the hill between the shrubberies he told himself it was absurd. How could bad luck be attached to a house? Bad luck was an ignorant name for coincidence. People had died in every house in more or less strange circumstances. He imagined the picnic, in a meadow in the evening, the girl ill for no reason. The idea of unexplained diseases made life seem unsafe. But surely nowadays there weren't such things. He was aware as he climbed the private road that his picture of the house had changed. He thought of it in yellower sunlight, the same shape yet contracted as if its bottom had shrunk but all its upper peculiarities remained, window-heavy like an illustration of a fairy story castle on a rock. The trees and bushes round were a darker forest-green. He told himself that he was hungry and depressed before lunch. He went the longest way and came up the front drive, past the tennis court and the lawn. Captain Cambridge was standing outside the French windows.

He was wearing the soft green hat and grey jacket he

had worn at the tennis party but with grey trousers instead of white flannels. He did well with a small wardrobe. No one seemed to have noticed his arrival except David who stood with him and seemed uncertain what to do; or perhaps others had noticed and gone on with what they were doing.

"Hallo, old fellow, how are you?"

He had the hearty phrases of a back-slapping army officer but not enough heartiness so that instead of being embarrassed you were angry.

"Hallo," said Peter. There was an awkward silence.

Peter said, "I'll go and see where everyone is." He went into the drawing-room and his father came quickly past him, not noticing him.

"Hallo, Hump," he shouted. "You've arrived have you? Come and have a drink. Peter, fetch some drinks."

*　　*　　*

The fine summer held, and streams of eight horse power family saloons, Women's Institute charabancs, and cream sports cars with two seats went down the two sea coast roads which passed to east and west of Rodenham. Occasionally buses which had strayed from these crossed the bottom of the private road with children leaning from their windows waving buckets. In the Beckford district colonels took off their coats to work in their gardens, disclosing braces and fawn shirts which suggested underwear. On the hillsides among the dry heather the smallest fir trees acquired an almost imperceptible dustiness which meant that though still green they were dead. And David Nicholas went for walks with Captain Cambridge.

They went for walks in the morning, and in the afternoon. In the evening they walked round the garden or sat on the edge of the window seat in the drawing-room, or went to David's room.

"Whatever do they do up there?" said Mrs. Nicholas, half laughing.

"Play cards."

"I should have thought they could have done that in the drawing-room."

At tea-time Captain Cambridge talked, often about politics, and sometimes they listened but gradually they ceased to bother. What he said seemed as wrong as what Mr. Nicholas said, but there was no temptation to answer, only to say, "Huh," with obvious disbelief; on the third day Mrs. Nicholas went out with the tea tray, forgetting that since no one else would listen he had been talking to her. For a moment he went on, speaking to no one, then he hesitated, turned a little in his chair, and spoke to Peter.

"That sort of thing isn't taxation, it's downright robbery."

"Certainly," said Peter. He went after Mrs. Nicholas into the kitchen.

She was at the sink, washing the tea china. "Where have they gone now?" she said.

"On to the lawn."

She placed the washed cups on the draining board and he began to dry them. "I do think David needn't spend the whole day with him."

"He never does the washing up?"

"Not only that, but he used to help me—you know—in the kitchen and things."

Dorothy arrived before supper to be there for David's birthday dinner next day. Her cotton frock showed her chest and much of her arms, making the largeness of the parts it covered apparent. She sat in a deck-chair in the veranda.

"Where are they?" she said.

"In David's room."

"What do you think they talk about?"

"The Hump is developing David's character," said Mrs. Nicholas half laughing.

"What do you mean?"

"I don't know. That's what he's told us."

Later in the evening Mr. Nicholas tried to telephone, but the number was engaged. He ran upstairs, cleaned his teeth, ran downstairs, and tried again. Peter hesitated in the kitchen, drinking orange juice, putting off going to bed. The room was grey and he noticed the shapes of the tins of silver polish and patent soap on the window-sill over the sink. He wondered if his father knew he was here. Through the closed door he could hear his voice echoing in the dining-room.

"What? What? Hallo?" A pause. "Thank you." A longer pause. "Hallo, could I speak to Mrs. Pawthorn?" When she answered he said, "Hallo my dear." It was an astonishing soft coo, quite unlike his normal voice. Peter finished his orange juice and moved to the doorway.

"Business first, my dear; all laid on with my bank . . . yes . . . the full amount."

Peter took a pace into the hall. He was on his way upstairs but he wouldn't hurry.

"How are you, my dear? Lovely to hear you darling . . . What? . . . What? Lovely to hear me, good . . . Lovely to hear you."

Peter took another pace, and saw Dorothy near the top of the first flight of stairs standing in a large white night-dress. She leant downwards, listening, and came down a few steps, and then went up. She was anxious to hear but did not dare to come nearer because she was clumsy. He grinned but she did not grin back.

His father was saying, "What are you doing, darling? . . . Knitting? . . . I don't believe you."

Peter went slowly upstairs, but when Dorothy was out of sight he stopped. He waited, listening carefully, ready to hurry up as soon as they began to say good-bye.

"And how is Homo Sapiens? . . . You don't know? . . .

You don't care, ha ha ha." It was their code name for some-one. "Tomorrow dear . . . I'll be there. . . . Right you are, darling, night-night, darling . . . Night-night." Peter went quickly upstairs.

Dorothy was going into the bathroom.

"Did you hear?"

"Not much," she said. "He might at least go out of the house to do it." She hated him for it.

From her bedroom his mother called, "Good-night," cheerfully.

"Good-night."

Owen was coming upstairs behind him.

"Where have you been?"

"In the drawing-room," he said, and grinned.

*   *   *

The hills were blue and hazy across the valley and there were more grey hills beyond, and then blue sky. Sitting on the edge of the tennis court, Peter drew them in his sketch book, but when the sun rose higher its heat made him dizzy and he sat in an arm-chair in the drawing-room. Anyway he didn't believe in sketching. Once he had sketched something it was finished, for if he painted the same subject later he did not remember it but copied the sketch. But if he did not sketch he ceased to notice things, the sudden unlikely arrange-ments of objects which excited him and made him despair of painting anything so good, the dog's copper-coloured head, for instance, over a chair arm, tilted at the same angle as the two chair backs, against the blue window seat—or perhaps he was now consciously discovering pictures.

Even in the drawing-room it was hot; the chair covers which seemed cool to his arms and bare feet soon became warm and when he moved were damp. As he sat he could see his mother's large back bent over her desk and hear her pen writing letters. There was no lunch to cook, for it was to be cold and light to leave an appetite for David's birthday dinner.

"Where's father," he said.

"At the Red Lion, I expect."

He sat up so that he could see her arm writing. Beyond it were the Fyffe's banana labels which she used to save for David, but now he had ceased to collect them.

"No, the Hop Pole, probably," she said. "That's where they seem to go." She went on writing as she talked. "I do wish he hadn't got in with this set."

"Who?"

"The Mortons and the Pawthorns, and Major Dale." He wondered if she was pretending, or if she really did not know.

The postwoman came across the lawn, walking with a slight roll. She wore no jacket and there were damp patches under the arms of her uniform shirt. Peter took the letters but there wasn't one for him.

*　*　*

At lunch time his father returned and Peter, coming downstairs, met him coming up, supporting himself by the wall and banisters. He grinned self-consciously.

"I'm . . ." he said, and paused while a hiccup threatened, retreated, and half came, "quite drunk." He moved up a few steps making several attempts to find each stair with his feet. Dorothy was watching from the hall and Owen came and stood at the workroom doorway. Mrs. Nicholas carried plates through the hall to the dining-room and pretended not to notice. Captain Cambridge came on to the stairs behind him and said very seriously, "Can I help you, Sir?" But Mr. Nicholas went up slowly, holding the banisters and wall, into his bedroom and sat on the bed.

From the dining-room Mrs. Nicholas called, "lunch is ready. Ask father if he wants any."

Peter went back to the bedroom doorway. His clothes

were about the floor and he stood on the linoleum in his vest and pants, swaying a little.

"Would you like some lunch?"

"Tell them," he said, "I've been celebrating David's birthday." He grinned and belched.

"No lunch for me old boy."

David and Captain Cambridge were standing in the drawing-room and Peter picked up a paper. "Jolly bad business," said Captain Cambridge.

★   ★   ★

"Don't you know the one about the Arab?" said Captain Cambridge. "You must know the one about the Arab, the Arab who lost a certain vital article of clothing? No? Well there was once . . ." He had begun telling stories in the drawing-room before dinner and since then scarcely stopped. At first from habit of politeness they had laughed at the conclusions but soon they had only made the effort to grasp each new plot near its end and ceased to laugh. Now they laughed continuously and each time he said, "Don't you know the one·about . . ." they were hysterical. Captain Cambridge was inspired by their laughter; he knew they were laughing at him and not at his stories, but believed they were thinking him funny not contemptible.

The candles flickered and reflected among the cutlery on the mahogany lid of the billiard table where they were dining for the occasion. Outside, the evening was just dark enough to justify them.

"What a pity," Mrs. Nicholas had said to Owen the day before, "that it's summer and we can't use the new candlesticks."

"Why not?"

"It'll still be light."

"When?"

"At supper time."

"Why not wait till it's dark?"

Mrs. Nicholas had smiled at him, accepting his fantasy with tolerance.

"Well why not?" Owen was becoming angry, and she realised, as she had feared all the time, that he meant it.

"We'd never get the washing-up done that night."

"So what?"

She had smiled at him, but without amusement, for he meant it.

And Owen had gone away saying, "Set bed-time, set time to get up, four set meals and four set wash-ups, no we mustn't alter them," so that she could hear.

And somehow during the day she had persuaded Mr. Nicholas that dinner at nine was a good idea. Anyway he wanted to use the candlesticks which he had just bought.

Wax dripped from holes that had been bored in their sockets to fit them for electric light bulbs. They had thick brass stems and five coiled brass branches.

"I'm convinced they're eighteenth century Continental," said Mr. Nicholas. He sat at the head of the table saying little, occasionally resting his head on his hands. When Mrs. Nicholas helped him to vegetables he said, "Not much for me, dear."

"Have you heard the one about the coppersmith?" said Captain Cambridge. "My dear lady, let me tell you the one about the coppersmith." Mrs. Nicholas turned from him and giggled at Dorothy. Peter had noticed her do it before; it reminded him of three female cousins who always giggled, when he spoke to them, at a joke he could not see, and he supposed that Mrs. Nicholas had once been as irritating; but the effect of taking Mr. Nicholas and her sons seriously for twenty-five years, and laughing logically at their jokes, had, except occasionally with Dorothy, cured her of spontaneous amusement.

She turned back quickly to listen, aware of her mistake and

132

forgetting that it was only Captain Cambridge. She and Dorothy had been cooking since five o'clock. The table was heavy with stuffed goose, sauce, gravy, and three vegetables, and fruit salad was on a side-table. She was conscious that she had made her contribution to the party.

David sat next to her. "Jolly good dinner," he said. "Lovely grub, to coin a phrase." He ate steadily, lowering his head towards the plate for each mouthful. At the start of the meal they had pulled one cracker and given him a pink paper hat which he wore seriously. You couldn't tell what he thought.

Peter poured out the wine.

"Only a drop for me," said Mr. Nicholas.

"It's good."

"Oh yes, I know Mr. Jones; he would only sell me a damn good wine. Now bad claret, you might just as well drink red ink. Burgundy, yes Burgundy's all right but it gives you a liver . . ."

"Yes," said Peter quickly. He looked for something to change the subject. He said, "Where did you get these?"

"I tell you, Mr. Jones . . ."

"No, the candlesticks."

"Well if you want to know, they're family possessions of Mrs. Pawthorn." He said it loudly, and Owen heard, and Dorothy looked up. David was eating. Captain Cambridge was making bird noises. He half filled his mouth with water and bubbled through it producing a high warble. Mrs. Nicholas was laughing at him but she probably heard Mr. Nicholas. Peter moved to the next glass. He couldn't think of another subject and wasn't going on with that one.

"So they're only borrowed," said Owen.

"No," said Mr. Nicholas. "I've bought them."

Captain Cambridge warbled, and Mrs. Nicholas giggled, and David gave a loud laugh.

"Do you know this one?" said Captain Cambridge.

"Smack my head." Dorothy smacked the back of his head, and he spat a sixpence on to his side plate. Everyone giggled. "And again," he said, and she went on doing it. After each time they watched him pick up the sixpence and put it quickly back in his mouth. They giggled hysterically.

"How much for?" said Owen.

"That's my business," said Mr. Nicholas.

Each time Dorothy smacked his head harder. She hated him. They doubled up and cried with laughter.

Later they drank David's health, and pulled the crackers, and put on paper hats.

\*   \*   \*

In the kitchen Mrs. Nicholas was making a cake, and Dorothy preparing vegetables. There were measuring scales, calibrated jugs, enamel plates of dried fruit, and packets of flour and sugar arranged round the mixing bowl on the table, and Mrs. Nicholas stirred and poured. When Peter came in she straightened her back and said, "Pff," pushing back her hair with her wrist. It was hot in the kitchen and her efforts had made patches of her face pink.

"Where are they now?" she said.

"Upstairs, I think."

"If only he would go."

"He won't do that," said Dorothy. She sat on the end of the table slicing beans into a bowl. "He's on to a good thing."

"David?"

"Free board and lodging."

"Surely," said Mrs. Nicholas, "there's some way to get rid of him."

Mr. Nicholas came downstairs, across the hall, into the kitchen. "Get rid of who?" he said. "The Hump? Isn't he going?"

"I don't think so. Not till his ten days are up."

"Ten days?" said Mr. Nicholas. "That's absurd, we should all go mad. Oh no, that wasn't the understanding; we asked him for David's party; after that he must look after himself." He stood at the open back door and the sunlit day made him feel well and energetic. He often invented understandings where there had only been misunderstanding.

"He's told David that he thought he was invited for all the time his landlady is away."

"Why does he send messages by David instead of speaking to us himself like any normal person? He's not David's guest. Oh no," said Mr. Nicholas, "that's absurd, and I won't have it. It would be different if he'd behaved himself, but after his conduct with David it's mad."

He walked about the kitchen with his hands in his breeches pockets. Mrs. Nicholas poured the cake into a baking-tin and Dorothy went on slicing beans.

"Anyway he's making mother miserable, and that's got to stop." He spoke loudly as if he hoped to be overheard.

Mrs. Nicholas said that *she* didn't mind, she just thought it bad for David.

"Of course, my dear. That's why I mind too. It's the worst thing in the world that could happen to a boy of his age." He walked up and down, increasing his indignation. "A normal person would realise he wasn't wanted and take the hint. I shall speak to him. Where is he now?" He went out of the kitchen, not waiting to be told.

Peter went slowly upstairs, and as he passed the closed billiard room door he heard his father speaking to Captain Cambridge inside. "That's not the point at all. You haven't understood my point at all." Peter found a book and came slowly downstairs. "I'm not going to argue with you about it. No, no, I won't argue." In the kitchen his mother and Dorothy were slicing beans. Presently Mr. Nicholas came down.

"What happened?"

"I told him he must go."

"What did he say?"

"At first he tried to bluff it out. Said he thought he'd been invited for the ten days. He didn't really think anything of the sort. Said that David had told him so, but I pointed out that it was usual to take invitations from your host, not his children. I was quite decent about it. I said that in normal times when one could get servants we should have been glad to let him stay, but these weren't normal times, and the extra work was simply wearing my wife out. Then he tried a sob-story, but I wasn't having that. Said he'd nowhere to go, so I said I'd buy him a ticket to any place in England he cared to name."

"What did he say?"

"He didn't like that a bit. He realised that he was caught."

"The trouble is," said Mr. Nicholas, "he has no money. Like a fool he commuted his pension. I suppose he makes a little out of his sporting prints. That's all his collection really is though he wouldn't admit it. A man with any guts would take a proper job instead of mouching about pretending to be a political lecturer, and sponging on other people's hospitality."

Captain Cambridge spent the rest of the morning telephoning, and eventually told David who told Mrs. Nicholas that he could go next day to stay with his sister in the North.

"The trouble is," said Mr. Nicholas, "he really has no friends."

After lunch David and Captain Cambridge went for a walk and at tea-time they had not come back. In the veranda Mrs. Nicholas poured out tea on the trolley and the others sat in deck-chairs.

"Where can they have got to?"

"Taking a farewell stroll."

"Having a last go at David's character."

They were aware of unusual unity; Captain Cambridge

was something they could agree about. Mrs. Nicholas brought her cake from the shade, cut it, and passed the plate, noticing who took a piece. It was too hot to eat.

"Did anyone notice which way they went?" she said trying to sound casual, and no one troubled to think if they had.

The dog was crouching and snarling, but even Owen had not the energy to play with it. Across the lawn the broom seeds snapped, and the tall green firs stood still against the cloudless blue sky.

"I hope they do come back," said Mrs. Nicholas. She gave a nervous laugh to hide the absurdity of her suggestion.

"They often stay out till half past four."

"It's gone five," she said.

The outer leaves of the rhododendrons drooped in the heat. From across the private road in the fir wood came the knocking of croquet balls and sometimes the sound of General Binforth's voice raised in organisation.

"Another piece of cake?"

"No thank you."

"More tea?"

"No thanks."

They came slowly up the drive, Captain Cambridge holding on to David's shoulder, leaning his head towards it, and limping, David supporting him with a hand round his back, but holding his head away and not looking at him.

"Oo," said Captain Cambridge as they came up the step on to the lawn.

Mr. Nicholas got up and went towards them. "What's the matter?"

"Oo," said Captain Cambridge, wrinkling his face to show pain.

"David, what's happened?"

"My leg," said Captain Cambridge.

"Is it broken?"

"No," said Captain Cambridge. "It's gone." Owen giggled. "First time it's done it for five years."

Mr. Nicholas came back and sat down.

"Happened at the bottom of Vale Lane. If it hadn't been for your son I should never have got home."

David had moved away from him and he stood with his weight obviously on one foot. There were no spare chairs and no one stood up.

"Extraordinary thing, first time it's happened for five years."

No one answered. Mrs. Nicholas poured out more tea for Dorothy.

David fetched a chair from the end of the veranda, and set it up, and Captain Cambridge, holding David's arm, lowered himself into it with a small cry.

"Didn't know your son was so strong. He's been supporting most of my weight as well as his own for the last hour. If it hadn't been for him I don't know what would have happened."

The sun moved over the tennis court, and shadows of the fir trees started to come on to the lawn. Peter sat on, drinking tea in case something happened. Mrs. Nicholas was restless to be washing up and preparing supper.

"Your son has kindly promised to give my leg a rub," said Captain Cambridge. He rose, screwing up his face and opening his mouth for pain, and limped in through the French windows; David went after him.

"I'm sure he made David do that," said Mrs. Nicholas.

"I'm sure it was David's kindness," said Owen.

"To think," said Mr. Nicholas, "that any son of mine should come to rubbing the leg of a retired army captain." He stood up and made a consciously dramatic exit, across the lawn, down the hill to the Red Lion.

"Did you notice which leg it was before he sat down?" said Owen.

"His right," said Peter; he felt sure.

"It was his left when he got up," said Owen; he was almost certain.

"He's fixed us," said Dorothy.

"How?"

"That leg won't be fit to travel tomorrow."

But perhaps it cured itself, or perhaps David's rubbing made it better, for it was all right in the morning, and Captain Cambridge, still limping a little, went with David carrying his bag down the hill to the main road to wait for a bus to the station.

# Chapter Eight

DOROTHY LEFT next day and on Friday Mr. Nicholas went to London. The windows were open, and the house silent and hot. David was upstairs in his room cleaning his shoes. Recently he had spent many hours a day cleaning his shoes till they shone like patent leather. Owen was on the hillside building a castle. He damped the sand, shaped it into rectangular walls, and let it bake hard in the sun. In the kitchen Mrs. Nicholas was cooking but there was no one to talk to and the sound of her knife cutting on the deal table came between intervals of silence. The excitement of the past days seemed to have passed. As he stepped into the taxi which took him to the train Mr. Nicholas had said, "There's no doubt we've cured our Hump trouble."

Mrs. Nicholas bent over a salad, decorating it with hard-boiled egg, and Peter coughed so that he should not startle her by being there suddenly.

"Hallo darling."

"Hallo."

"One piece too many, now where shall I put it?"

"I don't know."

"What are you busy with?"

"Nothing, really." There was a pause.

He said, "Why has father gone to London?"

"With Mrs. Pawthorn, I suppose."

"Did he tell you?"

"Owen heard them arranging it last night on the telephone." She cut slices of cucumber. "I really can't understand what he sees in her." She said it looking at what she was doing, as if she thought she was wrong to talk about it.

"No," said Peter. He went back on the remark, considering it apart from his mother. "No, I really can't."

"Owen can't stand her," she said. She was trying to excuse her dislike. "He says she flatters him."

"What does Mr. Pawthorn say?"

"I don't think he worries. Will you arrange these for me?" She passed him the slices of cucumber, and he began to lay them one at a time symmetrically on the salad.

"When will father be back?"

"By the eleven-two tonight."

He went on helping her with the lunch because he was suddenly aware of her loneliness, and didn't like to leave her in the kitchen, cooking all day to make nice things to eat for people who had ceased to care about her. He could remember Mr. Nicholas caring for her very much. He could remember standing beside the double bed in the early morning, asking his father to come shooting, and his father saying, "Coming, old boy, let Mummy and I have a last five-minute cuddle."

They had been defiantly in love. His father had often compared the successful way in which he loved his wife and his wife loved him with other people's failures.

After an argument, when he had got his way, he used to say, "Give me a kiss," and take her round the waist, leaning forward as she leant back smiling and let herself be kissed. "No, a proper one."

"I want a kiss," he would say, grasping her wrist and leaning towards her between courses at lunch.

When the servants laid them at opposite ends of the table he used to be angry. "I won't have it, I always sit next to my darling Mummy."

He had seemed to make a point of demonstrating his affection for his wife as a criticism of Peter's quarrels with Owen.

It was difficult to remember when these things had stopped. Even after his illness they had both slept in the double bed for

141

a time, until he complained that her snoring kept him awake. And when he was cheerful or drunk he still kissed her.

Peter watched her fingers making pastry. They were long with smooth lozenge shaped bulges from chilblains and too much washing-up.

"Shall we go to the air display tomorrow?"

"I don't know. We could."

Mr. Nicholas telephoned at eleven-fifteen, and Peter went to answer it, but his mother was there first. He could hear his father shouting at the other end.

"Hallo, is that you, dear?"

"Yes, dear."

"I'm ringing from the station. I've just missed the last train."

"Oh, bad luck."

"I shall have to stay the night in town."

"Yes."

"You see, I'm at the station and it's quarter-past the hour, and the last train went at eleven."

"Yes, what'll you do for pyjamas?"

"What? What? Oh I shall manage."

"When shall we expect you tomorrow?"

"I don't know at all. Probably in the evening."

"I see."

"Good-bye dear."

"Good-bye dear."

Owen was in the dining-room doorway. "Who was that?"

"Father," she said. "He was ringing from the station. He's just missed the last train." It did not occur to her to disbelieve him.

★ ★ ★

"Are we going to the air display?"

"Why not?" said Mrs. Nicholas. She was less tired and the problems raised seemed less insoluble. She began to think about Thermoses.

"Owen is asking Brian."

"Oh," said Mrs. Nicholas. She stirred the porridge.

"Is that all right?"

"I suppose so. You know he's had to leave his new school?"

"What did he do?"

"Well nothing as far as anyone has heard, but he's had to leave. I *am* sorry for Lady Binforth." She moved about the kitchen, frying and toasting.

"Perhaps he won't come," she said. "If he does it'll mean sandwiches for five. I could take the milk in a bottle, separate from the tea."

They started soon after breakfast, carrying picnic baskets. David had put on a clean shirt and suit.

"David," said Owen, "you haven't pressed your trousers."

"David," said Peter, "you've forgotten your umbrella."

David laughed. He never knew what to say. Sometimes when they continued to tease him he threw something, or pushed them, but usually he laughed. When he laughed there was no suggestion that he thought it funny.

The letters arrived as they were leaving, and David took them from the post-woman, and put one for himself in his pocket. Mrs. Nicholas watched him and tried to see it. She looked quickly through the rest and put one in her handbag. She was in the habit of recognising letters before she opened them, and anyway Captain Cambridge's writing was distinctive, very small and neat.

\* \* \*

The aerodrome stretched away to an indefinite farther boundary near low hills. There were no trees or bushes, and only occasional holes or pieces of broken building made the surface uneven. The earth was a faded purple, the colour of cinders and the few areas of grass were grey green as if ash had blown on them. Far across, where the concrete runways met, the massed bands of the R.A.F. were playing, "250

143

strong" according to the programme, but their music came so faintly that there was no tune. It was apparent because their position gradually shifted that they were marching, and presently they had disappeared, somewhere beyond the aerodrome towards the hills. Perhaps it was the barbed-wire round the edge which gave the aerodrome the atmosphere of an empty battlefield.

But this side of the wire pink and blue Coca-Cola bars and ice cream stalls were rising in the morning sun. Spectators moved thickly round them and scrambled to capture with their coats patches on one of a few low hillocks. Programme sellers shouted, and the broadcast system asked Mrs. Abrahams to collect her small daughter from the Wing-Commander's office.

Before it was too late they also found space on a sandy slope, among the outstretched legs of family men in shirt-sleeves, behind the rounded backs of summer frocks. The sun became hot and there was no shade. Children went in a continuous stream, tripping over legs, down the hill for bottled drinks. Beyond the stalls were marquees and then the aerodrome, with the planes now apparent in lines along its edge. "Daddy, when are they going to start?" A silver aeroplane began to circle and twist above. When it looped it seemed that it would not be able to level out before it hit the ground. It dived vertically at great speed, turning only very slowly, and the crowd watched. It came lower and lower still heading downwards. Several women stopped eating. The man with the large red growth on his neck was holding his breath. "Daddy when are they going to start?" It levelled fifty feet from the ground and flew across the aerodrome, its engine screaming.

"The pilots all get drunk," said Brian.

Presently Brian and Owen went to buy ice-cream, and David went away somewhere by himself, and Mrs. Nicholas read Captain Cambridge's letter.

"What does he say?" Peter asked.

"Thanks us for his visit."

"Did he enjoy it?"

"He says so."

"Does he mention leaving?"

"No." She put it in her bag. "He says he knows that he has his faults, and one of them is being too sensitive."

It was so unlikely that Peter could not help thinking again about it. It was the exact opposite of what his conversation suggested.

"I don't think he is," said Mrs. Nicholas.

That he thought this of himself should, Peter supposed, have helped to explain him, but it was impossible to understand in what sense it could apply to him.

"Do you?" said Mrs. Nicholas.

"I suppose not," said Peter.

Against the bright sky small fast aircraft circled and rolled. After a time their stunts were monotonous. It was obvious after the fifth or sixth loop that they never did hit the ground. On the shadeless hillocks men put newspapers over their heads and ate sandwich lunches, and their large white arms, unaccustomed to exposure, turned pink. In front the helicopters hovered, new types flew past at astonishing speeds, like tropical insects, bombs and rockets exploded, and several dozen Alsatian dogs jumped through a hoop. In the late afternoon two or three hundred four-engined bombers flew over in formation and the men and women on the hill-tops drank tea. When the boy came shouting among them they bought evening newspapers. The crash came unexpectedly, the plane seemed to slip sideways into one of the hills beyond the aerodrome. There was a heavy detonation and a thin column of white smoke.

Mrs. Nicholas looked at it anxiously. "Do you think anyone's hurt?"

* * *

They had supper on the lawn. The sun was sinking over the wood, lighting the house a curious orange, but the air was still warm. There were pink wisps of cloud in the sky which was blue above and green and yellow near the horizon. Somewhere in the valley a wireless was playing through an open window.

A taxi came up the drive, stopped at the front door, and Mr. Nicholas got out. "How much is that? . . . Here's something for yourself. Hallo dear. How's everything?" She stood up and they kissed.

"Having a picnic supper, are you? I see. Well, what have you been up to?"

"We've been to the air display."

"I see. Lots of thrills and excitement? I've just been reading about it in my paper. Some wretched fellow was killed in a smash. Bad business. Rather a good article by some journalist chap. The point he made was . . .

Presently Mrs. Nicholas said, "There's a letter for you."

"For me? Who from?"

"Captain Cambridge."

"Who? The Hump? Have you opened it?"

"No, I had one as well."

"Where is it? Let me have a look." But he could not be bothered with the writing.

"Mother, you'll have to read it to me." They went away with it.

\* \* \*

When Peter came to clean his teeth his father was filling the bath. He wore only a shirt which he held to his tummy with one hand; his thin legs were bent at the knees and his toes turned up.

"Has mother shown you my letter?"

"No."

"It's a disgusting piece of work. Fancy writing to your

host criticising his wife. He says he was forced to leave because mother was jealous of his influence over David. I explained clearly to him that it's quite unreasonable nowadays to expect people to give you indefinite board and lodging when they have no servants."

He tested the bath with his heel, and ran in more cold. "It would be different if he was a desirable little man."

"What else did he say?"

"Oh a lot of other nonsense."

Peter cleaned his teeth into the lavatory and Mrs. Nicholas came in.

"After you," she said cheerfully.

"Don't you agree, mother, that it's a disgraceful letter."

"Yes," she said sadly.

"It's time we took this matter in hand. I'm not used to being written to like that."

"I'm only afraid," she said, "that if we're too firm we may, as it were, drive David into the Hump's arms."

"I quite agree with you, my dear, but we can give him a damn good talking to; point out what a fool he's making of himself. Don't you think so, Peter?"

Peter said, "It couldn't do any harm." It sounded silly and was not what he meant.

"It'll do the hell of a lot of good."

"If it's done tactfully," said Mrs. Nicholas.

"I quite agree, my dear, but it's no good mincing words. It's absurd that a boy like David should spend whole days with a man of the Hump's age."

"Do they mean to go on?"

"He hopes," said Mrs. Nicholas, "that we won't put anything in the way of a friendship which has already had such happy results on both sides."

"Who's he to say that he's had a happy effect on David. You've only got to look at the boy to see it's not true. He's begun to have that curious transparent green look which comes from not going to the lavatory regularly. He's almost given up his cricket. He used to play me a decent game of billiards, but now he's lost interest. He mopes about at home with nothing to do. Don't you agree, Peter?"

"He does mope."

"Anyway," said Mr. Nicholas, "it's absurd that he should force that silly little man on *us* any more, I shall make that quite plain."

"Mm," said Mrs. Nicholas sadly.

Peter went slowly upstairs. Owen's light was on and he opened the door, and saw that he was in bed reading.

"Father's in terrific form."

"He usually is after a London week-end."

"I wonder if they go to bed together."

"I suppose so." Owen's bitterness surprised Peter, and made him realise that, since his father's behaviour had ceased to affect him personally it made him less angry. Sometimes he felt that he and Owen thought so similarly that there ought not to be this difference.

★   ★   ★

Mr. Nicholas spoke to David next evening.

"I think I put some sense into his head."

But after two or three days David began to go away after breakfast returning a few minutes before lunch, and go away after lunch returning a few minutes before supper. Sometimes he hesitated at the back door, holding it open and not going out, and said, "Well, I'm off," but often he went without saying anything. And it was obvious even before Mrs. Nicholas asked that Captain Cambridge had returned to the district.

"Where to?" she said, trying to sound casual, but she was much too concerned.

"To the town. I may go and have coffee with Captain Cambridge." He went slowly through the doorway, as if he was trying to think of something else to say.

"Has the boy no sense of family loyalty?" said Mr. Nicholas.

"The trouble is," said Mrs. Nicholas, "he thinks the Hump can do no wrong."

Peter went on to the tennis court and lay in the shade reading a novel. It had an intensity which made him want to read the second half all at once, and it was short enough. He thought it terrific. It was the sort of book which made him walk about with excited detachment, noticing things, and which he tried to lend to friends.

He became aware that Mr. Nicholas was on the court. He was walking about at the far end, occasionally bending. Presently he had moved to the near end. Peter went on reading.

"Damn these bloody ants." Peter could see out of the corner of his eye that he was blowing insect killer on them and he went on reading.

"This should do down the little devils." When there was no person he found something else to attack. *Fight the good fight with all thy might* was his favourite hymn. On days of National Prayer in the village church at their last home he had chosen God's advice to Joshua for the lesson, and read it with emotion. "Only be strong and of a good courage." Peter realised with annoyance that he had read a page without understanding it and began again at the top.

"It would be reasonable," said Mr. Nicholas, "if David had been a bookworm, but it's amazing that a thing like this should happen to a normal healthy boy."

"Mm," said Peter without looking up.

"It's as absurd as our Cousin Richard. We had him here to stay, you know. He did jolly well, made a good score and took a lot of wickets. The very next day he rushed off home because he was frightened by some cats in the night."

Peter marked his place with a piece of grass, closed his book, and leant on his elbow.

"Mm," he said.

149

"Well, old boy, do you want to come to the pub for a drink?"

"I don't think just now, thank you, Dad."

Peter finished the book, closed it, and sighed. Usually he was careful not to sigh in case he depressed other people. He walked slowly off the court towards the lawn. He felt as if he had suddenly been set back from the succession of daily events so that others in the past and future were in sight. On the lawn his mother was saying good-bye to Lady Binforth.

"It's so very kind of you," said Lady Binforth. "The General and I are so very grateful to all you kind people who do so much to help our poor soldiers. We do want to say thank you very very much." She wrinkled her powdered face into smiles and went away down the drive helping herself with a walking stick gripped among her rings.

"What did she want?"

"She was selling these for soldiers' orphans and widows." Mrs. Nicholas showed him a plaster plate about the size of a coffee saucer with a relief figure of an eighteenth century gentleman in the centre. His face was salmon pink without eyes or mouth, and some of the red paint meant for his long coat was on his white stockings.

"What are they for?"

"You hang them up," she said. "I think they're rather nice."

"I think they're horrid," he said. If he went on adapting his opinions to other people's he would cease to know what he did think.

"Oh are they?" she said sadly. "I suppose so."

She carried them into the drawing-room to hide in a drawer. Mr. Nicholas was coming up the drive, across the lawn. There would still have been time but she became aware that she was hiding them from him and stopped. She should have no secrets from him.

"Hallo, my dear, what have you got there?"

"Some things Lady Binforth was selling for soldiers' widows."

Peter waited for it. He had heard it so often before. "Dear old mother, can't say no. Just throwing money down the drain."

"What did they cost?" said Mr. Nicholas, and she told him.

"Charming," he said.

Peter went upstairs. The hours since breakfast and the heat made him exhausted, and he climbed slowly. The smells of the morning's cooking had risen to the top of the house, and he noticed them when he reached the landing. Owen was humming tunelessly in his room, as he did when he was making something. David's door was open and on his floor were his stamp albums and a dish of water with floating pieces of envelope, and some pairs of trousers which he had been pressing with a play-box, and scattered books. Peter went across the landing, into his own room and shut the door. On his desk was a letter from Julia.

He wondered who had put it there. He sat on his bed and read it quickly. She said that she was writing in the garden on a hot afternoon while some kind person played Bach next door; she described a walk in a wood and the trees and the smells, and how she had got lost; and she asked if he remembered looking for the castle in the moonlight. She said she was sorry she had not written before and still more sorry that she hadn't read any Kafka.

Peter lay on his bed and read it again, slowly. He went and sat at his desk. The sun was coming through the window and he half drew the curtains. After a time he began to write to her.

When he had finished he realised that he had not asked her to stay. He thought of adding it at the beginning, but there wasn't enough space, and of putting a postscript, but it didn't seem the right place for an invitation. Presently he licked the envelope.

Mr. Nicholas came slowly up the stairs on to the landing, thinking of things to say. He came with slow steps across the landing into Peter's room and shut the door. "Now then, Peter, what are we going to do about it?"

"About what?" Peter put the envelope on his desk with the address underneath, and didn't look up.

"It just can't go on. Your brother David is making his mother's life miserable. We've got to stop it. Have you heard the latest?"

"No."

"He's refused to go to Communion with her tomorrow because he's arranged to go with the Hump. Fancy preferring a creature like that to his own parents."

In a way Peter was flattered to be consulted, and he tried to think what to suggest, but he wasn't sure what he wanted to achieve let alone how.

"You see, I've talked to the boy, and it seems to have had no effect." Mr. Nicholas stood with his hands in his breeches pockets and Peter waited for him to go on. It was impossible to be in his company without being aware of his mind working and expecting something at any moment to be thrown out. But now he seemed not to know what to say, and honestly to· want suggestions. It was difficult to become accustomed to this.

"I should have thought the boy would have had more family loyalty."

"Perhaps I could talk to him." It was a stupid remark for it was a suggestion that he might succeed where his father had failed, but Mr. Nicholas, though not enthusiastic, chose not to be insulted.

"Well, good luck to you," he said. He went out letting in the smell of meat pastry. "Lunch is ready, old boy."

In the evening Peter went to David's room. He wanted to walk up and down, but there were too many books and clothes on the floor so he sat on the play-box and put his head in his hands. The bedside lamp made the evening outside the window seem black, but in the rhododendrons a blackbird was still calling in alarm. David sat in bed and his dressing-gown was too small so that several inches of his wrists showed beyond its sleeves. He had been writing in his diary.

"No one," said Peter, "understands what you see in the Hump." He wanted to explain that everyone thought him a silly little man, but he tried not to put himself out of sympathy with David.

"Mm," said David. He lifted his pencil as if he was going to go on writing, but let it fall. If only he would say something.

"I don't only mean mother and father who are prejudiced." Peter tried to imagine what David was thinking and looked up to see if he had been right.

"No," said David, and frowned. It was impossible to tell, and Peter waited for him to go on, but he didn't. You couldn't talk to him if he never said what he thought or admitted when you guessed. You could only talk at him, but that was what his father did.

"You may think that everyone misunderstands the Hump," said Peter, "but . . ." He forgot what he was going to say, and it did not seem worth remembering. He left the sentence hanging. He wasn't going to try to finish it. He put his head in his hands and waited.

"I think they do," said David.

"Well why?" said Peter.

"I just do."

"You must have some reason."

"Not necessarily."

"But of course you must or you wouldn't think so."

David didn't answer and Peter was aware that he had stopped him talking, but he didn't care. That sort of illogical argument maddened him. It made him despair of ever making contact with David.

"He's done me a lot of good."

"Ah," said Peter. That was typical: to deny obstinately that he had any reason, and in his next sentence give one.

"In what way?"

"Developing my character," said David. He had no idea of inventing his own phrases. Everything he said was a quotation. He seemed to struggle to find words to say what he thought till Peter wanted to help him, and then when he spoke it was obvious that he had been trying to remember somebody else's words. Often it was possible to realise that he was using a phrase familiar to himself though one had never heard it.

"In what way?" said Peter.

"Helping me to be less selfish and greedy."

"But you never were, particularly."

"Yes, I was. I mean greedy in the full sense of the word."

Peter could think of no answer. The conversation had gone in a wrong direction. He stood up and fiddled on David's mantelpiece.

"Must you go to church with him tomorrow? It's mother's birthday and she's very upset."

There was a pause. "The thing is, we've arranged it," said David.

Peter didn't answer. He tried to let David suggest something, but he didn't, so he said, "Could you go with her tomorrow, and him next week?"

David frowned. After a moment he said, "You see he says she can't get its full benefit if she goes every week and it becomes a mere routine."

"But this would only be two weeks."

There was a pause. "The trouble is," said David, "it's all arranged."

He was hopeless: when you came to the end of the argument he went back to the start.

"Perhaps," said Peter, "there's a second service tomorrow." He tried to let David make the obvious suggestion.

"There's one after Morning Prayer."

Peter waited, but David wouldn't go on so he said, "Couldn't you go with him to that, and with mother before breakfast?"

"Two Eucharists in one day?" David said, and Peter realised that he had said something ridiculous.

"Oh no, of course."

He stood near the mantelpiece, fiddling with an empty cartridge case. "Well, all I know," he said, "is that mother is very miserable." He was tired of interfering in other people's decisions, it was hard enough to make your own. He was sick of suggesting compromises while David didn't try. "Would the Hump approve of you making her miserable?"

David frowned.

"Would he?"

"I don't know. He once said, 'Oh don't bother about her, she's jealous,' but I'm sure that's not what he really thinks."

"How do you know?"

"I'm sure."

"But how are you sure?"

"I just am."

"But something must make you sure."

"Not necessarily."

Peter went away. "Oh," he said, and shut the door. He had tried to sound sarcastic, but when he was half down the stairs he was sure that David had taken it as agreement and wanted to go back.

Mr. Nicholas was on the landing. "What luck?" he said.

Peter didn't want to say. He felt guilty; the odds had been heavy enough against David and there had been no need for him to join. "Not much," he said.

"Did you tell him that he'd bloody well got to go with his mother."

"No," said Peter. He let the silence go on as long as he dared. "I tried to persuade him." It sounded pathetic and smug. He hurried on to prevent his father's contempt. "I asked him whether the Hump would approve of making mother miserable."

"What did he say to that?"

Peter hadn't meant to repeat it. He went on unwillingly. "Apparently he once said, 'Oh don't bother about her, she's jealous'."

"What did David answer to that?"

"I don't know."

"Damn it the boy's eleven stone. Couldn't he knock him down?"

*   *   *

It was light when Peter woke and there were sounds in the house. A door shut and steps went across the middle landing, down the stairs. Then they ceased and he recognised the second silence of Sunday before breakfast. In the valley the bell of the mission church was shaken two or three times; it was like a school dinner bell. Peter dozed. When he rewoke the house was still silent and he got up and dressed. David's door was open and he looked in but the bed was empty. Eggs were ready to boil on the kitchen table and the porridge simmering on the oven but no one was there or in the dining-room. He opened the back door and stood on the doorstep in the warm morning sun which only came on that side of the house for the first hours of the day. The cat near the door-mat looked up at him, stretched a front paw, and after a moment rolled on its back to be tickled. His mother was coming up the cinder-path, past the rhododendrons and the coal shed, with the sun behind her so that it was difficult to see her clearly, but when she came closer David wasn't with her.

"Hallo darling."

"Many happy returns."

"Thank you."

She came into the kitchen and began to boil kettles and make toast.

"Ready in a moment."

"David didn't go with you?"

"No," she said. "He'd gone when I got down. He left this on my plate."

The envelope was addressed to Mrs. Nicholas, Pine Knoll, Beckford, Nr. Rodenham. Peter took out the letter.

"I hope you will believe me when I say that it is not without great heart-searchings that I have determined that it will be for the best to act in this way. Only so can we show that we are determined that nothing shall come between our friendship.

"You speak about family loyalty and I am fully aware that I owe you a debt for many of the essential but unimportant things of life. But for almost all spiritual things I am in Captain Cambridge's debt. It has indeed been a very real awakening.

"I think you may not have realised how the events of the last few weeks have hurt Captain Cambridge, a man of a very real sensitivity, and I feel it my duty to do everything I can to show him that these injuries were the result of thoughtlessness, not actual malice.

"I must end now,

Your affectionate son, David.

"P.S.—I shall not return till this evening that you may not be tempted to answer in haste."

She was waiting for him to comment, but he didn't know what to say. He was annoyed by the idea that she was waiting to hear what he thought before she knew what she thought.

"Not a kind letter," he said, but he only said it to comfort her, and it did not sound genuine. It was obvious that David had not meant to be unkind.

She didn't answer, and he didn't go on. The cat came

157

slowly in at the open door, stretching its legs, smelling for food.

"How hard would you like your essential but unimportant egg?" she said and laughed but it was close to crying.

★   ★   ★

The hot Sunday morning passed slowly. Owen was in his room, and his continuous tuneless hum could be heard at the bottom of the stairs; Mr. Nicholas stayed in bed with the Sunday papers but got up in time to go to the Red Lion; and Mrs. Nicholas cooked the joint. When she basted it the smell of roasting meat and potatoes spread through the house, and towards lunch time came continuously from the kitchen. It was too hot to want to eat.

They started lunch without Mr. Nicholas. When he came in he said, "No sign of our son David?"

"No."

"Now then mother, what are we going to do about it?"

"His letter said he wouldn't be back till this evening."

"I know, my dear, I'm not talking about that. I mean that dirty little swine the Hump." He had had a good morning at the Red Lion.

"Mm," said Mrs. Nicholas sadly.

"It's not right that my friends should be asking me why they always see my son about with an old man." Mr. Nicholas chewed vigorously and put out gristle.

"It's time we took this matter in hand. We've tried talking to him sensibly and that hasn't worked. It's time we took a firmer line."

"I'm only afraid," said Mrs. Nicholas, "that if we're too firm we may make matters worse."

"How, my dear? He must bloody well be made to realise that we mean what we say." Mr. Nicholas emphasised his swear words as if defying someone to tell him not to use them.

158

"Mm," said Mrs. Nicholas sadly.

They had tea in the veranda. Mrs. Nicholas had made herself a small birthday cake. Mr. Nicholas in a deck-chair finished a Sunday paper and tossed it on to the grass.

"Well, no sign of our affectionate son?"

"I was wondering," said Mrs. Nicholas, "if we could arrange some—you know—tennis and things to give him some interest at home."

"Mm," said Mr. Nicholas. He had a headache.

"Because I think that's half the trouble, don't you Peter?"

"Yes," said Peter. He was too quick to have thought about it but she didn't notice. He wanted to say, "No I think it's about a tenth," but it was pointless, because she didn't mean what she said; she made talking futile; and she would have agreed sadly with him. Also it would have been a snub, and he didn't want to snub her.

"Perhaps we could mark out the clock-golf course," she said.

No one answered. Owen sat on the lawn, playing with the dog. Mr. Nicholas was aware of his headache. There were patches of sunlight in the veranda, ants crawled on the sand between the worn brick floor, and the air was hot.

"Have a piece of essential but unimportant cake?" said Mrs. Nicholas.

*　　*　　*

Peter was on the lawn when David came back a few minutes before supper.

"Hallo," David said cheerfully, with no cheerfulness.

"Hallo," said Peter. He didn't know what to say to him.

When they had started supper it seemed too late to say anything. They waited for what Mr. Nicholas would say when he came back from the Red Lion. It was impossible to imagine Mr. Nicholas ever thinking a moment inappropriate to say something. But when he came he had forgotten David.

"I stood up and told them so. They didn't like that a bit. It's no good their thinking. . . That's typical of these fellows with no proper education . . . So I stood up. . . .

"Of course I partly blame Major Dale. You can't have a club without matches and it's the secretary's job to arrange them. It's not for me. . . Part of the trouble is that he's a Scotsman. . . . Of course he gets the hell of a time from his wife.

"Anyway," said Mr. Nicholas, "there's a match in three weeks' time. Is that all right for you, Peter?"

"I'm afraid I shall be abroad."

"What about you, David?" It was nearly a threat.

"Oh, yes, I expect so," said David cheerfully.

"And could we have some tennis next Wednesday?" said Mrs. Nicholas.

"All right, my dear." Mr. Nicholas chewed his omelette. "The thing about these working chaps is . . ."

★    ★    ★

Next morning Peter and Owen marked the clock-golf course, and after lunch they played with David. There were small white clouds in the sky, but they did not come near the sun and there was no shade on the lawn. No one wanted to play.

Sometimes Owen remembered to try to make Mrs. Nicholas's plan succeed, but then he hit the ball intentionally as if by accident into the rhododendrons, cutting up a piece of sandy lawn, and looked round to see who was laughing. Because he himself disliked losing he did not want to make other people lose. When it wasn't his turn he played with the dog and forgot to come back.

David played because he had been asked. Perhaps he realised that it was a scheme to keep him at home, or perhaps not. There was a sluggishness about David's thought which made him fail to notice anything he was not told in words, which Peter almost understood. "That was a good one," David said. "This will be a tricky one."

Peter was not sure why he played. The idea of winning depressed him; it would impress no one he cared to impress; and he hated the automatic meaningless conversation not meant to be answered, and the waste of time. Perhaps he wanted to help keep David at home, but even if he thought it right to interfere between him and the Hump he did not know if this was the right way. He was reluctant to make up his mind about these things, for making up his mind meant an opinion, and an opinion meant trying to persuade people and watching them misunderstand and disagree and deliberately do the opposite. It was more comfortable to watch.

Then he was angry that he allowed himself to become so ineffective. He could imagine other people's contempt for someone who could not make up his mind. Without opinions it seemed that he ceased to be a person, and he tried to decide what he thought.

The game ended.

"Are we going on?" said Peter.

No one answered. Owen was poking an ants' nest with a pencil.

"We might," said David. For a moment Peter thought he was laughing at their failure and looked up quickly, but of course David never discovered his own jokes. He stood in his shirt-sleeves, one knee bent, his tummy forward; you could see the sun making him think about nothing.

"Whose turn to start?" said Peter.

"Are we going to play?" said Owen.

"I shouldn't think so."

"Actually," said David, "I haven't time." He put on his jacket, straightened his tie, and went down the drive and the private road.

\*　　\*　　\*

On Tuesday before tea they stood in the kitchen, in the warm air which came through the open windows bringing a smell of heath smoke, while Mrs. Nicholas buttered toast. "Father has got Sarah Horn and Doreen Briggs for tennis to-morrow," she said, and looked up, hoping for interest or enthusiasm from her sons. Owen was arranging four china egg cups in a tower, waiting for someone to tell him to stop.

"Who else?" said Peter.

"I'm afraid I can't be here," said David.

"Oh, but why?"

"We've arranged to go out to tea with a friend of Captain Cambridge to see his collection."

"What collection?"

"Rings and things."

"Oh dear," said Mrs. Nicholas.

They carried tea into the veranda where Mr. Nicholas was asleep in the sun in a deck-chair, wearing breeches, coat, waistcoat, and several pullovers, his canary cricket cap over his eyes.

"David's going out to tea tomorrow," said Mrs. Nicholas.

Peter said, "When was it arranged?" It was the obvious question, but he said it reluctantly because he could see clearly the next question whatever David answered. He pretended that it was interest in how David would escape the trap which made him ask.

"A long time ago," said David. He seemed unaware of the insinuation.

Peter paused to let someone else ask it, but they didn't so he said, "Why didn't you say so on Sunday night?"

"Yes," said Mrs. Nicholas, "Why not?" It was so un-expected that she should follow the argument that Peter stared at her, and she thought he was criticising her unkind-ness and added an incongruous smile intended for David but made accidentally at Peter.

"Anyway," said Mr. Nicholas, "who is this man that you should prefer going to tea with him to playing tennis with your own family?"

"When could I have mentioned it?" said David.

"On Sunday at supper." Peter felt that the argument was his and he must support it.

"When we told you about the tennis," said Mrs. Nicholas. "If you knew then that you were going out to tea why didn't you say so?"

"I don't remember," said David.

It was absurd, of course he must remember. "When you were asked about playing cricket," said Peter.

They had sat down except David who stood behind a deck-chair, picking at its rotten wood and frowning.

"Come on, old boy," said Mr. Nicholas. "Be honest with us, did you go off at once and arrange this tea party so that you needn't play tennis?"

"No," said David.

"Then it's very strange that you didn't mention it before."

"I couldn't."

"Because it wasn't arranged?"

"No," said David, "I don't remember." ·

Suddenly it was obvious to Peter that David was telling the truth and had not been listening on Sunday.

"You don't remember why you didn't mention it?" said Mr. Nicholas.

"In fact you did hear?" said Mrs. Nicholas.

"Come on, old boy, be honest with us."

Perhaps in a sense he had heard but he had still been thinking about the cricket match, or about something else before that. It was partly the idea of David being deceitful which was absurd, but also the idea of any deceit being so muddled.

"Of course, old boy, we aren't going to stop you going to your tea party, but in view of what has happened you might think whether it wouldn't be considerate to us to play the tennis we've arranged for you instead of going off with some stranger."

David didn't answer.

During the rest of the day he stayed at home, sitting doing nothing in the drawing-room or polishing his shoes in the work room, on and on till they were smooth and shiny like the shoes of old city gentlemen. When Peter heard him he invented a reason to go there, thinking that he would ask him casually what he had decided to do. He wanted to talk to him quietly, pausing between remarks, speaking carefully and trying to understand what he said. It was absurd that he should know so little of what David thought. But at the work room door he saw David polishing his shoes and frowning: what an absurd way to spend time! And he remembered that he had tried talking to him before but that it didn't work because David didn't answer. It was like hitting something soft, there was no reaction so he became a little angry and hit again, harder. And he realised that, although he had waited long enough for himself to have answered, David's reactions were slower, and that he was practising his father's trick of making his next remark before there had been time to answer the last. And this made him angry so that he went on speaking at David with shorter pauses, more unkindly, trying to provoke an answer, till he was stopped by a recollection of how he had meant the conversation to go.

"Hallo," said David. He looked up and smiled and went on polishing his shoes.

"Huh," said Peter, and went away.

And gradually, because David said nothing, it became certain that he would not play tennis.

"Let's invite the Hump instead," said Owen. Mrs. Nicholas laughed nervously. He was being funny.

"I think that's not a bad idea," said Mr. Nicholas. "No seriously, Owen has made a sensible suggestion. What harm can it do? We want to avoid driving this thing into a corner as you agree, my dear."

"Mm," said Mrs. Nicholas.

"If we can show him the little swine beside decent fully

grown people perhaps he may realise what a fool he's making of himself. What do you think, Peter?"

"Perhaps."

"I think Owen's idea is a damn good one. We'll invite him whenever he wants to come."

"Oh not too often," said Mrs. Nicholas.

"Yes, my dear, you don't see the point. . . ."

David agreed to take the invitation next morning.

★   ★   ★

Every now and then Owen and Brian appeared among the bushes and trees on the edge of the court, stood for a moment, and ran away into the wood with hysterical giggles. They were making Mr. Nicholas furious, and Owen knew it and didn't care. He enjoyed provoking and provoking till there was almost a row. They ran away just before Mr. Nicholas called at them, and once when he shouted after them they didn't hear. Rows were less embarrassing to Owen because it was never difficult for him to find words. Just as his father always had another argument Owen always had an excuse; and it was easy to imagine him denying that they had meant to be rude. But Mr. Nicholas knew that they were laughing at his tennis party.

Though Mr. Nicholas was angry he made efforts to control himself, aware that he had not the usual advantage with Owen. His other sons and his wife were always trying to pacify him so that he could be offensive and personal knowing that where he stopped they would. He was always increasing and they were always reducing the emotion of the argument, not its love or pity but its indignation or anger. But Owen did not care. "Old boy, stop picking your nose." So Owen tipped his chair. "Old boy, I've told you, these chairs won't stand it." "When? I don't remember." Owen always had the answer or the red-herring. Owen was always right or if not he sulked, making it obvious that he thought he was; and he did not wait to sulk till the second chance, or think it seemly to stop arguing or sulking because there were other people present. So Mr. Nicholas did not go after Owen and Brian, shouting into the wood, but concentrated on winning the game.

He made no attempt to hide his annoyance when he played with Mrs. Nicholas and she missed. "Mother's got a hole in her racquet today." "Mother dear, try to keep your wrist straight." "I'll start serving shall I?" That was the trouble with knowing him too well: you could have heard in his remarks his desire to win even if he had hidden it. And Peter, playing against him, began to want to beat him, and when he realised this and tried to do it casually and failed he tried to hit him with the ball.

Mr. Nicholas still called "Well played," if David won a point and said nothing if David's opponents played well, but this was less offensive. It was something left over from a past judgment, and Peter could hear the slight hesitation and lack of conviction with which it was now said; or perhaps he was discovering what he expected to hear.

The Hump, sitting beside Mr. Nicholas, also encouraged David, and presently they fell into competition.

"Damn fine shot," said the Hump, partly to the court and partly to Mr. Nicholas.

"Mm," said Mr. Nicholas vaguely.

"Well played David," shouted Mr. Nicholas.

"Mm," said the Hump, agreeing conditionally.

And David went on playing, saying nothing, apparently unaware that he was interesting.

He said little and what he said was so confused that it was often difficult to believe he thought. Of course he had feelings and prejudices, but they could not be like thoughts. Even his feelings were sluggish, late, and did not seem to include anger or dislike, so that his obstinacy, when discovered, was astonishing and annoying. It could be neither logical nor emotional. It seemed unreasonable.

Presently they had tea in the veranda, sitting in deck-chairs on the edge of the hot sun.

"My dear lady, what delicious cakes."

"Are they?" said Mrs. Nicholas. If anyone but the Hump had said it she would have been delighted.

"Where do you acquire them?"

"I make them."

"I'm most frightfully sorry, I thought . . ."

"You should think again." She was aware of the rare excitement of repartee. She was conscious of their surprise at her anger, of Mr. Nicholas grinning and approving, and she gave a little simper.

"Don't you know the difference between bought and home made cakes?" It was once too often. It had ceased to be genuine, and she was waiting to smile if she was smiled at. Even when genuine it had been a disillusioning break in her universal charity. Something had happened, she had lost the last of her family whom she had hoped to understand and be loved by, and she had ceased to think kindly; and it did not seem certain that she would ask to be forgiven when she said her prayers.

"Your tea," she said. Passing it with her left hand while she went on watching herself pouring out another cup with her right. The Hump came forward to take it on one knee, misjudged the distance, hit it with his upper arm, and the cup, tipping in the saucer, poured the tea in a steaming flow on to his coat and trousers.

"Oo," he said. He stood up, holding the hot cloth from his skin.

"Oo, oo," he said. He was watching the effect he was making, judging how much to be hurt, like a bad actor with an eye on the audience. He was so used to playing at guest that he did not seem aware of his new advantage.

After tea Peter sat on the dry grass slope near the edge of the court. Behind him a ladies' set was going on.

Sarah, whose face suggested the Admiral's, and Doreen who had the Commander's intonations, were playing the two not quite middle-aged ladies who were married to naval officers. Across the valley, on the dusty hill, the mortars were firing.

He became aware of another guest coming up the private road. She wore a white tennis frock, and at first the leaves and shadows hid her face, and then he did not believe he had guessed right, but when she came on to the drive there was no doubt. Mr. Nicholas came across and took Mrs. Pawthorn to sit by him at the court-side.

Peter was surprised that the orange tint of her face, which he had always supposed to be artificial, extended on to her large chest, but perhaps that was also artificial. His mother, further along the court, had stopped talking and was glancing sideways as she glanced at letters to read the postmark. She was hopeless at cunning. But probably she had known all the time that Mrs. Pawthorn was invited; probably Mr. Nicholas had told her. He was capable of it.

Owen and Brian were on the edge of the court in the bushes and Peter waited for them to turn and run away, giggling, but when Owen saw Mrs. Pawthorn they didn't, and Peter was aware of his anger. They walked across the court, between the players who waited to serve, and went towards the house.

"Owen," said Mr. Nicholas.

"Owen," he shouted. He stood up. "Owen."

"Yes." Owen made it clear that he had heard for the first time.

"What ever do you think you're doing, walking across a game?"

"But it wasn't a game. They were looking for balls."

"Don't be silly, of course it was a game."

As Owen passed Peter wanted to show his support. He wanted to say, "I think the least he could do is keep his mistress somewhere else." But he would have been suiting his mood to Owen's. And anyway Owen would have been tolerant, placing himself gently outside Peter's anger.

★   ★   ★

Peter sat in the drawing-room, his arms on the arms of the chair, trying to extract coolness from the cover, but unless he moved them continually they began to sweat where they touched. His socks were hot and sticky so he took them off and threw them through the French window on to the lawn. His father was angry if clothes were left in the drawing-room. They lay untidily on the dry yellow grass, making no shadow in the sun, taking the same bleached look as the pines and the weeds on the drive. People had given up talking about the weather. In the first week they had said, "Nice to see the sun for a change," and in the second, "What a lovely summer we are having," and in the third, "What a really remarkable summer we're having." After that their superlatives seemed exhausted.

Through the open drawing-room door, across the hall, in the kitchen, he could hear his mother talking to the dog.

"Did he want a piece of cake? Ah, the poor good doggie, well he'll have to wait a minute, yes he will, he'll have to wait a whole minute, while I cut him a bit. And a little fish paste? just to make it tasty? There now, was that nice for a good dog? What do you say? Say thank you. That's a good doggie. That's a good Sambo."

She went on and on. He could remember her talking in the same way to his brothers when they were babies and was annoyed to think that she had once done it to him.

David came downstairs and went through the drawing-room, across the lawn, taking letters to the post. For several days the Hump had been away and David had stayed at home, sometimes sitting doing nothing in an arm-chair in the drawing-room, more often in his room.

"If only he could find some other interest," Mrs. Nicholas had said.

"Stamp-collecting."

"But that doesn't really keep him busy."

So, because David had once or twice, out of kindness to his mother, shown interest in the lupins and peonies in her flower bed and in the heather she picked among the pines, they had bought him a pocket book of wild flowers. It was hopelessly obvious; he must have realised that they were not in a mood to give him presents without a purpose, and Peter had half expected him to laugh and throw it away, but instead he thanked them with improbable enthusiasm, exactly as he always thanked for presents. And sometimes he went down the hillside taking it with him, bending when he remembered to look for a flower, but usually walking slowly with a slight frown. More often he stayed in his room.

"What does he do there?"

"Sticks in stamps."

"Writes to the Hump," said Mrs. Nicholas; and it was true that about once a day he walked down the private road to the post office. Peter sat forward in his chair, trying to see the addresses of the letters he was carrying, but he held a green printed envelope in front of the white one which he had written, and went across the lawn before Peter could think of anything to stop him.

In the kitchen his mother was saying, "Was he hot and exhausted then? Did he want a little lie down?" Peter went across the hall, slowly upstairs past the open doors of his father's room, the bathroom, the billiard room. The house was hot and empty, even Owen was out. On the top landing David's door was open and Peter stood for a moment looking at the clothes and books on the floor; then he went in.

The letters were on the dressing-table and he tried to get to them and start reading before he could ask himself if he should, but the play-box got in his way. He stood still in front of the dressing-table, touching nothing, and presently he thought that it didn't matter so long as he did not make malicious use of them, but the other arguments were too obvious: how would he like it if it was done to him? So he thought, why pretend? He was curious, he wanted to know what they wrote to each other, why not admit it instead of deceiving himself? There was nothing wrong with curiosity.

On the top of a pad was an unfinished page in David's writing.

"I take up my pen to send a few words of explanation and apology. How could you doubt my happiness when you know my great fondness—yes, I may even say love— for you my friend, and my great debt to you without whose timely aid I might never have found myself? I am to blame for being so thoughtless and self-centred as to let you doubt this.

"Now is the time, 10.30 ——

"10.40. Though I have tried my hardest to concentrate on the beautiful thing, and really believe I have felt near to you, yet the wicked thoughts keep intruding. 'We are as straw in his hands.' BUT 'God so loved the world, etc.' I do not think it matters if one does one's best, for (Jesus said) 'I am the light.' I have thought a lot of what you were saying about temporal happiness . . ."

Peter moved the pad and paper carefully, noticing their positions, then carelessly, trying not to notice. If it wasn't wrong why try not to be found out? Or was it wrong? He could not remember which he had decided. Underneath was an envelope addressed in Captain Cambridge's small neat writing, and he took out the letter.

"Angel, for this is indeed what you are to me. Last night I was so happy in the great joy which has been granted to me. I went back to my little room and went to bed wondering if I should manage to sleep or if I should have my usual tossings and turnings, and then the thought of you came to me and I went off quite peacefully. When I woke hours later as it seemed to me and quite refreshed I looked at my watch and it was only twelve-thirty. Then I again began to worry about sleeping, and again I thought of you, and suddenly it seemed that there was a great light above my bed. The whole room was full of a beautiful white light and I felt more happy than I ever have in my life before, and I knew in some curious way that the light was in you and from you, was in fact you. The next thing I remember is waking at ten to eight, the exact time for 'Lift Up Your Hearts,' and I stretched out my hand to turn on my wireless. Then I felt behind my neck to see how my boil was—and what do you think? It was quite gone! (I had had the blooming thing for a fortnight). Do you wonder that I call you Angel. 'For He sent His ministers to minister unto them, and His angels to be a flaming sword'."

There was more, but the writing began to slope across the page and become almost illegible. At the end, fitted into the bottom corner was "R.L.F.G. your Humpy." Peter tried fitting words like "Love" and "God" to the letters but none seemed to work.

Near the back of the table on an open stamp catalogue was another letter in the Hump's writing, probably more recent because it was out of its envelope. He picked it up, and then stood still listening for a noise on the stairs, but it had ceased; he had probably imagined it. He read:

"Thank you indeed for your enclosure. It was very, very generous and another mark of your wonderful charity that you should send it, which again makes me feel my great unworthiness. . . .

It suddenly fitted with what Dorothy had once suggested, and with the green printed envelope. David was selling his Savings Certificates to give the Hump money. Peter was astonished, and began to excuse himself, thinking that he was only realising how shocked his mother and father would be. Really it was typical, like David's collected edition of John Buchan, half on the shelf and half about the floor, his Harrison Ainsworth collected in five or six sizes, it was untidy. He saved money then gave it away. Even his stamps were stuck in torn and left about in envelopes which he forgot.

Yet why shouldn't he be untidy? Why shouldn't he give away as well as save? It was logical to forget everything else to get the one thing he really wanted. Peter could understand and envy that. But what an absurd thing to want.

Peter went downstairs, past the hot empty rooms with small bright patches of sunlight on the carpets near the windows, across the hall, into the dining-room. His mind was full of what he had discovered and he looked on the lawn for Owen but could not see him. He went slowly into the kitchen.

"Hallo, darling," his mother said. "Lunch is almost ready." She moved about between the oven and the sink, stirring the gravy, draining the boiled potatoes. "Where's David?"

"Posting letters." Peter sat on the edge of the table facing away from the oven, towards the back door and the roller towel.

"To the Hump?"

"One was," he said, "but not the other." He waited but she said nothing and her silence made him angry. She must realise that he had more to say. She was hoping he would go on by himself if she did not interrupt but her unnatural silence was more interrupting than any question. It was infuriatingly meek. Or perhaps she was stirring the gravy, thinking about the peas; he wasn't going to look round.

"David sends him money," he said. As soon as he started

173

to speak he was angry with himself, knowing that he said it because it was comfortable that his father and mother should go on finding fault with David. So he said it casually, trying to disassociate himself from it, leaving it to make its own effect, and instead of thinking what it meant she took her tone from his and accepted it without surprise.

She should have been shocked. By all that he knew of her opinions she should have been amazed and indignant. She couldn't even see that he wanted her to be.

"Does he?" she said. She believed him, and did not want to ask the question which he had thought of as soon as he had said it: how did he know?

His father was coming up the cinder-path. "Lunch, lunch, lunch," he shouted, "who's ready for lunch?"

Peter got off the table and went away, out of the kitchen, through the hall. He sat in the drawing-room on the arm-chair, and felt empty without his secret and empty in retrospect because it had not been impressive. He could hear his mother talking in a low tone in the kitchen, presumably passing it on to his father. Then his father came across the hall, the metal tips of his heels striking the tiles. It was as if he was charging and Peter thought if there was time to escape on to the lawn, and did not realise for several moments that the charge was not at him.

"Peter, is this true?"

Peter wondered if he was sure it was true. He had been convinced and never reconsidered it. He remembered uncomfortably that the letter had not mentioned money, and could just possibly have been about something else. What had seemed certain to him might seem less certain to others. But the green envelope, that was proof. And then he realised that it could only have been an application and that David would not get the money for several days. How stupid not to have thought of that before. There might, of course, have been others, but there was no proof.

"I think so," said Peter.

"Did he tell you?"

"No." There was a pause. He had not the energy to think of an excuse, and anyway the pause had been hopelessly suspicious.

"I saw it in a letter."

His mother had understood, but his father wasn't listening.

"No, that really isn't good enough," he said. He walked up and down, working himself into anger. "I shall go and ask him straight out."

"Oh no," said Mrs. Nicholas. Now that she knew how it had been found out she thought they should not use it, but she spoke impulsively and wished she hadn't.

"Why not?" said Mr. Nicholas. "It's the honest, straightforward thing to do. If it's not true he can deny it, and no more will be said. I won't have this hole in a corner business."

★   ★   ★

Peter stopped painting and listened. The afternoon sun was hot and he had drawn his curtains to keep it out; they hung inside his open window, unmoved by any breeze. His father's steps were coming up the stairs, across the landing and he expected his door to open but they went past. He straightened his back and laid his brushes on the book shelf, carefully making no noise. It was easy to hear through the wall between his and David's room.

"Now then, old boy, let's get this thing straight. Your mother and I have reason to believe that you have been giving money to your friend, Captain Cambridge. Is this true?"

There was a pause and then David said, "No," slowly. Peter could imagine him frowning.

"Well either you have or you haven't."

"Mm."

"Well?"

There was a pause.

"Well which is it?"

"What?"

"Have you or not given him money?"

"No," said David. "I said no."

"All right," said Mr. Nicholas. "If that's what you say we'll leave it at that." He did not try to hide his disbelief. He seemed to be waiting for David to make an admission, but nothing was said and presently the door opened and his steps went across the landing, down the stairs.

Before supper they stood in the kitchen waiting for Mrs. Nicholas to finish frying.

"Have a drink, mother."

"Not for me, thank you."

"Yes, come on, it'll do you good."

"No really."

"Yes come on." Mr. Nicholas poured out sherry and drank his own quickly.

"I had a word with David," said Mrs. Nicholas. "He says it was to pay for a meal they had together."

"The boy can't even be straight with you now," said Mr. Nicholas. He poured himself another glass.

"Fancy a man like the Hump sponging off a boy of seventeen for his meals," said Mrs. Nicholas.

She took the less likely explanation because, thinking what she did of the Hump, it seemed most likely. And Peter wanted to suggest that David had only been sending his own share, but he realised that if he did this his discovery would again become a failure, and while he thought of this Mr. Nicholas said, "Have another glass," and the chance passed.

Two days later it was apparent from David's long absences that Captain Cambridge was again in the district.

\*    \*    \*

The heavy thunder clouds piled on the horizon and dispersed and piled again. Between his curtains, behind and above the pines Peter could see them, sometimes white and low, sometimes rising in black pillars to huge tops which spread over the sky. He laid his brushes on the table and moved back. It was not bad so far but his head ached and he must stop or he would spoil it.

That was the trouble now: there was always some reason for stopping or putting off, and he was always glad to find it; before lunch he was hungry, and after lunch sleepy. It had been different once, he could remember not wanting to come to meals, and being impatient to leave them to continue building a tent or fighting a battle. Owen had not changed and still came late when he was making something, and did not speak but went on thinking about it as he ate, and went away as soon as he had finished. But Peter was aware that he had to make himself paint, and that as soon as he began to paint badly he looked for an excuse. He went slowly downstairs; anyway it was nearly lunch time.

His father was standing on the lawn in the hot sun, so he stopped in the drawing-room, but he had been seen and his father came in through the French windows.

"Now then Peter, we've got to solve this problem."

The friendly "we" had once given him a warm excitement, but he had been led by it too often to forgetting his silence and hearing his ideas patronised, or contradicted, or altered into some form familiar to his father's mind.

"What?" he said.

"This problem of your brother. It's beyond a joke. It's time we took action."

His father was excited and Peter wondered if something fresh had happened; as far as he knew there had been no provocation for three days. But probably his father was ignoring this and exciting himself by remembering what had happened earlier. He stood inside the French windows, staring at Peter, watching for him to co-operate, and Peter was aware that he might say something which would redirect his father's anger at himself.

"Now I could get my solicitor to write him a letter. That should frighten him. I'm perfectly entitled to, oh yes, I'm responsible for David till he's eighteen."

"Yes," said Peter.

"Alternatively we must go round together and give the man a damn good thrashing. What do you think?" Mr. Nicholas waited for an answer.

"Yes we could." It was the sort of thing Mr. Nicholas really might do if someone opposed him.

"Of course we could. Why he's only half the size of a proper man. I agree he used to play a decent game of tennis but that needs timing not strength. I'm sure he's a coward."

Mr. Nicholas began to walk about.

"With a coward like that it's the only solution."

He walked across the French window and back, silhouetted against the thunder clouds.

From the kitchen Mrs. Nicholas called, "Lunch is ready."

"Right you are then, Peter old boy, tomorrow afternoon we'll go and do that."

★　　★　　★

When Mr. Nicholas did not mention his plan again that day or the next morning Peter was sure he had forgotten it and perhaps thought of another. Not that his father calculated at the time to forget his foolish plans or absurd opinions, but his memory genuinely excluded them. He had no petty consistency. And after lunch the next day Peter went to his room to paint. The thunder had gone away with the evening but to-day it was breaking in the distance.

Presently he thought that he would need thin shirts in Italy and would put them out so that he should not forget; and at the chest-of-drawers he remembered thin socks. He would just open a suitcase so that he could put in things he happened to think of; for instance, citronella oil against mosquitoes. He hunted for it on his washstand, in his drawers, and then stopped, leaving them open, and made himself go back to his painting. Tonight was the time for packing when the light would be bad. He was angry that his mind had strayed and began to mix a colour. After a moment he put down his brush and began to hunt in his drawers and on his mantelpiece; it was impossible to work while his mind was continually wondering where it could be. His father had opened the door before he heard him.

"Well, Peter, are you ready?"

He gripped a walking-stick and spoke dramatically. Like most of his father's emotions it was over-acted and seemed the result of determination to be angry rather than anger. Because he could think of nothing else to do Peter went with him. He had committed himself the day before; and he was less reluctant than he might have been, for if his father really was going to beat the Hump with a walking-stick he wanted to watch.

They walked down the drive, down the hill, on to the main road. It was hotter than ever; the sun seemed to strike with physical force in the patches between the trees, and on the main road the tar was soft with shiny black dribbles going towards the gutter. There was no wind, and the hot damp air made their eyes seem half open as if they had just woken.

His father said, "This money business is the last straw. I don't believe a word of David's story. The Hump put him up to that. It's perfectly clear that he's been supporting the little runt."

"Mm."

"After all, whose money is it? David's relations didn't give it to him to spend on charity to some broken-down retired army officer."

They walked between gardens of pine trees and rhododendrons, and curiously shaped houses built between the wars with verandas on black oak pillars and gable ends of planks edged with bark. There was shade on the rockeries and the gravel drives, but the sun shone on the main road, making them dizzy with its heat on the backs of their necks; and the cars came past disturbing the dust.

"Until David's eighteen," said Mr. Nicholas, "I'm responsible for him. What happens if he goes and gets himself into trouble? The court will say I should have looked after him better. It's not only my duty, but I'm legally bound to interfere if I don't approve of his friends."

"Mm."

"Damn it, whose son is he, mine or the Hump's?"

He repeated his arguments till their fallacies became obvious, but he didn't look for them. He wasn't concerned with their truth or logic. They were words to shout to help him win. Of course they must seem true and logical because then they were more effective, but it was for the other side to find their mistakes. It was easy, if you could step back and watch, to laugh at the self-deception, but it wasn't possible if you were caught up and swept along and expected to agree.

Nearer to Rodenham there were rows of brick houses and fewer trees; the Hump's road was a sandy track leading from a side road at the end of which builders were working. Number three was semi-detached with bow windows and tiles on its front, the sort of house that stands in lines along by-passes. In the sun it looked new and almost gay. The curtains of the front bottom room were drawn.

"Seems shut up," said Mr. Nicholas.

"May not be," said Peter. He wanted Mr. Nicholas to go on. It was his father who would have to meet Captain Cambridge, to avoid embarrassment, to think of words. He could follow and watch.

Mr. Nicholas rang the bell, and for a moment there was silence, then inside the house they heard a handle turn and steps, and Captain Cambridge came to the door. He wore no coat, and the cuffs of his shirt were kept up by expandable metal garters above his elbows.

"Oh, hallo," he said. "Come in."

They followed him into a small room full of furniture. There were two arm-chairs and a sofa covered in grey with a red flower pattern, two collector's cabinets, an ornamental table, several upright chairs, and a desk. Peter had to move into the room close to Mr. Nicholas so that Captain Cambridge could shut the door.

"Excuse me, but my landlady's having her rest."

The sunlight came through and between the curtains. On the desk was an empty tea cup and a plate with a sandwich, but nothing else was dirty. David was sitting at one end of the sofa and seemed not to know whether to stand up.

"Do sit down," said Captain Cambridge, but they didn't.

"Would you like some tea?" said Captain Cambridge. "It's rather early, but I think I could raise some." He looked towards the door, but made no move.

Mr. Nicholas stood close to him, consciously thrusting out his chin, looking a little above him.

"Now then, let's be quite straightforward about this business. You know what I've come to speak about. Well it's got to stop, do you see. I'm warning you. It's got to stop."

"I don't know what you mean?"

"Don't be a bloody fool, of course you do. This monkeying with my son David."

"I don't understand."

"What are you doing on an afternoon like this sitting behind drawn curtains?"

"That's because the old woman's always peeping in."

"But you said she was resting. Anyway, what are you doing that you don't want her to see?"

The Hump didn't reply, and Peter was aware that already he was wanting to answer his father's arguments. He wanted the Hump to point out their mistakes, and was annoyed when he didn't. He wanted to disassociate himself from his father's unfairness, not because he liked fairness, but because he was afraid that other people would be unfair to him.

"Anyway, that's beside the point. What matters is this business of David spending his days with you and treating his home like a hotel. It's got to stop, do you see. You're responsible . . ."

"In what way am I . . ."

"Don't interrupt me. I say you're responsible. If we thought anything of you as a person it might be different."

Mr. Nicholas tried to quarrel, to raise the intensity and make the Hump shout so that he could shout back louder. There was sweat on his upper lip where he shaved, and he gripped his walking-stick below the handle, holding its point off the floor. The Hump didn't answer.

"No one ever invited you to appoint yourself a moral tutor to my son. It's for me to say if I want that done. Anyway, I don't think you're suitable."

"If that's the attitude you take . . ."

"Of course it's the attitude I take. What do you expect if you set out to steal the affection of a child for his parents?"

The Hump didn't answer. He had moved back against the mantelpiece, standing on the low tin fender as if to equalise their heights, looking at his polished shoes, and it seemed that he was about to say, "Please don't be so rude," but didn't dare.

"Have you nothing to say?"

"Well, no . . ."

"I didn't expect so. Come on then Peter, we'll go."

They walked along the main road, between the rhododendrons and half-hidden houses. The sun was still uncovered but behind the trees there were heavy clouds and the day, instead of opening out towards a cool evening, seemed to be closing in and getting hotter. The thunder had ceased and there was the sort of absolute stillness in which one starts unconsciously to wait for a noise. Somewhere a long way below on the hillside tennis was being played.

"We shook him," said Mr. Nicholas. "He won't forget that in a hurry."

As they walked Peter had the impression that the retired officers and business men who lived in these houses had come out from their afternoon siestas, finding it too hot to sleep, and were standing in their gardens watching the road. Sometimes one was suddenly obvious among the rhododendrons where there had seemed only shadows, but most of them stood very still so that he never saw them.

"He didn't like it a bit when I said that he was responsible. You see, that's his game, to put the blame on David."

They walked past the Red Lion and the Baptist chapel, up the private road.

"We shan't get much more trouble from that little worm."

He had genuinely forgotten that they had set out to thrash him.

★　　★　　★

"When he saw me at the door his face went as red as a guardsman's tunic. I could see he was absolutely terrified. He hadn't a thing to say for himself."

"Mm," said Mrs. Nicholas, She carried hot buttered toast for tea through the drawing-room, on to the veranda.

"I gave him a bloody good talking to. I'm sure that we were right. When dealing with a little coward like that it's essential to go and frighten him."

It was the same conspiracy of success; they went on telling each other that what they had done was best till they believed it, agreeing to be deceived because they wanted to be, never allowing each other to think that they had muddled their lives or that anyhow they weren't important. Yet it was different, because Mrs. Nicholas was not quite part of it, seeming uneasily aware of the other point of view; she was confused that her family was not all on one side. But Mr. Nicholas did not notice.

"They were sitting there with the curtains drawn."

"No?" said Mrs. Nicholas. She stopped pouring tea and looked up; she was astonished and shocked; you could not guess what would shock her. "How did he explain that?"

"He couldn't. He had some ridiculous story about his landlady."

"What were they doing?"

"Your guess is as good as mine, my dear."

Presently David came back. "Come on, old boy," said Mrs. Nicholas. His father's phrase sounded absurd when she used it.

"That's right, find yourself a chair. Chocolate cake?" She was being tactful, asking to be snubbed. She avoided what David was thinking about so obviously that she insulted his intelligence.

When David didn't answer Peter looked up to see if he was missing something. Mr. Nicholas was drinking his tea with loud unembarrassed sips; it was impossible to associate embarrassment with Mr. Nicholas; he always had words to explain himself. Owen was watching; sometimes he and Peter were able to watch and laugh together but now his detachment was competitive, and when Peter smiled at him he looked away, suggesting that Peter was as much part of his amusement as the others. And David was sitting forward in his deck-chair, his elbows on his knees, holding his plate with one hand, looking at his cake as he broke it with the other. No one seemed to know whether he had answered; Mrs. Nicholas looked at him anxiously and seemed stopped by her uncertainty. He was about to say something and half-lifted his head to begin, but put it down again as if they were not the right words. And Peter felt that the silence hesitated between the moment when people surprise themselves by saying what they think, and cheerful talk about the weather.

After tea Peter went upstairs and tried to work. There was a piece he wanted to finish before he went away, but the thunder made his head ache, and after a time he came downstairs and stood on the lawn a few yards from the veranda, listening to it in the distance. It rumbled over the hills, not loudly but almost continuously. It was a huge storm wherever it was. Over the dark green slopes and grey tops there were low black clouds. But the sun was above them and still warm. Small strong gusts of wind were moving the trees in the valley and once one came over the hilltop, flapping the canvas of the empty deck-chairs but then they hung still. He looked across the lawn, up the bare trunks of the two Scottish pines to their tufted tops which almost touched seventy feet above and tried to see movement but they were still. He went through the drawing-room and the hall to the kitchen.

"Where's David?" said Mrs. Nicholas.

"I don't know. In his room I expect." He pretended not to notice her anxiety.

"Don't think so. I've called." He knew that she was anxious because instead of going on cooking or laying the table she stood waiting for him to answer.

"Perhaps he didn't hear. Perhaps he's in the garden."

"Mm," she said agreeing with him that it was an absurd fancy.

Through the kitchen window he could see the black clouds over the hills. The sun was going down behind them, making their tops red. He stepped out of the back door on to the concrete slab and it was like going from one warm room to another. It was so still now that a candle would not have flickered.

He heard Owen come into the kitchen and stepped back into the doorway.

"You haven't by any chance seen David?" She tried to sound casual and went on collecting food for supper.

"He went down the hill an hour ago," said Owen.

"He might have been going to the heath," said Peter.

"What for?"

"To find flowers. He sometimes does."

"We could go and look for him," said Owen.

"Yes," said Peter. He didn't think he was there, but they suddenly were agreed that it was a good reason for walking on the hills in the evening.

They crossed the main road and went up the sand track between pines and birches to the heath. The colour had gone from the light so that the buildings among the trees seemed no longer an intrusion on the hillside but part of it. They did not see the fire till they reached the top.

It must have been burning for some time for it was already difficult to tell its extent. The opposite hill-face was black, with thin wisps rising between skeletons of a young fir plantation. Close to them on the near hillside it was burning steadily but not fast up-hill among the heather. Here it seemed tame so that Peter felt on its side against the men who were beating it with fir branches, but in the bottom of the valley it was going with the wind, running from tree to tree, throwing the sparks as high as the sides of the valley with a crackle which they could hear though it was five hundred yards away. Of course it explained everything; David had seen the fire and stayed to watch it.

They looked for him among the nearest beaters and then went along the hilltop, downwind, looking for the dramatic place to fight it alone, running a little as if afraid it would be out before they got there. The burning heather made a line of light below them, becoming redder as the daylight faded and presently on their other side there were houses through the trees. Gradually they drew together so that they could see ahead the place where the fire had reached the hill top and was almost at the garden fences.

The gardens these enclosed were of gorse and heather with

186

thin strips of lawn near the houses, but the owners were protecting their chestnut palings as if they were the important place to stop the fire instead of the path which ran along outside them. One was making a trench; he dug down about a foot, unaware that an inch was enough, and that the fire would be in his garden before he had half crossed its front. Another stood behind his palings with a stirrup pump, his daughter or perhaps wife fetching pails of water, waiting for it to come closer, crouching a little as if accustomed to avoiding bullets.

At first it seemed that the beaters on the path were too many for it; but soon in one place, then another it had crossed, creeping along the peaty soil or jumping with sparks, and Peter and Owen began to help.

The heat was intense, and sudden gusts of wind made it impossible to come near enough to reach the flames. The smoke made their eyes water continuously and blew thickly over them so that they had to bend to breathe. The effort of raising and beating with long fir branches was surprisingly exhausting. But the danger to the houses, the excitement of being heroic yet safe, made them enjoy the discomfort and feel that they could go on for hours.

Farther along the path the fire was already into one garden, burning round the bottom of a small black summer house. The sparks were flying and they could see what would happen for about ten seconds before it did. Then the thatch caught on several sides at once, and flared high as the tree tops, lighting the path and gardens. In the next one Peter recognised Mrs. Pawthorn.

She was wearing a long flowing dress or perhaps nightgown and held a wine-glass. It must be her cottage. Presently he recognised the figures with her: Major Dale, Mrs. Morton, and Squadron Leader Morton. They all held glasses and walked about, clearly interested in the fire but doing nothing to stop it. Major Dale was nearest and offered his glass to one of the beaters. When Peter went closer he saw the bottles on a card table near the house. So that was where his father's money went. He supposed he should have felt angry.

A top window in the house opened and Mr. Pawthorn leaned out. In the half light his face seemed featureless, his pale hair and eyebrows all part of a pale round knob.

"Let me out," he shouted. "Let me out, let me out, let me out."

Mrs. Pawthorn walked about the garden, swinging the bottom of her nightgown. After a moment she shouted, "Be quiet you silly old man," without turning her head.

Peter walked on and climbed the fence. He had lost Owen and peered closely at one or two figures to see if they were him, or perhaps David, but they weren't.

"Let me out, let me out, I shall be burned," shouted Mr. Pawthorn.

But the fire in this direction seemed now to be stopping, as if it meant only to show what it could do by entering the gardens.

Beyond the trees, in the valley below, he could still hear it and he went on round, following its edge. He no longer felt support for it; on this side there were long stretches where it was burning unchecked, and even the occasional beaters were leaning on their branches, exhausted by the impossibility of stopping it. He was angry with them for not trying. Everything was possible if you thought it was, and anyway what an opportunity for a gallant failure; but they didn't want to be gallant and presently some of them were going away; it was past their bedtime. He hated them for it, recognising his own calculation, his own inability to get excited, and desire for comfort and routine. On the burnt heath behind the fire a small animal was running with its coat alight. It ran in curious unabrupt curves as if it was on a track, squealing.

Half down the slope he found a party of boy scouts cutting a clearing through a thicket to make a fire break. They worked with hatchets and penknives, exerting themselves without reserve, talking to each other.

"Let me take over, Bill."

"That's O.K., Allan, I can keep going a little longer."

It wasn't the way they usually talked, they used an unnatural number of words, explained too carefully, were too considerate. You could hear the phrases of adventure films, the admission that they thought themselves heroic.

The scoutmaster walked about organising his troop.

"Run to the camp and fetch the sharpener."

"Is it in its usual place in your tent, sir?"

"Of course."

He was as excited as the rest but tried to hide it by unnatural curtness. Presently he became aware of this and advanced through the bushes to the fire where he could be seen beating alone, exhausting his excitement without the absurdity of words. For a time Peter helped them but their enthusiasm sickened him. Why couldn't they enjoy it without talking?

Moving from party to party, sometimes helping, sometimes watching, he came gradually to the bottom of the valley. Here the fire had burned through the fir wood and come to the edge of an area of bracken, bramble bushes, and long dry grass enclosed by ten or a dozen oak trees. It lit the undersides of these with an orange light, and an effect of sinister beauty.

A fire brigade was there when he arrived, but the bushes near it began to burn and the firemen climbed on to their lorry and bumped back across the clearing. They had been to too many fires in the last weeks, and knew that they could not stop them. Everything was too dry, so that, though the flames were put out and the heather damped, in an hour, or six hours, or a day there would be new smoke and a new fire. Peter was no longer angry but exhausted and sat on a log.

The fire here seemed to have lost its urgency. He could hear it crackling in other places, continuing to burn down the valley, and the darkness above was thick with smoke, but

it seemed to have avoided this place. Occasionally a patch
of bracken flared but then it became quiet and the only light
was the flame from an old pine tree whose resinous trunk
was burning. Presently Owen came there; he had been round
the other sides of the fire but hadn't seen David. They might,
of course, have missed him, but it was much more likely that
he hadn't been there. They had never really thought he was.
He and the Hump were probably in a train together, or in
bed—no, Peter didn't believe that.

But why shouldn't they be? The whole idea of forcing a
code of behaviour on David because he happened to be a
member of the family suddenly seemed wrong. It was the
same as dirty shoes for tennis, with only the difference that
Peter disapproved of one and not the other, didn't even
disapprove, but was unable to understand anyone else approving of the Hump. It was astonishing that he had not seen
this before, and allowed himself to join in the same bullying
he had suffered. He was pleased to find reasons for supporting
David, and told himself without quite believing it that he
had wanted to the whole time. He was anxious to be home
so that he could establish his new attitude, and uneasy that
he might forget the argument.

It was three o'clock when they came slowly up the cinder
path. The moon was rising over the hills and the fir trees in
front of it were pointed black shapes. There was no light in
the house, and they went quietly in at the back door, and up
the stairs, but their mother was awake. She called to them as
they passed her door and they went in. She lay under a sheet
with only her face showing. She probably had not been to sleep.

"Is David back?"

"Yes, he came in about ten. He'd been on the heath. You
must have missed him."

"Was he fighting the fire?"

"I don't think so. He didn't mention any fire."

*　　*　　*

When Peter came down in the morning breakfast was over and his mother washing up. He came into the kitchen and saw her before she heard him, washing up slowly. Normally she created such a splash and hurry that you forgot she was alone. She stood with her head over the sink, taking out the soapy china piece by piece, thinking of something; because she usually was adjusting what she said to your meaning it was easy to forget she had her own thoughts. She heard a noise and began to hurry, thinking he was still out of sight, ashamed to be found pessimistic. When he coughed she looked round and said, "Hallo darling, shall I make you some breakfast?" cheerfully.

"Thank you," he said. "Where's David?"

"Oh, he's gone again. He left that."

He wanted to laugh, but it wasn't funny for her. He was always trying to withdraw to a distance so that he could understand both points of view, and then he ceased to understand either. He took the letter from the kitchen table.

At the top was written, "Not to be shown to father unless absolutely essential."

"Dear Mother, I am writing to you to explain my absence in case it should cause you undue anxiety. I have told Captain Cambridge that I will have tea with him this afternoon and shall not return till this evening. I do not think you have fully understood our friendship. I have not until the present time. It is quite impossible for it to end now. Nor can I think that you should be anything but pleased by this, were it not that you were moved by considerations of jealousy. I can only beg that you ask yourself once more whether this is so.

"I remain your affectionate son, David.

"P.S.—I have put this in the cutlery drawer where I do not think father often looks."

191

"Has father seen it?"

"Yes, he wants to get his solicitor to write to the Hump a legal letter, but I don't know if that would do any good."

"It might."

"I'm only afraid that it may, as it were, drive him into the Hump's arms."

Mr. Nicholas came across the hall into the kitchen. He never waited to see if a silence was part of a conversation.

"Well, Peter, isn't that the most abominable letter you've ever seen? How any member of my family could write such a thing! I can only suppose that that little devil dictated it to him."

Peter did not answer.

"Anyway it's time we took definite action. This thing has been going on too long." His voice became for a moment thick with emotion, but he cleared it quickly. "Now I think a solicitor's letter may be the answer, unless you've any better plan."

"No," said Peter. "No, I don't think so." It was the moment to explain what he did think and he almost began but they would not understand. They no longer started from the same place. He went slowly upstairs and began to pack. In a few hours he would have left Beckford, in two days he would be a thousand miles away, and he began to be conscious of how it would seem from there. The phrases began to form in which he might, when a little drunk, explain it to his friends. "My parents trying to rescue my brother from a dirty old artillery captain."

# Chapter Nine

THE SUN was hot and the small early breeze had disappeared when Peter carried his suitcase up the private road. Though the thin grass under the pines was green, showing that the drought had broken, it seemed to him that there had been no interval, that this new fine weather was the same that he had left six weeks before. His suitcase was heavy and he sweated and made himself go slowly and change hands. He was impatient to be at the top.

He had been impatient since Florence, where he had at last arrived and collected his letters. There had been two from his mother, about Sambo, and the cat, the rain which had been so badly needed, and a concert by the Rodenham Music Society; the third had been from Owen, written in pencil, and short.

> "Thank you for your postcard. This will not be a very good letter as I am too tired. Home is if anything worse without David, and father threatened to beat me yesterday for picking my nose at lunch, but it's no good arguing. I hope you are having a nice holiday in Italy.
> "Love from Owen."

He had held his anger anxiously as he travelled, sometimes reminding himself of it in case it had ceased. For a day and a half he had been in Italian and French trains, eating rolls and salami, moving fast for hours through valleys of vines and olives, the Alps, then green monotonous farm land; and at each station they had been a little later. At Dieppe in the hot afternoon they had stopped on a bend and all the efforts of the engine would not move them. He could hear it somewhere out of sight breathing and blowing like an exhausted animal, and French guards and porters ran about shouting at each other and bicycled along the platforms looking for a new engine or the station master, and the passengers leaned out of the train windows, watching. The boat train had been three hours late, the customs slow, and when the train eventually arrived at Victoria he had missed his last connection, so he had stayed the night in London. But because he had not wanted to forget his mood he had slept little. As he climbed the hill he felt his mind going fast, trying to accelerate, as if he had been drunk the night before, and his knees seemed insecure.

His mother was in the kitchen.

"Hallo, darling." She was surprised and delighted, she could never remember not to show it. She came at him and kissed him and he was almost persuaded; but what was the good of meaning to be indignant all the way from Italy if he forgot it in the first minute?

"Hallo," he said and let her kiss him.

"How are you, darling? Have you had a good crossing? What a surprise this is. Have you had a meal?"

"Quite well," he said.

"Come into the drawing-room." She tried to take his case from him but he held on.

He said, "Where's David?"

It was much too soon and he was aware of the familiar feeling of giving, not taking offence. She had turned away and for a moment he thought she was angry, and looked up from the floor for the first time, but of course she wasn't. She was nearer crying and he tried to think of something to say to stop her but couldn't.

"In Norfolk, we think."

So it was true. His indignation had been restrained by the suspicion that it wasn't, and now it came on him fully. They had hidden it from him, treating him like a child. The whole business of consulting him had been a pretence, for as soon as he went away they didn't even tell him what happened. And because he was aware of his own pettiness he became more angry.

"Why didn't you say so when you wrote?"

"Father said we shouldn't mention it in letters going abroad."

"Why not?"

"They open them, don't they? I don't know."

There was no point in explaining to her. She would never judge for herself, because she didn't want to.

He said, "Where's father?"

"Outside, chopping trees."

"What trees?"

"In the wood."

This was the real thing. He felt a little ill with anger. There was a lump in his throat and tears behind his eyes so that he couldn't speak. He wanted to say, trees can't be put up and down like houses, it takes thirty years. He wanted to say, you might have let me have a chance to ask you not to do it. And then he didn't want to say anything because words could not hurt as much as he wanted to hurt. He wanted to kick where the skin was close to the bone, and knock against a corner of brick.

He thought that perhaps only a few trees had been cut down, but the wood was ruined, he was sure of that. He didn't want it to be anything else. He wanted to go on feeling hatred and his stomach turning over and his throat and eyes full of angry tears. And he was relieved that he had a genuine grievance and need no longer be angry with himself. He went upstairs to his bedroom and locked the door.

His mother had made his bed with clean sheets, and put lavender in a jar on the mantelpiece but he didn't want to look at it. He lay with his face in the pillow and when he thought of the wood he cried. He was surprised and satisfied that he felt so strongly.

195

Someone turned the handle of the door and his father's voice said, "Peter." He lifted his head out of the pillow and listened. He could hear the slight movements of feet on the landing boards. The handle turned again. "Peter." He felt a delightful safe excitement. His father called twice more and he could hear his anger increase. Then he went away.

Peter lay and watched the hot day passing outside his window, and tried to discover some suggestion of autumn in the weather but couldn't. At first there was silence in the house, and then his mother called, "Lunch," and doors were opened and shut. After that there was silence and he imagined them eating. He was disappointed that no one had come to call him.

Presently he heard his mother's steps on the landing. She didn't touch the door because his father had told her it was locked and she believed him.

"Peter."

He waited a moment. "Yes."

"Are you feeling ill, old chap?"

He paused. "A little."

"Shall I bring you some lunch?"

"No thank you. I'm all right."

"Would you like some medicine?"

"No thank you."

She stood outside waiting for him to say something more.

"Just tired, are you?" she said.

"Not particularly."

After a moment she went away. He was angry with himself for accepting her excuse.

Sometimes during the afternoon he dozed, and sometimes he watched the blue sky through the window, and sometimes he remembered Italy. He remembered the wine in Amalfi and the ice-creams in Rome; and he remembered the Cloister of San Agostino at San Gimignano where he had sent a post-card to Julia. He had written, "Italy is fun. I wish I knew the

Italian for 'the sun is shining,' but I don't." After a pause, he had written, "Love from Peter." It had been easy to put that since he no longer felt it. He had realised that they had never understood or been at ease with each other. They had never told each other what they thought, and he had always put on an act, a profound, thoughtful act. And he remembered his relief that he no longer wanted to invite her to Beckford.

Finally he fell asleep.

When he woke it was evening and he unlocked the door and went downstairs. He could smell his mother's cooking from the kitchen, and his father was there talking to her. He came down quietly and stood in the hall.

"Damn it whose house is this?"

"Mm," she said sadly.

The dog barked, and ran out of the kitchen into the hall and began to lick him. They realised he was there and his father stopped talking, and drank the rest of his sherry, standing looking at the table.

"Hallo, darling, are you feeling better? What would you like for supper?"

"I don't mind."

At supper he sat silently, and presently began to be afraid that they really thought he was ill and didn't realise he was sulking. So when his mother asked him cheerful questions he replied shortly and almost rudely till she sighed. If only she would be angry, but she just sighed. Owen was in his own mood and Peter didn't look at him. His father was eating silently, the silhouette of his jaw going up and down against the grey window. And Peter waited for a chance to explain his attitude but none came. After supper he walked alone in the half dark evening on the lawn and then went up to his room. The key had been taken from the door.

For a moment he did not believe it and looked on both sides and on the floor. Then he shut the door, and went to his nail box and found a garden nail, and hammered it through the door into the door post. His hand shook with excitement and drops of sweat fell under his arms on to his ribs. He was aware that he was almost enjoying the game; but it hardly seemed to be his doing. The next move had come to him with peculiar impersonality as if it had been supplied from outside. And he knew that the courage to do it did not really belong to him. It was the way Owen and his father lived, doing what they wanted first and then looking for the consequences. His hand shook so that he hit the door, taking out a splinter of cream-painted wood, and he didn't care.

They must have heard him downstairs but no one came up. He lay on his bed, reading and listening for them. For about an hour he could not concentrate on the book. He began a sentence meaning to understand it but halfway through found himself thinking about what had happened and what might happen. At last he became interested; and after an hour or two went to bed.

In the morning the sun shone through his windows and he woke early and dressed and pulled out the nail with pliers and came down the sunlit stairs, walking quietly past the closed bedroom doors. Little noises of enamel plates from below told him that his mother was about, but otherwise the house was silent. When he reached the last flight he was surprised to see her standing still at the bottom, facing away from him. She held the heavy cut glass jug which they used for lunch, and it was full of water. She seemed to have hesitated about which way to go, and never decided. He came down quietly, and couldn't think what noise to make, and then he was too close. She started violently and the jug fell and shattered on the tiles.

She said nothing but got down at once on her knees and began to pick up the bits. He knelt beside her and helped, and when he saw that she was crying he put his arm over her back and kissed her on the cheek. It was soft and he did not dislike it. He wanted to say nothing, just to help her and be sorry for her. He felt as if suddenly, for the first time for years, they had made contact.

She sat back on her heels, sniffing and wiping her eyes with her apron.

She said, "Why must you all quarrel?" and he was aware that the misunderstanding had begun again.

*  *  *

The sun came round the corner of the house, leaving the back door in shadow and shone on the veranda, making the red brick floor bright, and in through the windows of the drawing-room and billiard room. On the lawn the dew dried and the shade of the pines shortened. The magpies in the wood near General Binforth's vegetable garden screeched to each other as they ate his fruit. And Peter waited for the familiar, "Come and speak to me, old boy," and the familiar sinking excitement. This time he was prepared and almost looked forward to it. But the morning went, and though there were opportunities his father did not take them. By the afternoon he had ceased to expect it, and gradually as the hot day passed he became aware that he was ceasing to want it.

When he went on to the tennis court he became indignant again, but not as he had been the day before. The young beech trees along the top lay on the grass, their leaves hanging down and discoloured. Many of the chestnuts lower on the slope had been cut, and the trunks of some of the larger trees had been chopped a quarter through as if to make sure they could not be saved. But he had to explain to himself in words how destructive and pointless it was before he could feel the same anger. He tried to think himself back into not knowing about it and discover it for the first time, and it worked once, but not again.

After tea he sat in the drawing-room, waiting for the day to become cold. He was surprised and a little satisfied that he had made his protest and nothing terrible had happened, and also uneasy. Always before there had been a scene and a reconciliation. It was like starting down an unfamiliar path which seemed safe but he was not sure. Beyond the tennis court someone was using an axe, hitting regularly, faster than he could imagine doing it himself as if the swing was hurried. His father had all the answers, he just went on doing what he wanted.

Peter went slowly upstairs, sweating from the cups of hot tea, and opened Owen's door. He was making an aeroplane and the bed was laid with small pieces of balsa wood tied together with cotton so that the glue would stick. Peter was aware of Owen's anxiety that he should not come near them and stood against the wall near the door.

"What will it be?"

"A glider, not a model." Owen went on working, kneeling on the floor.

Peter said, "How's mother been?"

"Much the same. She works too hard and no one makes her go to the doctor. The whole house without any help, the cooking, the Mothers' Union and the Women's Institute. I suppose she wants to, so that she can forget things." He was annoyingly understanding, as if he was a little bored because one ought to know.

"David?"

"And us."

"How did it happen?"

"He just went away one morning and didn't come back."

"What did father say?"

"He wanted to go to the police but mother persuaded him not to."

It was all right, talking to Owen. They had to be careful at first not to take offence, each giving the other a chance to please himself by something he said. Then they ceased to want to take offence.

"How's father?"

"Much the same. Ranting against women, classical music, the wireless, you, me, the government. Most week-ends he goes to London."

"With Mrs. Pawthorn?"

"I suppose so."

"What does mother think?"

"I don't know. She goes on bottling it all up."

Peter went to the window. From the other side of the house came the sound of his father chopping.

"When did he start on the wood?"

"About a week ago."

"Why?"

"Don't know. Not enough to do, I suppose."

Owen laid two struts on the eiderdown to dry.

"Has he threatened you any more?"

"No." Owen did not want to talk about it and Peter was annoyed to be deprived of the chance to be sorry for him.

★　　★　　★

"Mother dear, we must do something about Owen, his manners are perfectly abominable."

Peter sat at the end of the table and his father and mother were eating lunch beyond the candlesticks against the light from the window. He realised that he no longer listened to what his father said but looked for the fixed opinion which made him say it.

"It's most unfortunate that he ever met that Binforth boy."

"Yes."

"This reading at meals, we must make a rule about that, it just isn't civilised."

When Owen came down and began to look at a magazine he said, "Now Owen, old boy, we've made a rule about that. We're not going to have any more reading at meals."

Owen went on reading till Mr. Nicholas was about to

shout, then closed it without looking up. He ate slowly, saying nothing.

"Why don't you help us do the crossword, old boy?"

"I can't do crosswords." It was exactly the right slightly pathetic tone.

"Well join in the conversation then?"

"There isn't any other conversation."

"That's rude, old boy.

"Old boy, I want you to apologise for that.

"Owen, I'm waiting for you to apologise to your mother and me.

"Owen, old boy, I think you'd better go away if you aren't going to have the manners to apologise."

Owen pushed back his chair and went out leaving the door a few inches open. No one spoke and sometimes they could hear him beyond the hall, doing things in the work room. A light summer breeze came in through the open dining-room window and every few seconds the door jarred.

"Shut that bloody door, will you Peter?"

After lunch Peter heard his father talking to Owen in the billiard room.

"You see, old boy, when you get to my age and have a house of your own you'll be able to say what happens. It's not right that you and Peter should be continually arguing with what I say. You see, I'm older than you and I've learned a few things in my life which you don't know yet."

He paused and Owen didn't answer. "Another thing, old boy, I don't want to have to tell you again about cleaning your teeth in the bathroom basin. You've only got to turn round to use the lavatory."

Owen said, "Soon we won't be allowed to wash our hands." He was always saying the things that Peter didn't dare say, and surprisingly getting away with them.

"Old boy, I won't have you speaking to me like that."

There was silence for a moment. Then he said, "Old boy,

202

I think it's time you stopped seeing that red-headed friend of yours. He's not the sort of person your mother and I want you to know. If I'd brought someone like that into my father's house he would have had us both turned into the streets."

After a time Mr. Nicholas went across the lawn to the wood and Owen came upstairs, and Peter, standing halfway, wanted to speak to him, but saw that he had been crying and let him pass, pretending not to notice. He hated his father. Always before that there had been a restraint, a sense that he ought not to feel in that way.

In the evening Mr. Nicholas went to a meeting at the Red Lion and came back late for supper. No one was speaking when he came in and he began at once to say what had happened. He always had confidence that others were equally interested in himself.

"The trouble with dear old Major Dale is that he's all things to all men. You won't get anywhere in this world if you're like that. I never wanted to make him secretary in the first place, but I was over-persuaded."

Peter felt that it wasn't true, but was just not able to be sure.

"Anyway, Peter, I've got you a place in the team for our last match."

"Ah, thank you."

"You see this silly fellow Wheeler had put his name down as reserve; but I know he doesn't really want to play; and anyway he's a useless bat. But the dear old Major insisted that we should ask him first. It's bloody foolishness to try to run a club like that. It's most important that we should have a good team for this last match. They're a damn good bowling side, Of course I'm sorry in a way for the old Major. He has the hell of a time from his wife. She's a hard woman, Mrs. Dale."

He took a mouthful of omelette. "Anyway, I made him put you in."

Peter said, "If it's difficult I don't mind . . ."

"Oh no, no, that's right, you're to play."

"What did the others think?"

"Oh they were all on my side."

★   ★   ★

Peter sat in the drawing-room, looking through the open French windows at the shadows in the silver birches and the lawn lit by the after breakfast sun. When his father came in he began to look at a paper. Mr. Nicholas was never restful; he walked about with his hands in his breeches pockets, thinking, trying to find some new way to get hold of life, to attack it and hurt it. He had endless vitality. He was full of new, intelligent ideas which made one want to think and answer.

"It's no use Major Dale pretending he never had that money."

He didn't wait for you to look up but began talking, expecting attention.

"The trouble with the Major is that he's too easy-going. You must be business-like with money. You can't just say you expect it will turn up. He has a most disorderly mind."

It was suddenly clear to Peter that it would be the same with Major Dale as it had been with Captain Simmons, the second-in-command of the Home Guard, and Graham, the treasurer of the Working Man's Club at their last home. There was a period of extreme favour and then a row. One never heard their point of view, they just weren't mentioned again.

"The landlord isn't the sort of man to make a mess of a thing like this; I know old Belcher, you can trust him about money. If he says he gave it to Major Dale he did. He wouldn't be a pub-keeper if he made mistakes like that."

"What does Major Dale say?"

"The Major? He says he remembers nothing about it, but

that's ridiculous. Eight pounds isn't the sort of sum you forget."

"What was it?"

"The subscriptions, and the bus fares. The landlord collected them, that was the most convenient arrangement, and handed them over to Major Dale. If old Belcher says he did that you can take it he did."

"What has the Major got left?"

"Nothing."

"Has he had expenses?"

"Eight pounds for the motor-coach. And two pounds eighteen for a pair of wicket-keeping pads. That's another piece of wasteful stupidity. Any wicket-keeper who's any good can use ordinary pads; but our wicket-keeper is a little funk; he'd be useless whatever pads he had. And Major Dale can't say no."

"Then he ought not to have any left."

"He certainly should. What's happened, I should like to know, to the ten pounds I gave them to start them off? The Major admits he had that, he could hardly deny it, there were plenty of witnesses."

Peter didn't answer and Mr. Nicholas walked up and down looking out of the French windows.

"It's no good going on making a fuss about it now. I shall know better next time. I've got the Major to agree to resign. I shall make someone reliable secretary."

He went into the hall, shutting the door. The sun on the lawn was bright, but the weather was less hot and sometimes there was a wind which bent the bushes for a moment before they became upright and still. Peter went into the hall. His father was talking to his mother in the kitchen in a low tone and he had to stand still to hear.

"You see, even allowing two pounds eighteen, say three pounds for the pads, and eight pounds for the coach that leaves seven unaccounted for . . ."

Peter went quietly upstairs.

When he came down before lunch his father and mother were standing in the drawing-room, drinking sherry. She seemed to have been made to come there to be like his wife, and was trying to be, but half her mind was on the food she had left cooking. They had been talking, but had stopped before he came in.

After a moment his father said, "Do *you* know, Peter, what would be the right price for a pair of wicket-keeping pads?"

"I've no idea."

"Would two pounds eighteen be reasonable?"

"I should think so."

Mrs. Nicholas drank her sherry and went into the kitchen.

"The first way to ruin a club, " said Mr. Nicholas, "is to have a muddle about its finances, and a man like Major Dale should know that. He's been in the regular army."

His father stood near the French windows. "I've never met a man with such a muddled mind as the Major. Partly I agree it's his wife's fault. Oh yes, I've been there and heard her. She doesn't let him think straight. As soon as he starts to talk she chips in and contradicts him. The man doesn't dare to open his mouth in his own house."

Peter didn't answer.

"It was a most foolish thing ever to suggest him as secretary."

Presently his father said, "Tell mother I don't want any lunch." He went into the veranda, out of sight. After a moment he came into sight, going across the lawn without his coat, carrying his axe.

Peter opened the drawing-room door. The hall was dark after looking at the bright lawn. He went into the kitchen where his mother was bending over the table, placing slices of egg on a salad. "Almost ready," she said.

"Father doesn't want any." He waited for her to be incredulous and offended.

"I was afraid so," she said. He was always surprised when

206

she showed how carefully she must once have known him.

"I wish they could have the meeting, and get this business settled."

"What good will a meeting do?"

"Mm," she said, agreeing sadly as if he had made a statement, not asked a question.

"What's the meeting for?"

"I'm not sure," she said. "To make Major Dale resign?"

"But he's done that already."

"Oh has he?"

From the other side of the house, beyond the tennis court, came sounds of Mr. Nicholas working in the wood.

"When is it?"

"Next Saturday evening," she said. "I wish it was over. You know how he gets worried about things." She loaded dishes on to the trolley. "I've been noticing some of the old symptoms."

*   *   *

On the following days Mr. Nicholas worked at the wood till the sweat ran down his face and he leaned on his axe, panting carefully as if afraid of the exertion. He said little at meals, and as soon as they were over went across the lawn. "I'm tackling a brute of an old oak." In the evenings he did not go to the Red Lion but sat in his arm-chair reading, and went to the dining-room to pour himself another glass of sherry which he drank in quick gulps, tipping back his head. Soon after supper he went upstairs.

Sitting in the drawing-room they heard him moving between his bedroom and the bathroom. Then there was silence and he was presumably in bed. Half an hour later they heard his dressing-gown brushing the banisters and taps were turned in the kitchen; presently his dressing-gown brushed the banisters as he went upstairs again. He had probably come down for whisky and hot water to make him sleep. After an hour the drawing-room door opened. He had made no noise so that it was uncertain how long he had been outside. He stood in the doorway and seemed about to say something.

Mrs. Nicholas looked up from her knitting. "Hallo darling," she said in her bedside voice.

"Hallo dear." He cleared his throat. "Are you all coming to bed soon?" He paused. "It's no use my trying to get any sleep till you do."

At breakfast on Saturday Peter and Owen knew that Mrs. Nicholas was aware that the meeting was tonight because she didn't start making plans to fill a vacant day. She was glad that it had come but anxious that it should be a success.

She went upstairs for Mr. Nicholas' tray and came down quickly with it, and tried to carry it into the kitchen before they saw.

"Hasn't he had any?"

"One piece of toast. He's left all his nice porridge."

When she came out of the kitchen she had controlled her disappointment. "I don't think he slept much. He wants to get some more before this meeting."

Presently she went to the town, and Owen went to school and the house was silent. Peter went upstairs to fetch his sketch book, and came downstairs, quietly, past his father's closed door. There was no sound from inside. His shoe accidentally touched the wainscot.

"Peter."

He went softly downstairs.

"Peter, is that you, Peter?"

"Yes."

"Come and speak to me, old boy."

The sun outside lit the silver birches and rhododendrons but his father's windows were shut. The room was full of warm air with a human smell and Peter stood near the door, breathing as little as possible. His father lay under a sheet, several blankets, and an eiderdown, holding them together with one bare arm which came out near his neck. He lay with his head on its side on the pillow and didn't turn to it speak.

"Peter, will you do something for me?"

"I expect so."

He paused and Peter half thought he was going to be angry.

"You see, old boy, I'm not at all well. I've had no sleep. I shan't be able to go to this meeting tonight."

He knew what was coming; his father was going to ask him to go instead. The idea was too unreal to be alarming and he waited to see if he was right.

"I want you to take the message to them."

"I see. Can they hold it without you?"

"They must manage as best they can." His father kept his head on the pillow and spoke without looking at him.

"Surely you might get some sleep before then."

"No, no, please don't argue, old boy. Anyway I've got my doctor coming to see me."

Peter waited. After a moment his father closed his eyes.

"Who shall I tell?"

"Mr. Belcher, the landlord."

"Right you are." Peter began to go out.

"Old boy."

"Yes."

"Will you try to stop Owen banging doors. You see, I'm not at all well."

★   ★   ★

When Dr. Andrews stood against the drawing-room mantelpiece he reached it with his shoulders so that his thin pink head appeared among the willow-pattern china. His pointed black shoes on the fender suggested an office clerk, but had probably been professional thirty years ago. Without

209

his overcoat he seemed incompletely dressed, with too much thin wrist and black-socked ankle exposed. When he leaned back his short black coat came apart showing his small pot-belly inside his waistcoat.

"A hot bath last thing at night is very helpful."

"Yes," said Mrs. Nicholas.

"There are one or two other symptoms, but on the whole nothing that a good night's sleep won't cure. No one feels well if they haven't had rest."

"No."

"The first thing is to end the insomnia. After that every-thing else may disappear. I have given Mr. Nicholas a pre-scription. One or two capsules last thing at night should be ample."

Dr. Andrews came away from the mantelpiece and took up his overcoat and gloves. As he went through the French windows with Mrs. Nicholas Peter heard him say, "I don't know if he has ever tried Horlick's."

The next day Mr. Nicholas got up after breakfast and went across the lawn to the wood, where he could be heard all morning. The sun was hot but there was a small cool breeze. Twice Peter heard the snapping crash of a falling tree. But when he came into the drawing-room before lunch his father was sitting in an arm-chair, reading.

"Peter, old boy."

"Yes?"

"Shut the door, will you."

Peter shut the door and came back.

"Did you take that message for me?"

"Yes."

"What did he say?"

"I can't remember. Nothing interesting."

His father sat with his book on his knees, looking over it at the carpet.

"Peter, could you do something for me?"

"Yes."

"Could you go round and ask what they decided at the meeting?"

"Yes, or I could telephone."

"No no, old boy," His father looked up with alarm, and sat up in his chair so that his book shut and slipped between his knees, and he grabbed at it but missed and it fell open on the carpet.

"Old boy, please do what I ask."

"All right."

It was always the same, he couldn't talk without emotion, but emotion of his own sort on his own terms. Anyone else's he ridiculed.

"Why not?"

His father sat looking at the book on the carpet.

"Wouldn't it be quicker?"

"You don't understand, old boy. You don't know who may be listening."

"Oh, all right." If his father really thought that, the only thing was to make an allowance. Or perhaps it was the sort of fact about life which one was continually learning, which seemed absurd at first but later one accepted; what his father meant when he said, "You see, I've lived a little longer than you." Anyway it was no good arguing.

He sat down and began to look at a paper. After a moment he became aware that his father had not picked up his book and was waiting.

He said, "Will after lunch be all right?"

"No, old boy, you don't understand. It won't be all right."

When Peter came back they were in the dining-room and had started eating.

"Where's father?"

"He's taken his lunch upstairs. He thinks he may have strained himself with those trees."

Peter went slowly upstairs. His father was sitting on the edge of his bed with the tray on his knees.

"Hallo, old boy, I'm having mine upstairs. My clock-work's not very good." It had the tone of an excuse, like making a joke to the master when you hadn't done his work.

"What did the landlord say?" He stared with alarm and impatience.

"Nothing, they decided not to hold the meeting."

*　　*　　*

The sun shone in at his window in the early morning but he turned over and when he woke again it was covered by clouds, and clouds covered the sky except for small shifting patches of blue. The fine weather had broken and it was almost with relief that he saw spots of rain. Its rattle on the glass between gusts of wind was strange yet familiar. On the landing he could hear his mother's broom knocking the walls and the legs of the chest of drawers, and her dustpan moving on the boards. She began to brush the stair carpet; six quick strokes, a pause, then six quick strokes a little farther down. You became used to her pathetic devotion, so that it ceased to seem pathetic, just stupid. Peter lay and watched the white and grey clouds carried quickly across his window by the south-west wind. Presently the rain became steady.

His mother brought him the letter as soon as the post came.

"Breakfast's ready, darling," she said. She found a conventional reason for coming up, to hide the other.

"I've just got this."

She opened it and he was afraid she was going to read aloud, and said quickly, "May I see?"

But when she gave it to him, willingly, refusing to take offence, he only glanced at it. He did not want to become entangled again, to let his generalisations be muddled. He recognised familiar phrases: "Your jealousy," "Our friendship." Others, like "Our action," were new. It didn't seem to propose anything, or indeed to have any purpose and there was no address.

"It really is the limit, "she said.

Her reactions were ceasing to be original, settling into a pattern. She was developing a set of clichés for the subject. She had no sense of having said a thing once, but went on repeating it, expecting it to have the same meaning.

"It was addressed to me in disguised writing," she said. "Shall I show it to father?"

"I shouldn't," he said. "Perhaps you ought to." He had no opinion. It didn't seem to matter what happened to it or if it had never been written. It was an unnecessary addition to an episode which should have ended. He had already thought of it as a whole, judged the performances, and did not want another scene. He was astonished that something which meant so little to him should go on being important to her, and caught himself concluding that it meant equally little to her; but that was forgetting who she was.

"Perhaps I'd better not," she said. "It might upset him more."

"It might," he said.

During the next fortnight Dr. Andrews began to come regularly. He went up to Mr. Nicholas' room, shut the door behind him, and stayed for half an hour or sometimes two hours. Often no one saw him arrive, but his black overcoat on the arm of a drawing-room chair, and the sound of Mr. Nicholas talking in a low voice behind his closed door showed that he was there. Perhaps Mr. Nicholas had come down in his dressing-gown and taken him up; or more probably he had come through the French windows and found his own way.

He seemed to have few other patients. Before he went he usually led Mrs. Nicholas into the dining-room.

"Mr. Nicholas has a nasty cold, a very nasty cold. I wonder if you could make him some black-currant tea?" It was surprising that these were his only conclusions after so long.

"The first thing is to cure the cold. Perhaps you have a friar's balsam inhaler?" He seemed to have little confidence in his medicines, and gave the impression that recovery was something one must, of course, hope for but not speak about.

The weather was grey, and sometimes rain fell. A wind blew over the hill, stirring the surface of the rhododendrons like water, moving the pine tops, and windows which had been open for weeks were closed. At first Mr. Nicholas got up in the afternoons and sat in his arm-chair which was taken up to his room, but when he caught cold he stayed in bed, reading. He read quickly, and without comment, books about the war, *Life and Self*, by Si Yan, *The Pickwick Papers*, and the works of Arthur Bryant.

Sometimes Dr. Andrews didn't come.

"Peter, old boy, will you do something for me?"

"Yes?"

"Will you go and fetch my little doctor?"

"What shall I say?"

"Say I'm not at all well."

★   ★   ★

At breakfast Peter sometimes tried to think of a new phrase or a new intonation. It had become a routine and he was frightened of routine because it could be mimicked and then he would be aware of himself being summed up, classified, credited with a fixed opinion. But there seemed no other words so he said, "How's father?"

"A little better, I think," she said. That was half why he did not like asking. He hated her routine optimism.

"Did he sleep?"

"Not much, but he seems a little more cheerful."

"Did he sleep at all?"

"I don't think so."

"How many pills did he take?"

"Two," she said. She refused to admit that she had been

snubbed. "I think if he would get up a bit," she said, "he might do better. When he lies in bed all day he doesn't get tired so he hasn't any—you know—want of rest."

"Have you suggested it?"

"Yes, but he says he's too ill."

"What with? The doctor can't find anything, except a cold."

"Mm," said Mrs. Nicholas.

"Well what does he say?"

"I don't know. Just that he's too ill. You try talking to him."

She was offended at last and a little sulky. He never meant to do it, but as soon as they talked he became annoyed. She would never give an opinion and he tried to make her. Even when she seemed to he was aware that it was what someone else had told her, or was a guess at his own opinion. He drank his coffee and went slowly upstairs to his father's room.

He was lying on his back looking at the ceiling.

"Hallo, Dad." The word embarrassed him and he tried to avoid it, slurred it, and left off the last consonant.

"Hallo Peter."

"Would you like a paper?" He had picked it up in the hall. It was his conventional reason for coming up. He needed one just as she did and just as she wanted to hide her concern for David, he wanted to hide his concern for his father. He tried to hide his feelings whatever they were, his fears and desires, because they would be ridiculed or remembered, even his acts of kindness because they showed a weakness. That was growing up: learning to curl up smaller, to leave exposed only what could not be hurt and didn't matter.

"No thank you, old boy, I've got my book if I want to read."

He was relieved that his gesture had been refused.

"The papers are so full of gloom, I don't like to see them." His father often said that, but this time he did not want to go

215

on talking about not wanting to read them. He lay on his back, looking at the ceiling.

Peter stood near the chest of drawers, looking at his father's books: *The Years of Endurance, English Saga, The Duke*. He had got into the room without embarrassment but now he could not think how to make his suggestion. The longer the silence went on the harder it became. The embarrassment of saying anything seemed to increase each second.

"When are you going to get up?" he said suddenly, without thinking how it would sound, and waited with excitement.

"You don't understand, old boy."

"What don't I understand?"

His father didn't answer. He lay on his back and let his eyes close, then opened them quickly, but his head didn't move.

"If only the weather was decent. This rain, rain, rain, day after day. You can't call it summer."

"But you can't wait for fine weather to get well. The drawing-room's warm."

His father didn't answer.

"Why not sit in the drawing-room. Surely that would be pleasanter?" It was the best he could do for enthusiasm. He didn't feel much. He hadn't enough for himself and what he had he hid. It was another exposure.

"Anyway my little doctor wouldn't let me."

"Are you sure? Have you asked him?"

His father didn't answer.

"He doesn't seem to have done you much good so far." He felt conviction in his words now that he was depreciating.

"Perhaps you should try doing something that he doesn't allow. He admits there's nothing wrong with you. Why not believe that?" He paused. "How will staying in bed help?"

"He knows best," said Mr. Nicholas. There was a suggestion of how it might have been said, of the finality it might have had and the snub it might have been. It made Peter aware that he had talked too much. But there was no follow up, no labouring of the victory. His father lay on his back and let his eyes close.

Peter stood near the dressing-table. He lifted a book to see the one below and put it down again. He picked up the stone-age axe head which was a paper-weight.

"I didn't know you'd found this again."

"Which?"

"The axe-head."

"Yes."

"Where was it?"

"What? I'm not sure. In the billiard room. Please put it down, old boy."

Peter put it down and stood with his back to the bed, not trying to talk.

"You see, old boy, I've done a very terrible thing."

"Yes." Peter turned round slowly, not to disturb his father and prevent him going on. He became intensely curious; he wondered if his father meant Pussy Pawthorn, if in some curious way he had become frightened or was sorry about that; he waited for him to speak, not daring to ask.

"A really terrible thing."

Peter stood still, looking at the ground, listening for the first syllable. Then he became afraid that his father's mind had already gone on, and that he wasn't going to speak, and lost patience.

"When?" he said. It was a compromise, but it was hope-lessly obvious. Its evasiveness emphasised his curiosity.

"What?"

"When did it happen?"

"A long time ago."

Peter said softly and as casually as possible, "What sort of thing?"

"No, it doesn't matter, old boy."

He had asked too much and spoiled his chance of knowing. He stood looking sideways at the dressing-table, determined not to speak again. Lying beyond the books, near the wall, he noticed his own Colt .32 and remembered that it had not been in his room when he came back from Italy. His father had probably borrowed it when he heard of some local robbery, for he liked to talk of shooting burglars. It was surprising to remember that. Peter stared at the dust on the black oiled metal and waited, hoping that the silence would make his father go on. Then his mother opened the door and came in, carrying a tray with tea and biscuits.

The dog came behind her, wagging its tail, curling its neck and back, its feet pattering with excitement and friendliness on the linoleum. It knew it should not be there but no one had told it to go, and before she could put down the tray it had jumped on to the bed and run up the blankets, its tongue out, trying to lick. Mr. Nicholas pushed the sheets at it, climbing back on to the pillow, holding his head away turned sideways against the wall, keeping it off with both hands outstretched.

"Get him away mother, get him off my sheets, mother."

He caught his breath rhythmically, almost as if he was laughing but there was no suggestion of mirth. The dog licked at his hands but presently he caught it by the loose skin at the side of the neck and held it tight so that it stopped licking and yelped. Mrs. Nicholas took it on to the landing and shooed it downstairs.

Peter said, "I must go and work."

He took his cup and went up to his room. As he went he heard his father say, "Mother darling, you must try not to upset me in that sort of way."

When Peter brought down his empty cup his father's door was open a few inches and through the crack he could see him standing on the linoleum, his open hands holding his dressing-gown to his tummy; and he knew by the noises of the bed being moved and feet walking behind the door that his mother was changing his father's sheets.

*　　*　　*

Peter woke suddenly. The room was black, and the night black for he could not see the shape of his windows. Some-body had said his name. He had been asleep but he had heard it, and hearing it in his sleep it had had no direction. He wondered where they were and how close to him. He tried to clear his eyes but the room was so black that he could not tell if they were clear. He could not think how long he had been asleep, or connect the moment with any yesterday. He lay still with his hands under the bed-clothes.

"Peter." For a second he did not recognise it. Sweat broke out on his legs and the back of his neck. Then it was his father's voice.

"Peter, where's the light?"

"On the wall to the right of the door."

He could hear his hand moving on the wallpaper. When the light went on it was bright and he half closed his eyes. His father was standing in his pyjamas near the door. His feet on the linoleum were bare and he held up his pyjama trousers with one hand leaving his ankles exposed. In the other hand he held the Colt.

"Peter, can you help me?"

"Yes?"

"I think I've got a round in the chamber."

"Yes?"

"Will you help me get it out?"

His father came to the bed and gave it to him. The butt was damp from his hand. "Be careful," he said. He was glad not to be holding it. He stood beside the bed, not looking at what Peter was doing, facing half away. Peter took out the magazine, and worked the slide. There was no round in the chamber.

He put back the magazine and held it out to his father.

"It's all right now."

"No, you look after it, old boy."

"If you like."

His father went to the door.

"Shall I turn out your light?"

"Yes thank you."

He shut the door and Peter could hear him outside, feeling his way across the landing. He put the gun on his chair, and laid his head on the pillow. After a moment or two there was a sound and he lifted his head to listen. The door opened.

"Peter."

"Yes."

"I want to take another pill."

Peter waited.

"Could you come and help me?"

Peter got up and went with him down to the bathroom. He opened the green cellophane capsule, poured the white powder into a medicine glass, and added water. His father stood watching him.

"Did you wash the glass?"

"Yes."

"In hot water?"

"Yes."

His father took it with him to his room.

"Thank you, old boy."

"That's all right."

Owen and his mother had almost finished breakfast when Peter came down.

"How's father?" He felt a genuine curiosity this morning.

"I think he slept better," said Mrs. Nicholas. "Anyhow he didn't wake me."

"Does he usually?"

"For the last fortnight."

"Every night."

"I think so."

"What for?"

"To say he hasn't been to sleep and ask for another pill."

She went on hiding her sacrifices; there was no need to tell anyone because God knew; and when they were discovered by chance you wondered how many were never discovered. It had gone on so long that you ceased to believe in a time when she could bear no more.

"He woke *me* last night."

"Did he? What for?"

"Another pill."

"Mm," she said sadly.

"And to unload his pistol."

She didn't understand about guns and waited, trying to tell from his tone how alarmed she should be.

"It's so hard to know what's wrong," he said. "If you reassure him about one thing he thinks of another."

"It all started," she said, "with the row about Major Dale and the club."

"But why work himself into a state about that?"

Owen listened saying nothing. He made Peter angry; he seemed to say, you are becoming involved, almost excited about this thing, I wonder why. He made Peter want to ask him his opinion, but that would have been an admission, and anyway he would have avoided an answer. After a time, Owen fetched his bicycle and went to school.

Peter washed up in the kitchen and his mother carried through the china and fetched his father's tray. She stood beside the sink, drying the plates, her hands working briskly.

"Hallo," she said, "a car." They could hear its tyres on the gravel of the drive.

"Who is it?" He went on washing while she looked out of the window.

"Two policemen."

"I don't believe you," he said, but he did. It wasn't the habit of the house for people to say untrue things for fun to see what other people would reply. They would have been taken seriously and the joke would have had to be explained. "He's being funny." "Are you being funny?" "Of course he is." "Now come on, old boy, seriously, are you being funny?" . . .

She stood near the window. "What can they want?" she said. "Will you go and see? My overall is a disgrace." The vanity was surprising and she admitted it with apology.

"I suppose so." He began to dry his hands.

The kitchen door opened and Mr. Nicholas came in. He wore his dressing-gown round his shoulders but no slippers. He was staring with alarm. Peter had never before realised that people were wide-eyed with terror. His eyes were astonishingly open, and his lips pressed forward in a pouting expression so that they seemed to shake a little. He said, "What have they come for?" speaking with difficulty.

"I don't know; we haven't asked them."

The bell rang above the kitchen door setting a red and white disc swinging in its aperture. Peter went out beneath it, across the hall, and opened the front door.

"Good morning."

"Good morning, sir. May we speak to Mr. Nicholas?"

They were wide men with red faces and there was a joviality about their tone as if they assumed that the upper middles classes were on their side. It was like the big ally to the little and contained a hint of threat.

"I'm not sure. He isn't well. I'll go and see."

Peter went back into the kitchen.

"What is it?"

"They want to speak to you."

"What for?"

"I didn't ask."

His father moved about beyond the kitchen table, without purpose. He felt trapped; he wanted to hide but there was nowhere.

"Tell them to come back later."

Peter said, "It's probably something unimportant like a dog licence."

He saw alarm grow on his father's face.

"Mother did you get that licence?"

"Yes dear, I gave it to you."

He remembered, but he didn't say so. His mind was already finding a new fear. He sat on the laundry basket, his bare feet off the floor, shivering with alarm, or perhaps cold.

"I can't possibly see them now, I'm not dressed."

"They'll wait." The laundry basket was tall and sometimes he reached his toes down to the tiles and sometimes raised them from the floor and sat with his whole feet shivering.

"Peter, old boy, draw that curtain, will you?"

"It's all right, you're not in sight. The window's too high."

Peter stood near the door, waiting for an answer.

"Why not speak to them now and get it over."

His father got off the laundry basket and stood against the opposite wall, under the clock. There was not enough space and he had to bend.

"Old boy, will you go and ask them what they want?"

"But if I do that it will show that you could see them."

His father didn't answer.

"If they go away now they'll only come back."

His father didn't answer and Peter went out of the kitchen, across the hall. As he went he heard his father say, "Fetch me a rug, there's a dear girl." The two policemen had their large backs turned to the doorway and were looking out of the porch at the rain which had started to fall on the hillside. When they turned, their faces showed no impatience.

"I wonder whether you could leave a message?"

"Well, no sir, we shall have to speak to Mr. Nicholas personally, but it isn't urgent. It's about his cricket club; but we can call again sir. A matter of something owing to Home Counties Coaches Limited. But there's no urgency, sir. We'll call again, and we hope Mr. Nicholas will be better. Good morning, sir."

Mr. Nicholas stood against the kitchen wall under the clock. He had put the rug on top of his dressing-gown, leaving his ankles and feet still bare.

"What did they say?"

"They'll call again."

"What's it about?"

"I'm not certain."

"Did you ask them?"

"They said it wasn't urgent."

*   *   *

Dr. Andrews was speaking to Mrs. Nicholas in the dining-room, and except when the wind blew round the house making a noise in the trees, Peter, standing in the hall, could hear them. She listened to his suggestions about laxatives and to his explanations about bulk and liquid content, sometimes understanding and sometimes not, but agreeing. Presently she would let him go away. She never tried to direct the conversation, or make him answer her questions. She could never discover the deceit or evasion of what people said to her for herself, though if someone else explained it she listened and agreed.

They came into the hall to go out through the drawing-room, and Peter began to move, but not soon enough, and he was aware that Dr. Andrews knew he had been there.

"Peter," she said, "will you go with the doctor to fetch the medicine?"

Peter followed him through the veranda, across the lawn,

towards his car. The wind slammed the French window behind them and blew spots of rain in their faces. Though it was only five o'clock the afternoon was dark. Dr. Andrews opened the car's back door and took out a bottle of pills from a leather suitcase.

"Here, give him this." He was irritatingly sensitive, and aware of Peter's hostility.

"Does he know how many . . ."

"Yes, he knows." He was abrupt to Peter in a way that he never was to his mother. He walked round the bonnet to the car's front door.

"Are they sleeping pills?"

"What? That's right."

He opened the far door and sat in the driving seat, tucking his coat round his knees with his leather gloves. Peter opened the opposite front door and bent down.

"Are they bromide?"

"Yes." He sat with obvious impatience, looking ahead through the windscreen.

"Are they the same as before?"

"No."

When Peter could not think of anything else to say he shut the door and went back into the house. His mother was in the drawing-room.

"I do wish," she said, "I thought that Dr. Andrews did him more good."

They had agreed about that already and he suspected that she was repeating his own words. She went on saying it but she did nothing.

"So do I."

Normally it needed several unkind remarks to convince her that they were intended but she noticed this at once and went away into the kitchen, sulking a little. Owen was right, she was terribly tired. It was obvious in the way she spoke to the dog when it got in her way under the kitchen table. It wasn't surprising, if she was woken every night, and got up every morning at seven to clean the house.

She was aware that her children thought her a fool. It was hard to know what she felt about Mr. Nicholas. She had loved him once, and perhaps still did. She had a conviction that she should love and obey him which she held strongly, so strongly that it did not seem right to distinguish between it and something else which she really felt. And it was probably too simple to suppose that he had become just another opportunity for martyrdom. But it seemed so; and the Christian societies which she organised were easily explained as a way to forget that her happy family had been a failure.

Owen was back from school; Peter saw him through the drawing-room go past the French windows on his way to the front door, and because he did not want to be found standing doing nothing in the hall he followed her into the kitchen.

She was cooking supper, leaning against the draining-board, stirring eggs in a bowl, and she didn't turn round or speak.

"You see," he said, "I do think it's time we did something about Dr. Andrews."

"Mm." She moved to the gas cooker and poured the mixture into a frying pan. It slopped over and sizzled on the hot metal.

"Don't you agree?" he said.

"Yes." He was startled by her annoyance.

"What's the matter?"

"Nothing," she said. She stood by the gas cooker, leaning her stomach against it. She said, "I've such a pain."

She moved quickly away, out of the kitchen, across the hall. He could think of nothing she needed to fetch. He heard her feet stumble, and the dog yelped, then the noise of her fall. It was astonishingly heavy, so that the boards under the linoleum echoed, and some part of her smacked the tiles.

He knew that he should run and see, but waited a second

and then felt a great reluctance. He didn't like to think of what he might find. Beyond the hall he could hear Owen opening the front door, and above the kitchen ceiling his father was getting out of bed. The wind in the garden was bending the trees. He went quickly into the hall.

She was sitting on the floor in the dining-room doorway, rubbing her knee with both hands, crying quietly, Mr. Nicholas was standing at the top of the stairs.

"What's happened? Peter, what's happened?"

"Mother tripped over Sambo."

"Has she broken anything?" He stood on the stairs, staring with alarm, not wanting to go nearer.

"I don't know."

Owen stood by the drawing-room door, watching.

"I should think we'd better take you to bed," said Peter.

"No, I shall be all right." She dried her eyes with the back of her hand and tried to stand, lifting herself by the oak chest, but it hurt more than she expected.

"Yes, take her to bed," said Mr. Nicholas. He stood still, holding his dressing-gown together. Even now he could not forget his habit of letting nothing be done unless he gave an order.

Peter and Owen helped her upstairs, and Mr. Nicholas came up behind.

"That bloody dog," he said, and Peter was aware of its danger.

"It wasn't his fault," she said. She was already blaming herself for giving way to pain and running out of the kitchen. They helped her into her bedroom.

"I'll get into bed and have a little rest," she said.

"Can you manage?"

"Yes thank you."

They went downstairs. Mr. Nicholas was standing in his bedroom doorway. "Is she all right?"

"Yes."

"That bloody dog."

They went into the hall.

"Peter, are you sure there's nothing broken?"

"I don't think so. I'm going to ring up the doctor."

"Yes, ring up my little doctor."

Peter tried Dr. Andrews' number, but he was out. He would be back in about an hour.

Owen said, "What are you going to do?" and Peter noticed his alarm. It was so long since he had been like this that Peter had almost forgotten it.

"Wait and try again."

"Supposing there *is* something wrong. Are you sure her knee isn't broken?" He was almost tearful. It reminded Peter of times when he had climbed trees which Owen had thought unsafe and Owen had stayed on the ground calling to him not to go higher.

"I don't think so. No, I'm sure she hasn't; she'd know if she had." He was enjoying himself, taking charge in the crisis. "Anyway she had a pain before. That would be the only reason for hurrying." It was stupid to have told Owen.

"Couldn't we ring Dorothy?"

"What good would that do? She's in London." It was quite unnecessary to panic, and Peter was angry with Owen for spoiling his sense of control, making him wonder if things were all right. He said, "If Dr. Andrews is still out, presently, we'll try another doctor."

"It might be appendicitis."

Peter had not thought of that. After a moment he went, with a show of reluctance to telephone. The woman who answered at Dr. Andrews' house suggested Dr. Duncan.

Dr. Duncan answered briskly and said he would come.

He was about thirty, and tall with thick tortoise-shell glasses. He listened while Peter explained what had happened and his fear that it might be appendicitis.

"Where is your mother?"

"Upstairs, I'll show you."

Dr. Duncan went in to see her alone. When he came out he said, "She must stay in bed. Your father's ill too?"

"Yes."

"Is there anyone who could look after them?"

"I suppose we could."

"Have you any relations who live near?"

"We have a sort of aunt, a friend of our mother's, who lives in London. She might come." Dr. Duncan didn't answer. "I could telephone and ask her." Dr. Duncan said nothing, making Peter aware that he was leaving him to decide whether this was sensible. They went downstairs.

"Let me know what your mother's friend says. I'll ring Dr. Andrews this evening." It was impossible to tell whether he resented being called.

"Is there anything we should do?"

"No. I've told your mother to rest."

Dorothy Mariner arrived by the last train that night and stayed for a week. When Dr. Andrews came he could find nothing wrong with Mrs. Nicholas except tiredness, and she quickly got better. He prescribed Horlicks, which Dorothy brought to her in a large hot cup each night and she drank, leaning on her elbow. Then she lay under her blankets with only her face showing, seeming after all surprisingly small, and smiled, and looked comfortable, and went to sleep.

Dorothy also looked after Mr. Nicholas, taking him meals and his sleeping pills. She said to him, "You are not to wake your wife in the night."

She knew what she would say if he answered, but she did not expect him to.

"If you want another pill and can't get it yourself come to me."

She was kind but firm, and yet, surprisingly, this was not irritating. There was never any suggestion that she based her behaviour on some moral code and so you did not

229

feel that she was aware of her goodness; and you did not suspect that she made it out to be a little more invariable than it was.

She would go away and tell the story with skill to her friends in London, but what she would say would not be inconsistent with what she did while taking part in it.

Mr. Nicholas did not come to her in the night. Sometimes he could be heard running taps and knocking things in the bathroom; more often he seemed to stay in bed. But he did not sleep. When she or Peter asked he said so, but he did not try to tell them. Every day he could be heard behind his closed door, telling Dr. Andrews.

"When your mother is better," Dorothy said, "you must go with her to Dr. Andrews and insist that he does something. Otherwise this will all happen again."

\*     \*     \*

Clouds were blowing across the sky outside, and occasionally the sun showed, and sometimes rain fell. Dr. Andrews stood against the drawing-room mantelpiece, looking down at his pointed shoes on the fender.

"I suppose," he said, "that he could consult a psychologist." Psychology was something invented since he was trained.

Peter said, "Would that do any good?"

"It might." Dr. Andrews implied that there was no need to be violently opposed to it because its general failure was proved. "In a way there's nothing specific to consult one about."

"But Mr. Nicholas isn't well and he isn't getting better. There must be something wrong."

"Yes." Dr. Andrews admitted it reluctantly.

"Then there must be something to be done."

Dr. Andrews looked down at his shoes and said nothing. He let it be obvious that he didn't agree.

He seemed to resent this interruption to the routine he had

established. Medicine wasn't a matter of sudden magical cures, but of gradual, not easily explained recovery.

"Of course, we can do nothing without his own consent."

"He'd give that if you advised him."

"Yes, he might." Dr. Andrews turned to Mrs. Nicholas who stood near the sofa. "Have his bowels opened to-day?"

"A little," she said. "He finds that medicine very hard to swallow—you know, very dry and chuffy." She was absurdly unconscious that he was changing the subject.

"Have you tried it a little at a time?"

"No," she said, "that might be better."

Peter said, "Do you know a psychologist?"

"Yes." He paused and Peter expected him to go on about laxatives.

"I think I should warn you that they aren't cheap; and I have known cases where they haven't helped much. But of course if he wants to see one I don't want to stop him."

Peter had the impression that he honestly didn't want to stop him. The idea of Dr. Andrews as an evil little man, keeping his father ill for his own purposes, suddenly ceased to be believable. It would have been easier if it had been. There would have been someone to oppose and be angry with. But his helplessness was genuine; he was just old and tired and rather lost.

★   ★   ★

Mr. Nicholas sat against the cushions in the darkness of the back of the car, his knees and feet wrapped in a rug, not speaking, and Mrs. Nicholas, sitting next to him, and Peter, sitting in front next to the driver, did not speak. They felt as if they were holding their breath, that any word they said might make something go wrong. They had never expected him to come so far and could not quite believe that he would go the whole way.

The wipers made half-circles of clear glass on the windscreen, but as soon as they had passed it was covered again with thin rain, and drops gathered and ran, and gathered and ran off the bottom. It was pointless to watch them.

Presently Mr. Nicholas said, "Does the driver know where to go?"

"I think so."

He sat forward. "Driver, driver, do you know where to go?"

"Yes sir."

"Dr. Evenlode's. Not his clinic but his private address. What is it? What's the address? You know it mother. Mother what's his address?"

"Three Cannon Road."

"Three Cannon."

"Yes sir."

Peter watched the windscreen wiper and the gathering drops.

A maid showed them into a rectangular, cream-painted room with metal framed French windows, and beyond a garden with a stone pond and a lawn recently grown from grass seed and small shrubs and newly creosoted board fences. The rain fell lightly on it, and the expanse of glass let its chill into the room. There was a table with magazines and, at one end, a passage without a door led away. Presently a young man came from this and they stood aside to let him tidy the magazines or switch an electric fire, but he stopped when he came near them.

"Mr. Nicholas? I'm Dr. Evenlode. Would you like to come through?"

Mr. Nicholas went with him down the passage. He spoke first to Mr. Nicholas alone, then to Mrs. Nicholas, then to both of them, while Peter waited. The house was cold and silent, and the maid, wherever she was, made no noise. In the room at the end of the passage they were presumably talking, but he could hear nothing; perhaps they were sitting in silence. He was depressed by the idea of anyone living always in this house.

Yet already, though nothing had been done or said, his father's illness seemed less impossible. By only seeing other people he became aware of how it would appear to them, not as a unique problem, but as typical of some disease. The doctor would give it a name, put it in a category, suggest a treatment. There was a comforting routine for illness. It was only when one put oneself outside it and tried to take one's own decisions that one could think of no way out and became frightened. It was only when shut up with people who were emotionally involved that one became dramatic.

The door opened, they came down the passage into the room, the doctor behind, and Peter went with them to the front door.

"We'll see what we can do then." Dr. Evenlode shook hands with Mrs. Nicholas. He had no confident bedside manner. He was trying too hard to put himself in sympathy with depression.

"Good-bye." He shook hands with Mr. Nicholas who held out his hand but did not look at him. They got into the taxi and drove round the grass circle, down the drive.

"He's a nice young man," said Mrs. Nicholas. She was determined to think so and persuade Mr. Nicholas, but he sat in the darkness of the back seat, not answering. He did not trust young men.

"I thought he seemed very sensible," she said. "What . . ."

Peter looked round to see why she had stopped. Mr. Nicholas had nudged her and he was holding one finger against his lips, signalling her to be quiet. Peter noticed that the driver was watching in his mirror.

Dr. Evenlode telephoned next day to say that he would have a bed at the week-end; they were to let him know if they did not want it. Peter, on the upper landing, could hear his mother telling his father when she took up his lunch.

233

"You see, my dear, I can't go."

"Why not?"

"It's impossible."

"Yes, darling, why?"

"I never told him about my last nervous breakdown."

"That doesn't matter."

"Of course it matters. He would never have consented to treat me if he'd known."

She said nothing for a moment. She was so used to believing him that she could not contradict him.

"But are you sure?"

Peter could not hear any answer; perhaps he was already thinking about something else, about where the tray should be put. He heard it placed on the dressing table and she went downstairs.

When Peter came to lunch she said, "Father says he won't go."

"Why?"

"Because he didn't tell the doctor he'd been ill before."

Peter put down his knife and fork and went upstairs. He could have waited till after lunch but he was aware again of excitement. He could no longer think of his father just as a nervous case who needed treatment. He might refuse it. There were decisions which one had to take and persuade others to take.

When he was excited he saw what things to do and did them, not waiting to look for reasons against which would have been confusing, and which he knew could not be enough. Sometimes he was sure that it was the only way to live. Outside his father's room he paused and emptied his mouth. He did not want to admit that he had come in the middle of lunch.

His father was reading and had not touched the tray on the dressing table. He let his book fall on to his knees.

"Don't you want your lunch?"

234

"Peter."

"Yes."

"Close the door."

Peter closed it.

"You see, old boy, they get things out of you."

"In nursing homes?"

"They give you drugs to make you talk."

Peter said nothing.

"Isn't that so?"

"I don't know. I shouldn't think so. I suppose they ask you questions."

"And when you're asleep they listen. You're bound to say something sooner or later. And then they just pop you round the corner." His father signalled sideways with his thumb and, opening his eyes wide, gave a sudden grin. Peter wasn't sure what he meant.

"It's only two streets away."

He meant the asylum. Peter said nothing.

"You see, old boy, I'm perfectly convinced they make you tell them things."

"But they wouldn't pass anything on. It's in confidence—isn't it? Yes, I'm sure it's in confidence."

His father took down his plate and began to eat his meat pie. He seemed curiously aware that he had been impressive.

"Anyway, what is there that you want to hide?"

"You don't know, old boy."

\* \* \*

They had arranged about the taxi in Mr. Nicholas' hearing.

Peter said, "Did Dr. Evenlode mean Saturday or Sunday?"

"Saturday. I should think the afternoon would be all right," said Mrs. Nicholas. "Time for a nice lunch first."

"I'll ring up for a taxi," said Peter.

And Mr. Nicholas had lain still, saying nothing.

They half expected him to be ill on Saturday, or to refuse

to dress but he didn't. He had lunch downstairs, saying little, and only at the last moment, when the taxi had come said, "Mother dear, I can't do it."

"Come on," she said. "I'll go with you." She ran upstairs for her coat and they drove away together.

She came back two hours later.

"How was he?"

"A bit unhappy to be left you know. I saw his room. Quite nice, rather plain but quite nice."

"Mm."

"And I talked to his male nurse. He seemed very sensible. Do they always have male nurses in these places?"

On Sunday after tea, Peter packed his trunk ready to travel to Oxford on Monday. He was already a week late for term and another day would not matter. Sweaters for the winter, packets of sugar and jars of jam which his mother had given him, the heavy work books from the college library which he had not opened. Presently the telephone rang in the hall.

He could hear his mother answering, but not what she was saying. She came to the bottom of the stairs and called, "Peter."

"Yes." He came on to the landing.

"It's the nursing home."

He ran downstairs.

"Is it father?"

"No; someone with a message from him. He says he must come home at once because he has something very important to tell me. What shall I say?"

"Can't he tell you now?"

"I don't know." She went back to the telephone.

"Hallo, I wonder, would it be possible perhaps for my husband to speak to me on the telephone?"

She waited, holding the receiver. "They've gone to ask him."

After a moment a voice in the receiver said, "He won't do that."

"I see," said Mrs. Nicholas. "Just one moment." She turned her head. "He says he won't."

"Ask them why not," said Peter. "Ask them how important it is. Couldn't he write?"

"Hallo," she said. "I wonder if you could possibly find out for me how important it is."

"He said it was very important." The voice in the receiver was loud and brittle, like a short range wireless set.

"Tell them you'll come to see him," said Peter. "Tell them you'll come to-morrow."

"Hallo," she said. "Hallo." There was no answer. "I think we're cut off."

"Surely he can't have anything important to say. If he once comes home he'll never go back."

"He's probably coming now," she said.

"Ring them again and say you'll visit him to-morrow."

She dialled for the exchange and the receiver began to buzz regularly.

"They can't have treated him yet. They can hardly have seen him."

She held the receiver to her ear listening to its continual ringing.

"It's absurd to come away after one day. What could he have to say?"

"He may be very unhappy," said Mrs. Nicholas, and Peter was aware that he had forgotten that.

The receiver crackled and she gave the number. When it answered she asked for Mr. Nicholas, and for several minutes there was no sound.

"They're looking for him."

Presently she listened. "I see," she said. "Thank you so much." She put down the receiver. "They can't find him."

"I'll go and see him," said Peter. He was aware that he was being dramatic, and tried to under-emphasise it.

"Not now?" she said.

"Yes."

"But it's miles."

"I can bicycle. I'd quite enjoy bicycling."

"No," she said, "you must have a taxi."

The nursing home stood at the end of a gravel drive and was built of black-red bricks and tiles, with large windows and large pointed gables. Wide steps led to the front door and Peter stood on them, shivering in the cold wind. It was half dark so that it was difficult to tell if the sky was a misty blue or white clouds. Already he was aware of the hospital smell of disinfectant.

His father's room was on the first floor, and immediately he knocked his father's voice said, "Come in." He was standing in the centre of the room on a coco-nut mat. It was a large room, and the low bed and white painted wash-stand and small polished wood dresser all seemed close to the walls and floor, leaving most of it empty. The white bed-spread was without wrinkle, the towel was folded, and no books or papers or even hair-brushes were to be seen. The coco-nut mat was square on the floor and his father stood in the middle. It was impossible to guess what he had been doing.

"Hallo, old boy."

He could not have been expecting Peter yet he showed no surprise.

"Hallo."

"Don't shut the door, old boy, just close it."

"All right, why?"

"Because then they don't come and listen. I've discovered that. If a door is open they don't think it worth while."

"Have you ever caught them listening?"

"You see I've been discovering things about this place.

238

For one thing there aren't any baths. Not a single bath in the whole place."

"Are you sure?"

"You see, I find things out from Joseph."

"Who's Joseph?"

"He's my servant. He tells me things. They all hate it here. The fact is," he lowered his voice to a whisper, "the whole place is run on the cheap."

"What do you mean?"

"There isn't any butter for breakfast."

"Oh."

"Marmalade, but no butter. You see they don't want you here. They want to get rid of you or push you off. . . ." He signalled sideways with his thumb. He grinned, put his lips together, blew out the front of his face, and nodded solemnly.

"Have you seen the doctor yet?"

"Not yet." He seemed to lose interest in the conversation. "They only come twice a week. I'm due to see one of them to-morrow."

"Do they give you anything to do?"

"Some of them play bridge. There's a golf course. Joseph is going to teach me to play."

"Is he?" said Peter. He was aware of the silliness of the remark, but could think of no other. He stood opposite his father, embarrassed by the silence. There should have been something to say to give the interview shape, to connect what they had been talking about, but he could not think of it. He looked up, hoping it would come, but it didn't so he said, "Good-bye," and they shook hands.

"Good-bye, Peter, thank you for coming to see me."

On the stairs he stopped, remembering that he had not asked his father what he had wanted to tell his mother, but it was too late and he went on down.

# Chapter Ten

RETURNING AFTER AN INTERVAL Peter found reasons to hate
Oxford. He was sickened by the conversations which went
on till he felt empty of laughter. As long as he took part he
was convinced that he enjoyed them, and gradually as the
term went on the memory of the last conversation began to
fill the interval till the next, and if there wasn't a next he
began to look for one, till the time became continuous
talking; but at first there were gaps when he felt exhausted,
and on the day he arrived he did not want to talk cheerfully.
But beneath the superficial funniness there was genuine
friendliness, and absence of hatred; and anyway he liked
Oxford. It was reading law which he hated.

His mind began to argue about it impersonally, the deduc-
tions following automatically, as if the words had energy, so
that he was frightened of where they would lead him because
he felt responsible for their conclusion. If he was reading the
wrong subject he should start reading the right one. If he
thought his father would object he should ask him. He had
intended to at the start of last vacation, but he had never
expected to. If he intended something he should do it. He
began to imagine the interview and the words he would use.

Law had been his own choice, but he was no longer ashamed
of that. He had not known what it meant. He had made a
mistake, that was the unembarrassing phrase to use. Everyone
made a mistake sometimes.

His father would say that changing schools meant an extra
year which he could not afford. But it was no good answering
that yet. He must first make it clear that he did not like law.
Then the objections might disappear, or might not.

His father would say, "When you start a thing you should

see it through. Try hard and you will become interested."
It was probably true, but he did not want to become interested. It was not law but becoming a lawyer to which he
objected; the slow way their minds worked, their attention
to what was said, not what was meant, their inability to jump
to a new subject without an explanation; nothing could be
left unsaid. Of course some were different, but he knew that
he would become like this. He could feel himself changing,
was aware of his mind developing their habits. It was his
own weakness that he was afraid of.

His father would ask what he wanted to read instead. Law
led somewhere, to a solicitor's office or the bar. English led
nowhere. But the argument was becoming difficult, and he
ceased to admit his father's unselfishness. His father was only
interested in being able to say, "My son, who is reading for the
bar." It was not possible to say, "My son, who wants to be a
painter."

His mother's first letter came after a week. It was short,
and said how busy she was and what horrible weather they
were having. At the end it said, "Father came home on
Sunday. I think they have done him good."

Her second letter came two days later, and was shorter.

"Dear Peter, I hope you are settling down all right at
Oxford and are having better weather than we are. I am
worried about father and wish I knew what to do. He
seems to get no better. I suppose we must go on hoping.
Let me know if you have any ideas. Lots of love from
Mother."

Peter packed a suitcase and went home by train in the
afternoon. Anyway he wanted to speak to his father.

He telephoned from Rodenham station and then took a
taxi. Behind the pines there were light edges to the sky but
there were black clouds overhead and a few heavy spots of

rain. The taxi turned off the private road on to the drive and he could see across the tennis court and the valley to the hills and the dark sky. As he stood on the gravel paying the driver he saw through the glass top of the front door his mother and Owen, waiting for him in the hall. They stood and smiled, but they did not come out. When he was closer his mother opened the door.

"Hallo darling, what a surprise. Let me take your case."

"Hallo."

"Hallo," said Owen.

"Hallo, Owen."

His father came across the hall. He had been standing there out of sight all the time. "Peter, come and speak to me." He spoke very low, a combination of a whisper and a mutter, and he glanced about the hall.

"Oh not yet," she said. "He's only just arrived."

He was aware of his father trying to wait.

"Did you have a good journey?" she said.

"Not bad."

"I'm afraid your bed may not be quite aired."

"Never mind."

His father said, "Come with me Peter, will you." He led him across the hall, along the passage towards the downstairs lavatory. He turned the corner and stood in the small space between the passage and the lavatory door, where the stairs passed overhead so that it was too low to stand upright. He seemed to hesitate to begin.

"Peter, come here." They were already too close. Peter moved forward a short pace, but it was absurd and he shuffled back. His father was frightening him and he resented it.

"What do you want?" He tried to speak normally but in contrast to his father's whispers he seemed to shout. Terror came into his father's eyes. He looked behind him into the lavatory and sideways to see if anyone was coming down the passage but could not see round the corner. He reached for the curtain of the small window opposite and pulled it half across but it caught on its rail.

"Don't speak so loud." He was angry and peevish but without authority.

"Why not?"

"Because it's most important that no one should hear."

"Why?" Peter refused to whisper. He could see the pain in his father's eyes every time he spoke aloud. He said, "There isn't anyone listening."

"You don't know."

"But who could be there?"

His father didn't answer.

"What is it you want to tell me?"

His father stood still, his head bent under the low ceiling, not answering, and for a moment Peter thought he had gone too far and was annoyed because he was curious.

"The ammunition." He whispered it so low that Peter was not sure if he had heard.

"What?"

"You know."

"In my box?" Peter had collected revolver and automatic bullets in a cigar box. He had had about two hundred rounds of various sizes.

"I've taken it to a friend."

"I see."

"Did you have a licence for it?"

"I don't suppose so."

"You can get it back if you want to." His father was almost cringing. "I've given it to my friend General Binforth. He'll give it back to you if you want it."

Peter was surprised that he felt so little annoyance. Usually he was angry if his possessions were touched and it was an effort to think them unimportant, but now he thought so at once.

He went upstairs to see if the packet of .32 which he kept

243

behind the books in his bookcase or the 9 mm. in the bottom tray of the Meccano box had gone.

His mother followed him upstairs into his room. He was aware of her timidity, but it was less than usual. His father had become something they could talk about.

"When did he come home?" He knew but he wanted her to tell him.

"On Sunday. He rang up at lunch time and said he was coming, so I said I would come in and see him and I got a taxi and went at once but by the time I arrived he had gone. Apparently he never got my message. Our taxis must have passed on the road."

"How has he been since?"

"When he got home he found no one here but I'd left the key in the flower pot in case Owen came back, so he got in and rang up Lady Binforth who said she would come and sit with him till someone came home. He says that she went and looked at his papers."

"Where?"

"On his desk in the billiard room."

"But how could she if she was sitting with him?"

"When she went to make him some tea."

"How does he know?"

"He says she was away a very long time."

Peter began to take the books from his top shelf, but he remembered not to do it while his mother was here, and put them back one at a time.

"Did they do anything for him at the nursing home?"

"I don't think so, except give him some new sleeping dope called paraldehyde. Not pills but medicine."

"Does it work?"

"Sometimes."

"Does Dr. Andrews come?"

"Yes, he sent for him the next morning. He comes almost every day."

"I'll go and see him," Peter said.

He went downstairs and opened his father's door. It was light outside but the curtains were drawn, making the room dark with everything visible. His father was lying dressed on his bed.

"I'm just getting a little rest, old boy."

"Oh, sorry." Peter shut the door. He was relieved because he realised that he had nothing to say, and went slowly upstairs. After a few steps the mortars on the range fired. They were louder than usual and the windows on the stairs rattled. In his room he took the books from his top shelf and found the cardboard box of .32. Every three minutes the mortars fired, and he could imagine how each explosion was shocking his father who was trying to sleep. The box of 9 mm. was gone from the Meccano tray.

In the evening when Peter came to the bathroom to clean his teeth his mother was at the basin and his father standing close to her, watching her pour out his medicine. It was colourless and viscous like liquid paraffin with a strong sweet smell which filled the bathroom. She poured two teaspoonsful into a glass and added water.

"There now," she said and made her face into a smile.

"Did you wash the glass?"

"Of course I did. Do you think I'd give you medicine in a dirty glass?"

Her little pieces of anger gave her away. They were never calculated because she was too busy criticising herself to criticise others. They escaped when she could bear no more. He tried to interrupt her to agree, and before she had finished drank it, tipping back his head. He went past Peter, out of the bathroom, across the passage, misjudging his doorway and jolting himself on it. Peter heard him in his room get quickly into bed.

His mother screwed on the cap and put the medicine bottle in the cupboard.

"Does he wake you at night now?"

"No," she said. "That's supposed to be enough." He thought she was snubbing him but perhaps she was just too tired.

He went upstairs to bed. Definitely to-morrow he would speak to his father.

*   *   *

There were movements on the boards of the landing outside his doorway, but this time he wasn't frightened; it had happened before; like everything it became a habit and a bore. He heard the handle turn, his door was opening slowly and the movements were on the linoleum. They were soft like socks but he could not make them correspond with steps. They seemed to have no direction but were moving about near the foot of his bed. Then they stopped. He told himself that this time he wasn't frightened.

"Peter."

"Yes."

"Peter, there's someone in the house." He felt his heart thump. It was stated so definitely that he did not disbelieve it. He felt the sweat start and the sudden clearing as his eyes came wide open in the dark. He was angry because he had wanted to remain calm and half asleep.

"Peter, will you come and see who it is?"

"All right." He got out of bed and felt for a sweater. "Turn on the light." For a moment he was dazzled by it, and half closed his eyes. He found his pistol on the dressing table. His father was standing near the door in his pyjamas, holding up the trousers with one hand. He went past him and reached his hand on to the landing to turn on the light. The bulb was dim and lit it a dirty yellow and the stairs beyond were black. He went quickly across and switched on the light of the middle landing. It lit the stairs, and he went down slowly, holding his pistol, and his father came behind. There was no

one on the middle landing. He went across to the switches
but didn't touch them remembering that there was not one
for the hall.

"Whereabouts?" he whispered.

His father didn't answer. He did not seem to hear.

"Inside or outside?"

His father stood on the stairs, swaying slightly. It seemed
to take him a long time to hear. It was probably the effect of
the medicine. He said, "inside."

Peter hesitated, then he went on down into the hall. He
had never grown out of his fear of the dark, the fear that
something might suddenly touch him. He said to himself, I
don't believe there is anybody in the house. I'm doing this to
satisfy my father. He felt the sweat running under his arms.
His grip on the gun was tight and wet. Halfway down he
stopped and whispered, "Which room?" His father was a
few steps behind but he didn't answer.

The lower stairs were completely dark, and he was aware
of moving into the atmosphere of the hall, the coldness from
the tiles, the clock ticking. His foot scraped the carpet, and
frightened him. He stopped and listened, but there was no
sound except the clock. He went down the last stairs. As he
stepped on to the tiles, a few feet away behind the kitchen door
the dog barked.

It began with loud rapid barks but they became connected
and drawn out into a long howl.

"Be quiet, Sambo."

"Shut up, you bloody dog."

They turned on all the lights and walked round the house,
looking in all the rooms, but there was no one.

"Well," said Peter, "I suppose we'd better go to bed." He
tried to hide the implication.

His father went along the passage towards the downstairs
lavatory, and Peter went after him. There was no one in the
lavatory. His father stood outside and drew back the curtain

of the little window at the bend under the stairs. It was open.

He did not say anything. He just looked at Peter.

It was useless to argue. It was useless to suggest that it might have been left open by mistake. His father knew better.

His father shut it and went upstairs. Peter put the dog in the kitchen, turned off the lights, and followed him. When he came on to the middle landing his father was in the bathroom, and the strong sweet smell of paraldehyde had spread out of the door.

"Good-night."

"Good-night, old boy."

★   ★   ★

It was a fortnight later one day at lunch that Peter decided that if he waited till his father was well he might wait for months. Some days he seemed better and sat in the drawing-room, and once Peter saw him open the French windows when he thought no one was looking but the wind took it out of his hand and he snatched at it and missed and went away, out of the drawing-room, up to his bedroom, leaving it swinging. On other days he stayed in bed. To-day he had come to lunch wearing his breeches suit and a woollen scarf, though it was mild and wet. He sat saying nothing, spreading his depression. Owen didn't try to talk. His mother made cheerful plans about food but presently even she became silent. When the front door bell rang his father put down his knife and fork and stopped eating. Owen went into the hall to answer it and Peter stopped in the dining-room doorway where he could see.

A large lady was on the doorstep, and several paces behind to one side was a little man. They both wore khaki mackintoshes with belts.

The lady said, "Nicer a little to-day, isn't it?" and laughed and the little man laughed.

She said, "Are you interested in God?"

"No," said Owen. He closed the door.

He watched them for a moment going down the drive and then came back into the dining-room.

"Who was it?"

"Jehovah's Witnesses."

"Oh yes," said his mother, "they've been before."

"What happened?" said Mr. Nicholas.

"She asked if I was interested in God, so I said no."

There was silence and they went on eating but Mr. Nicholas did not pick up his knife and fork, and after a moment he went upstairs.

"Aren't you feeling well, darling?"

"Come and speak to me will you?"

She sighed, and spooned fruit custard on to a plate and went after him with it. She was gone about ten minutes and came back still carrying it.

"What's the matter?"

"He says he has a headache."

"Was that all?"

"He wanted me to tell him that it wasn't Lady Binforth at the door."

After lunch Peter went upstairs and opened his father's door. He was sitting on his bed, propped against its head, with his feet under the eiderdown, reading. Even now Peter couldn't think what to say. He went in and shut the door.

"Old boy, I do wish Owen would be more careful."

"What do you mean?" Peter enjoyed defending Owen. Owen was everything that Peter liked to be and could be defended without embarrassment.

"That kind of behaviour does me no good."

"What behaviour?"

"I wish he would realise that for a person in my condition shocks are the worst possible thing."

Peter didn't answer. There was no point, and anyway he

wanted to talk about something else. He waited, letting the pause lengthen so that the other subject could die away. He thought of phrases: Could we talk . . . , I want to speak . . . , This may be a surprise to you. . . . They were none of them right. The interval was long enough now.

His father said, "There's a law about tree-felling, isn't there?"

"I'm not sure."

"You must have a permit from the Town and Country Planning Committee."

"Someone told me so, but they may have been wrong."

His father said, "What about the wood?" He looked at Peter for the first time, and there was a satisfaction in his alarm, as if he said, "Now I'm in a real hole, you can't argue me out of this one."

"But I'm not certain about the law."

"There is, I know."

"It may only apply to some counties. I can't remember. Why not ring up and ask?"

It was obvious that his father would refuse, and Peter knew that he should offer, but could not make himself. He could not think what to say. It was spending so much energy on something which did not matter. And yet it did matter, because it was typical. As you got closer and understood better everything mattered because everything was typical and then it was suddenly a shock to find yourself screaming about a collar stud. Peter said, "Let me ring them up."

"No, old boy, don't do that."

"Why not? It's the obvious thing. You want to know, don't you? They can tell you. Then ring them up." He tried to let his words work him into an opinion. "They can't blame you if you didn't know." He knew he was wrong and that ignorance was no excuse.

He said, "I'll just ask what are the regulations about tree-felling." He moved towards the door.

"No, no, Peter, Peter boy, Peter please."

"All right, all right." He was pleased to have produced the genuine alarm. At least that was familiar.

He stood by the dressing table, looking away from his father, but aware that there was sweat on his face and he must be sweating with alarm under the eiderdown. He was excited himself and before he could subside he said, "Could I speak to you some time about Oxford?"

"Yes, old boy."

He waited, wondering if his father meant him to go on. He might start at once whatever his father meant and then even if he stopped him there could never be the same embarrassment. He tried to think of the phrase, but could not remember it, or had he never decided?

He said, "Do you mean now?"

"No, old boy, not now. Wait till I'm better could you please."

"All right," said Peter. He could never say no. And anyway it probably was unfair to speak to his father when he was ill. But he couldn't wait. He had already waited too long, and soon it would be too late.

He said, "I suppose so."

He left his reluctance hanging, waiting for his father to reply to it, but he didn't. He tried to think how to make it more obvious but no words came. His father shut his book and lay down, pushing the eiderdown with his feet. His eyes shut and opened again quickly.

"Peter, old boy, do please try to make Owen more careful."

"Mm."

"Draw my curtains will you, old boy. I'm going to try to get some sleep."

$$\star \quad \star \quad \star$$

The days became shorter and the virginia creeper at the end of the house above the rockery turned crimson and dropped its leaves on the drive. The wind blew over the hill top, clearing the thin silver birch branches and bending the pine tops, and there were cold grey days and days of heavy rain. The birds ate the rowan berries dropping bits on to the gravel beneath so that it was stained red. And Peter stayed at home; he could not leave his mother with his father.

Doing what other people would approve became a sort of religion; not any people, but the people he admired. Often it was Dorothy, and at other times friends at school and Oxford. As soon as he knew them well there were questions on which he did not care about their judgments, but together they formed an opinion which was close to a moral code. Sometimes he thought that because he chose his friends it was his own, but at others he knew that it changed as his friends changed.

At the beginning of December he thought one morning that he ought to do more for his father, and suggested that they should go for a walk. The sun was bright for the first time for weeks, shining on the leafless branches which were damp where it had melted the frost.

"Would you like to walk round the garden?"

His father sat in his arm-chair in the drawing-room, reading. After a pause he said, "All right, old boy." He implied that it was a serious decision which he was taking against his real judgment.

"Fetch me my overcoat, will you?"

They went through the French windows, down the rockery. The air was fresh and had an autumn smell of burning leaves. When there was a small cold wind his father took his hands from his pockets and held his overcoat collar close to his neck.

They stood at the bottom of the rockery and his father made no effort to go on. Peter thought of moving down the hillside but he could see Owen and Brian there, and his father disapproved of Brian; he thought of going towards the tennis court, but the wood was there and the illegally felled trees. Everything began to have unsafe associations.

His father said, "I think I'll go in now."

"We've only been out a minute. Let's go round the house and in by the back door."

Peter began to move along the path, past the rhododendron hedge, and his father came after him, walking very slowly, holding up his coat collar.

Peter tried to think of conversation but he could hear the artificiality of what he said. He hadn't enough genuine cheerfulness for himself. They came up the cinder path, past the coal shed, in at the back door, and his father went and sat in the drawing-room. He was too exhausted to take off his overcoat.

After lunch he agreed to play chess and Peter went with him to his bedroom. Normally he could beat Peter; games of all sorts roused his combative instinct and he played them well enough to win or despised them and refused to play. But this afternoon it was difficult for Peter to avoid winning. He had to fail to notice chances to take his father's pieces; and his father did not notice that they had been in danger. He could not concentrate. Sometimes he seemed to make an effort, frowning at the board, but then he gave it up and moved a piece anywhere, and looked away. He sat on the edge of the bed not watching what happened when it was Peter's turn. He gave the impression that he did not want to be disturbed from thinking about his illness. After half an hour he said, "Finish it off with Owen, will you, old boy."

"But Owen doesn't play."

He sat back on his bed, looking at the blankets.

Peter said, "Come on, you can't stop just when I look like winning." It was hopelessly insincere. He could not put himself in sympathy with someone who wanted to win games, and think what they would say.

"All right, I'll try a little longer." His father shifted the responsibility.

They went on, but his father became slower and slower. He was trying now, hesitating between moves, unable to decide. When he held his hand over the board it shook, and he pulled it back, and put it out half taking hold, and pulled it back upsetting the piece. It was as if he was putting on an act to make the game impossible.

"Old boy, I really can't go on."

"All right." Peter folded the board, slid the pieces into the box, and went away. No one could say he hadn't tried. He went slowly downstairs. He was a few steps from the bottom when the explosion came.

It was loud and frightening, apparently just outside. It seemed to catch him with his breath out, and he was angry as if he had been punched. It came from everywhere so that he was sure it had been as loud all over the house. Looking back he saw his father at his bedroom door; the skin of his face was grey and his hand by his side twitched. Peter went on down. If his father spoke to him he would shout. He went across the hall to the kitchen where his mother stood upright, holding a fork she had been using.

"What happened?" she said.

"I'm not sure."

"Was it a bomb from the range?"

"I don't think so."

"What was it then?"

"Can't you guess?"

He went out of the back door, round the house, down the hillside. Owen and Brian were at the bottom of the rockery, alternately giggling and looking at each other with wide-eyed amazement at their success.

"There was a real sheet of flame," said Owen.

"And a real mushroom of smoke."

"It was the sort of bang you feel as well as hear."

They went down the slope to measure the distance apart of the pieces. The largest had moved a yard, the two smaller fourteen and eight yards. They could see the tracks they had torn in the bilberries.

"I never knew you could have a real sheet of flame."

"How much did you put in?"

"We just poured till the hole was full." They looked at each other and sat down and giggled.

"I shouldn't tell them at home; they will think it was a stray mortar bomb."

Owen explained how the important thing was to bore a deep hole, and pack it tightly, and use the clay as a wad. They hunted for other pieces, and examined the scar, and found the burned fuse.

After a time Brian went home and Peter and Owen went up to the house. Mrs. Nicholas was in the kitchen.

She said, "I do think you might be a little more thoughtful, Owen." She was surprisingly annoyed.

"What?"

"Father's in a terrible state. He says he won't sleep for a week and that this will probably be the end of him. It was you, wasn't it?"

"The tree, oh yes, that was us. Did you hear it?"

Peter said, "You haven't told father what it was?"

"Yes, of course."

★   ★   ★

Perhaps it was because of the explosion, or perhaps because the paraldehyde was becoming less effective as he went on taking it that Mr. Nicholas slept worse. He made Mrs. Nicholas give him larger doses, and went for more himself in the night. His hands shook so that he spilt it behind the basin on the floor, and the bathroom smelt permanently of it. Mrs. Nicholas said that sometimes in the morning he was quite silly when she took up his breakfast; and once he upset his porridge into his sheets.

They hoped that when Dorothy came for Christmas she

would know what to do, but she didn't. He refused to have another doctor; and even if he could be persuaded to go to a nursing home he would probably come away again. He seemed to have ceased to want to get well.

She said to Peter, "I wish I could think of a solution. Your mother won't stand much more."

"Won't she?"

"You should know. It doesn't look like it to me."

She seemed right when he thought about it. He did not notice when people looked ill, assuming that he had mis-remembered them; and he did not often look at his mother, but talked to her looking at the carpet.

"I think someone should tell you Peter, how well we think you are coping."

"Am I?" It had not occurred to him. He had not solved the problem; but perhaps it was insoluble. He began slowly to adjust his opinions, hunting for reasons to be able to agree with her. Usually Dorothy was critical, noticing his selfish-ness and unkindness, but occasionally she said something personal and flattering which pleased him more than all his mother's love.

*　　*　　*

On Christmas morning they had always come with their stockings to the double bed where their father and mother slept, and when their father and mother had ceased to sleep together and the double bed had been put in the spare room they had come there. When Peter found out about Father Christmas they had continued to do it for Owen and David, and when Owen found out, for David, and when David found out they had just continued. This year it didn't seem possible, and Peter said so to his mother, and Owen said, "Then it'll be just like any other day," and they could hear the tears in his voice. So his mother put presents in two football stockings, and laid them by their beds, and on Christmas morning when it was still dark Peter and Owen carried them downstairs and woke her and went with her to the double bed in the spare room where Dorothy was sleeping. They wished each other a merry Christmas in whispers so as not to disturb Mr. Nicholas whose room was next door.

They put their feet under the eiderdown and ate chocolate and opened envelopes containing book-tokens from obscure aunts. And Mrs. Nicholas said, "Somebody start eating their tangerine. It doesn't seem like Christmas till I smell tangerine." She said that each year.

They blew up balloons and let go of their ends so that they flew about the room making vulgar noises, and they rolled a new ball for Sambo who chased it under the bed and over the bed, but they stopped quickly when he wanted to bark. It was difficult so early in the morning to be continuously cheerful.

Peter said, "I wonder what David will send us? A holy text on jealousy?"

"I shouldn't be surprised," said Mrs. Nicholas. She gave a short laugh. After a moment she went out of the room and they realised that she was crying. Dorothy went after her. He had meant it as a joke. All his jokes were at someone's expense. Because she never showed it he forgot that she went on feeling about David.

"I suppose we'd better get ready for church." They always went to church on Christmas morning. For several years he had wondered whether to refuse. It was a choice between hurting her by telling her and going insincerely to please her. Sometimes he thought that she understood anyway, but in the end he always went, not because it was kinder but because he could not face the immediate embarrassment.

He tidied coloured paper with Owen, and they collected their presents and went upstairs. It was dark and cold in his room, and outside the windows it was still night with only a suggestion of dawn. He turned on the light and drew the curtains. His mother was coming up the stairs. Now he must apologise.

She said, "He won't let me go."

"Where?"

"To church."

She stood in the doorway, trying not to cry but every now and again she shook with a sob. She stood there waiting for him to do something. Then she went away, realising that she should not expect anything to be done.

He followed her to the banisters. He said, "Why don't you just go?" It was a silly suggestion because he knew she wouldn't. He went slowly downstairs into his father's room. He didn't know what he was going to say, and he didn't care.

His father lay under piled bed-clothes with only his head showing. When he heard the door shut he moved it an inch or two to see who it was.

"Hallo, Peter."

"You won't let mother go to church."

"You don't understand, old boy, I'm very ill."

"You think you are." He hadn't the patience to be kind and persuade. He only wanted to say something that hurt. He went out and slammed the door. It was probably three months since a door had been slammed in the house and it gave him a shock to do it. The echo sounded downstairs in the empty kitchen. He could imagine Owen in his room looking up with a shock of curiosity, his mother in her room looking up with shocked anxiety, and the sweat running off his father under his piled bed-clothes.

In the afternoon they opened more presents in the drawing-room and ate Christmas cake. Mr. Nicholas sat in his arm-chair, opening the books he had been given. She had forgiven him, and poured out tea cheerfully and tried to be gay, and Peter tried to join her, but it wasn't possible when he was afraid to make sudden movements.

\*　　\*　　\*

Dorothy went away at the new year, and a week later Owen went to a crammer. The school had said that otherwise he would never pass his exam. One didn't realise till he went how comforting he had been. Because Peter now saw no one to whom he said what he thought he ceased to put his thoughts into words and they began to seem unreal; and the house seemed more silent because there was now no chance that anyone would sing or be foolish. Grey days came in succession with no rain or snow but a cold wind, and his father sat in his arm-chair in the drawing-room wearing his scarf. He had found David's collection of Harrison Ainsworth and was reading through it. A few days later the dog was put down.

Peter did not know till it had been done and when his mother came back from the town he asked where she had been.

"Taking Sambo."

"Where?"

"To the vet."

"What for?" He guessed but he wanted to be sure.

"To have him put to sleep."

He said nothing. Silence might make her guess at his anger. If he said things she would think she had its measure. He turned his back and walked away.

"It *is* very difficult," she said, "having a dog in a house when someone is ill."

He walked out of the kitchen into the hall.

"He was rather a mongrel," she said. He could hear her nervous smile behind him. She followed him into the hall, but he went upstairs not looking back. Half-way he said without turning, "What about the cat?"

"What?" she said. "What did you say?" but it was too silly to repeat.

That evening Mr. Nicholas had a cold in his head and went to bed, and after that he did not come downstairs.

He only got out of bed to go in his dressing-gown to the bathroom. On Friday Peter found him there standing in front of the basin.

"I've got an infection in my eye. What shall I do?"

"I don't know. What sort of infection?"

"Shall I bathe it?"

"That couldn't hurt."

"Help me, will you, old boy."

He fumbled with the key of the medicine cupboard and Peter opened it for him. He stood in front of the basin holding the eyebath.

"Bathing couldn't do any harm, could it?"

"I don't see how."

He held it under the tap to fill it. His hand shook so that it tapped against the china. The hot water rushed into it and out the other side in a fountain, down his dressing-gown on to the floor. He moved it to the cold tap, leaving the hot running. He leant away and tried to turn the tap but it only dripped. He gave it a jerk, drawing himself back but it went on dripping. Then it came with a rush, out of the basin on to the floor.

"Shall I do it?"

"Yes, old boy, do it will you."

Peter filled it with warm water.

"Is that the right temperature?"

"Try it with your finger." Peter held it out to him but he hesitated.

"Wash your hands then. There's no hurry."

His father washed his hands and dipped one finger a tenth of an inch.

"Is that all right?"

His father didn't answer.

Peter put down the eye-bath, washed his own hands, tested the temperature, gave it to his father and went away. At the top of the stairs he heard his father pour it down the drain.

After lunch his mother was in the hall, ringing up Dr. Andrews.

"Why are you doing that?"

"Father wants him. He's got rather a nasty eye."

When Dr. Andrews came he prescribed drops and washes, and left cottonwool swabs. Peter heard him talking to his mother in the dining-room.

"That's really a very nasty conjunctivitis. Wash it out with lukewarm water four times a day and then put in the drops." He seemed to grasp this tangible illness with relief. Peter waited for him to say, "The first thing is to cure the eyes."

"And don't let him use them too much."

"Yes."

"I'll also give him a new sleeping-draught. That stuff they used at the nursing home seems to do him no good." The implication was obvious. Peter went out of the hall, not wanting to meet Dr. Andrews.

After that his father didn't read any more. He lay in bed with the curtains half-drawn thinking of his illness, and of when his eyes would next be washed.

*　*　*

On Sunday after breakfast Mrs. Nicholas was to be allowed to go to church. She hurried about upstairs, dressing, telling Peter how to bathe his father's eyes, telling Mr. Nicholas that Peter would do it, giving him unnecessary chances to change his mind. At last she went, down the cinder track, into the mist, and Peter waved from the kitchen. He made himself some coffee and drank it slowly and went upstairs.

His father lay on his side, and when Peter came in he said, "Hallo, are you going to do my eyes?"

"Yes." He could only be polite, for the idea of touching his father revolted him. He filled the enamel bowl with luke-warm water, and sat on the chair by his bed. His father pushed back the bed-clothes from his chest and lay with his head on the pillow, blinking at the ceiling. Peter dipped a piece of cotton-wool and leant across, trying not to breathe his father's smell. He started to wipe one eye. His father blinked and twisted his head. It was pink and inflamed and there was pus in the corners and on the lids which he tried to move. Some of it had dried and had to be repeatedly wetted before it would come away. He felt nauseated. He thought if his fingers touched it he would be sick.

After ten minutes he had finished. He put in the drops, left the bowl with the used cotton-wool on the landing, and ran downstairs. He felt exhausted. The thought of what he had been doing made him shudder.

He put on a coat and stood in the front door porch, breathing the fresh air. A damp mist obscured the valley and covered the hillside so that he could only see fifty yards among the pines and rhododendrons. A car was coming up the private road. He heard it turn into their gateway, and in a moment he could see it coming up the drive. It stopped opposite him and he recognised Pussy Pawthorn.

"Hallo, Peter." She sat in the front seat and spoke to him through the open window.

"Hallo."

"I hear your father is ill."

"Yes."

"May I say hallo to him?" She said it casually as if it was not important.

Peter stood, looking below her eyes at the door of the car. After a moment he was aware that there was a child in the back. It seemed to come up from the floor and began to lower the window but this would only go down a few inches so it looked at him with its eyes over the edge of the glass. He wondered whether it was hers and realised how little he knew of her because he was not sure if she had a child. He could not think what to answer. He said, "Just a moment, I'll go and see."

"No, you can't ask your mother, she's at church. Make up your own mind."

It was difficult to associate her directness with what he remembered.

"Why do you want to see him?"

"To tell him to get better."

"But he may not want to see you. It may upset him."

After a moment she said, "Hurry up and make up your mind."

He did not know what to say. He would have allowed her if he had not been afraid that his mother might come back. The child had forced its head at an angle into the window space. It was a little girl. His mind kept imagining what would happen if the window was wound up.

Mrs. Pawthorn relaxed and lay back in the driving seat. She heaved her breasts and gave him her large plain smile, and he remembered her.

She saw her mistake at once. She sat up and said, "I will be there half a minute, thirty seconds, no one will know."

Peter stood saying nothing. He wanted to be able to go on saying nothing and see what would happen. He resented being made to decide. When he looked up she had turned away apparently bored with him.

"Half a minute?" he said.

"That's what I said."

"All right."

He saw her lean forward and expected the door to open but she was taking off the brake, for the car began to move away down the drive, past the rhododendron hedge, out of sight towards the back gate. He looked round and his mother was in the hall behind him.

"Hallo, darling, who was that?"

"Pussy Pawthorn."

"Oh," she said. She half smiled. "Did you deal with her?"

"Yes," he said. He went past her into the hall. His father was standing at the top of the stairs in his pyjamas.

"Who was that?"

"What?"

"That car in the drive?"

"What?" He pretended to be confused.

"Was it a mistake?"

"Yes," he said, "it was a mistake."

"Had they got the wrong house?"

"Yes."

His father said, "Peter, was it the police?"

"No, it wasn't the police."

Peter put on his coat and walked across the lawn on to the tennis court. The ground was hard with a black frost and there was a cold wind and grey clouds. Looking down the hillside, through the felled trees, between the trunks of the pines that still stood at the foot of the hill, to the white walls of Mr. Belvene's house, he could see no difference to show that he had now died.

When his mother had told him at breakfast Peter had not remembered who Mr. Belvene was.

She said, "The man who lived at the bottom of our hill."

"And asked us to cut down the wood?"

"Yes."

"And came up here one day before breakfast?"

"That's right."

"What did he die of?"

"No one seems to know. He couldn't eat anything; he was always sick; eventually he broke something inside."

Peter looked down the hillside to the green lawn and white-washed house between the trees. There was no one moving and the windows and doors seemed shut, but they usually were. Perhaps he was lying there, or perhaps they had taken him away.

It made his father's illness appear to him again as a problem. That was the trouble, he could only see things as problems when he could see solutions, and so they had ceased to be problems. Otherwise they became a succession of events of which he was a part.

He went into the house and found his mother in the kitchen, sitting on the edge of the table, preparing vegetables.

"It really is time we did something."

"About father?"

"He gets no better. I know his eyes are, but now he's so frightened to use them he won't read. He just lies there."

She said, "I wish I knew what."

"We must get another doctor."

"Mm," she said, agreeing sadly, as if he had said, "I wish I was rich." It was a nice idea.

"I'll go and telephone." He didn't mean to. He wanted to make her believe that he was serious.

"But who?" she said.

"I don't know. The man who came when you were ill, Dr. Duncan."

"Anyway you can't—can you? It's not professional? He wouldn't come."

"We'll tell Dr. Andrews. We'll call it a second opinion. There's nothing wrong with that."

"Mm," she said sadly. "Father would never agree."

He walked away into the hall. He must control his annoyance and remain detached. He must not support his idea so strongly that if he was persuaded it was wrong he would go on supporting it.

He was amazed that one could take decisions about life from the same small motives that one decided about getting out of bed or going to a party. He had imagined that before important decisions there would be a warning and he would be able to prepare himself to be impartial, to stop being mean and petty, but there was no warning. And no one was watching so no one could ever know that what he had done or not done had made his father recover or not.

Logically he was sure that he was right. Dr. Andrews was useless; another doctor could not be worse. But his father might not want another doctor, and what his father wanted might be best.

He went back to the kitchen. He said, "If we ask father what would he say?"

"I don't know," she said. She honestly didn't know. She knew what he would feel but she thought Peter was asking some other more logical question. When she spoke to him she tried to forget her emotional opinions because she thought he was not interested, and as they were the only opinions she had she became lost.

He said, "I'll go and ask him," and didn't wait for her to answer.

He went upstairs and opened the door. His father was out of bed in his pyjamas, kneeling at a chair. His bare toes were on the linoleum. When he heard the door he turned and began to stand up.

"Just a minute, old boy, I'm saying my prayers."

"Oh, sorry." Peter went out and shut the door.

His mother had come up the stairs after him. She said, "Let me do it."

"He's busy now."

"What's he doing?"

"Saying his prayers."

"See that nothing boils over will you?" She opened the door quietly and went in.

In the kitchen Peter could hear their voices through the ceiling but not what they were saying. His father was never embarrassed. Even now he had had the words ready to explain what he was doing, a little too ready, as if it was an act. But it probably wasn't. He never went to church, and disliked the parson, and sometimes talked logically about religion so that you almost imagined that he had none. Then suddenly he became aware that his intellect was leading him instead of he using it, and was obstinate about a prejudice. Of course he believed in God. His father had.

The voices in the bedroom stopped and his mother came downstairs.

"What did he say?"

"He agreed. He was quite sensible about it."

Dr. Duncan came that afternoon. He saw Mr. Nicholas for half an hour and then came down to the drawing-room.

He said, "I must speak to Dr. Andrews, I shall probably find him at six." He stood, apparently looking at Mrs. Nicholas' knees, but it was difficult to see behind his thick glasses. He seemed not to know how to say good-bye.

She said, "What do you think about him," nervously, as if she thought she should not ask.

"Of course, its absurd for him to be here." He muttered rudely so that he seemed to criticise them, not Dr. Andrews. "I'll ring you to-night to say what's happened."

He was brisk and efficient; he made plans and gave confidence. It seemed to Peter that his father's illness consisted of calling in people with new energy who expended it and gradually lost confidence.

Dr. Duncan telephoned after supper. He said, "I've spoken to Dr. Andrews and he has asked me to see if there is a bed in the Weatbridge Psychiatric Hospital. I've been on to them and they say it can be arranged."

"Supposing he won't agree to go."

"We'll think about that if it happens. Say nothing to him to-night. Just get his things ready so that he can leave at once. I'll be round to-morrow at eleven."

Mrs. Nicholas put down the telephone and went upstairs, and Peter went to help her. He was frightened by the success of what he had started. It seemed to have got out of his control, and he wondered if he had been right.

She found a suitcase and put in his tooth brush and paste. When she carried it they rattled to the bottom. She found a spare pair of pyjamas in the airing cupboard. There didn't seem to be anything else.

"Razor," she said. "I almost forgot."

"Will he be allowed it?"

They stood on the landing, talking in whispers but Mr. Nicholas heard them.

"Peter, what are you doing?"

"Nothing. Looking for things."

"Is mother there?"

"Yes."

Mrs. Nicholas whispered, "Writing paper," and they went into the billiard room. The yellow light over the table with its large shade left the ends of the room in half darkness. The whole surface of his desk was a confusion of papers.

From across the landing he called, "Peter."

"Yes."

"Come here, will you a minute, old boy."

Peter went into his room.

"Peter will you close my window, the curtain's flapping?"

He was made restless by their unusual movements, like an animal when someone is leaving. It was difficult to know what he guessed.

★   ★   ★

The grey light came slowly in the morning, but Peter could not sleep. He had been too hot all night. He pushed off the bed-clothes and stood on the coco-nut matting, noticing when he properly opened his eyes that it was darker than he had thought. Though both his windows were wide the air was warm. He dressed slowly, staggering a little. He remembered that to-day his father was going away, and tried not to be satisfied at his achievement. He might still refuse to go.

As he went downstairs he could hear his mother's noises in the kitchen; she had probably been up an hour. Otherwise there was a curious silence; the traffic on the main road seemed a long way off. On the middle landing he was surprised to see his father's door a few inches open.

He supposed his mother had not noticed it. She had probably gone downstairs when it was still dark, and not used the light because the switch made a noise. There was no sound inside the room. He pushed the door gently till there was space to put his head round.

His father was lying still, apparently asleep. The curtains were across and it was difficult to see him clearly. Peter was about to go out, glad not to have been heard, when he noticed his father's hand hanging over the edge of the bed on to the floor.

He went across the room and drew the curtains. His father lay on his back with the sheets and bed-clothes pushed back from his neck and shoulders. There were red cellophane capsules in his open mouth and in the folds of his sheet and pillow. Some he had broken with his teeth, and the white powder was on his lips and in a streak down his chin, and his eyes were open.

Peter ran downstairs. He stood in the kitchen doorway.

"Hallo, darling, you're early."

When he didn't answer she looked at him and he saw her alarm. He supposed he was white. "Father," he said.

He went into the dining-room and telephoned to Dr. Duncan who said he would come at once. He heard her go upstairs and went out through the French window; he did not want to be there when she came down. He went across the lawn to the tennis court.

He thought, I have tried to take all decisions honestly. He remembered what Dorothy had said to him; but he could no longer pretend to himself that she was a fair judge. She didn't know the facts. She didn't know why he did things or in detail how he did them. He was aware now of what had been missing. He had never felt or shown any love. He had been dutiful, that was the word, the awful word.

He was aware of relief. Now that his father was out of the way he could do what he wanted. And because of it he realised that his own impatience with his father as much as his father's impatience with him had caused their quarrels.

Anyway his father had won in the end. They had tried to make him better because it was a convention to get better. They hadn't even the courage to show that they didn't want it. And the ultimate triumph of his father's bigness over their littleness was that he had refused to get better.

His father had won all the time. He had made his sons what they were, intellectual, ineffectual. They wanted to win as much as he did, and when they couldn't they had adopted a device which told them that they deserved to. Their father didn't care. They hadn't even made his life uncomfortable. It was quarrelling and winning which he enjoyed.

Peter looked down to his right, where between the pines he could just see Mr. Belvene's house. To his left, beyond the valley was the line of hills which hid the range. From here, when the sun had been shining, he had seen David and Captain Cambridge standing together on the lawn, looking up at the martins' nests. The tracks of Mrs. Pawthorn's car were on the wet gravel of the drive; or perhaps they were Dr. Andrews'. It was all much too confused. It was silly to blame.

As soon as things were cleared up he would go away somewhere, perhaps abroad. His mother could stay with Dorothy.

When he looked at the house again his mother and Dr. Duncan had come on to the lawn. He must have come up the back drive. His mother came forward towards him.

She said, "He's been very sick. He's still rather dopy but the doctor says there's no danger. We must give him lots of black coffee. I've rung Dr. Andrews."

Peter said, "Have you? Why did you do that?"

"He wanted him."

There was nothing to say or do. He didn't want to do or

say anything. He turned his back and walked away across the tennis court and sat on a fallen tree beyond its edge.

The day got lighter for a time and then no lighter. There were grey clouds and it was warm as if it would rain.

Presently he went across to the house. There was no one in the hall, and he went upstairs. His father's door was wide open, his bedside lamp alight, and he was sitting up looking at a book.

"Hallo Peter."

"Hallo dad."